D E A T H   T R I C K

DEATH TRICK

A MYSTERY NOVEL BY

RICHARD STEVENSON

ALYSON PUBLICATIONS

LOS ANGELES

This book is fiction. All the characters are made-up. References are made to public officials in Albany, New York, but the characters who fill these offices in the
book are not meant to resemble the people who fill the offices in real life.

Manufactured in the United States of America.
Printed on acid-free paper.

This trade paperback is published by Alyson Publications Inc.,
P.O. Box 4371, Los Angeles, California 90078.
Distribution in the United Kingdom by Turnaround Publisher Services Ltd.,
27 Horsell Road, London N5 1XL, England.

First published by St. Martin's Press: 1981
First Alyson edition: 1983
Second edition: September 1996

5 4 3 2 1

ISBN 1-55583-387-X
(formerly published with ISBN 0-932870-27-9)

Library of Congress Cataloging-in-Publication Data
Stevenson, Richard.
      Death Trick
      I. Title.
      PS3569.T4567D4
      813'.54   80-29318
                                                         CIP

For Chuck
for Fred, David, Bob, Ralph and George
for H.
and for Robert Berndt

1

THE WOMAN'S VOICE WAS FULL OF THE MUSIC OF BUSINESS.

"Donald Strachey?"

"Yo."

"Mr. Stuart Blount is calling. One moment please."

I hung up.

Cars were double-parked on both sides of Central Avenue, and I watched an Albany police cruiser negotiate the course like a Conestoga wagon up the Donner Pass. By Thanksgiving it could be in Schenectady.

Again. "Donald Strachey?"

"Speaking."

"We were—disconnected, sir. Stuart Blount will be with you in just a moment."

I hung up.

The sky over Jimmy's Lounge was slate gray and a cold wind chewed at the crumbling caulking around the windowpane next to me. Five weeks after Labor Day and already winter was sliding across the state from Buffalo like a new Ice Age. I found some masking tape in the back of my desk drawer. I ripped off a long strip and pressed it against the grime where the pane met the frame.

Ring, ring.

"Strachey."

"Mr. Strachey, this is Stuart Blount. I've been trying to reach you."

"The damn line's been tied up. What can I do for you, Mr. Blount?"

"My attorney, Jay Tarbell, tells me you've handled missing-person type situations, and I seem to have been, ah, saddled with one. Perhaps you've seen it on the media."

I said yes, I had.

"I'd much appreciate your getting together with Mrs. Blount and me to discuss the situation. You probably understand that the matter could develop into an extended time frame. Are you available?"

1

I pitched the *Gay Community News* I'd been reading for the past hour onto the sooty stack of *Advocates* and *GCN*s below the windowsill. Down on Central an old blue Pinto was stalled sideways in the middle of the street, and the midday traffic was backing up on both sides. A foot patrolman glanced over his shoulder and ambled into Jimmy's.

I said, "I'll do what I can to clear out a block of time. How does next Thursday look?"

"In point of fact, Mr. Strachey, I was thinking hopefully we could do business sooner than that. I could work something out for this afternoon. As you know, we've got one hell of a problem situation over here."

It was that, though Blount spoke in the tones of a man who hadn't exactly been unhinged by it—if when all about you are losing theirs, grace under pressure, or whatever.

"I'll make some arrangements," I told him. "Where's your office?"

"Twin Towers, but why don't we make it at my residence? Mrs. Blount will, ah, wish to be present." He gave me the address. "Say, one-thirty?"

"I'll be there."

There were two banks within close walking distance of Twin Towers on Washington Avenue. I phoned my lover's ex-roommate's ex-lover, who worked at the Mechanics Exchange Bank. He called back five minutes later with the information that there was no danger of my depleting Stuart Blount's checking account anytime in the current century.

I walked down to Elmo's at Central and Lexington and ordered a diet Pepsi and a roast-beef sub with extra meat. I wrote Elmo a check for the $2.93 and made sure I had a State Bank deposit slip with me for after I'd paid my call at the Blounts'.

They lived in a three-story neo-Romanesque brownstone on State Street overlooking Washington Park. The place was in the middle of "the block," which I knew well enough, if only from the street. The buildings had a solid Edwardian propriety about them, the sort of neighborhood Lady Bellamy might have visited if the *Titanic* had made it across. Those houses that hadn't been carved up into roomy high-ceilinged apartments for professional people and upper-echelon state bureaucrats were still occupied by families that were rich and, by and large, straight. In recent years my close contact with both groups had been relegated to mainly business.

The heavy oak door had a big oval of glass in it, beveled at the edges, with the name "Blount" engraved in the center in a fancy script. The Blount family was not new to State Street.

I rang the bell and stood shivering on the stoop, wishing I'd worn a sweater under my corduroy jacket. I looked at my reflection in the polished glass and checked my tie, a pricey tan suede job that had been a gift from Brigit's mother back when she still referred to me as "our Donald" and not "that sneaking fairy." I'd once tossed the tie in a Goodwill box, then bought it back a month later for thirty-five cents; it was the only one I owned, and it helped clients like the Blounts meet their need to take me seriously.

A muscular brown woman in a black dress and white apron led me through the foyer, past a ticking grandfather clock into a pale yellow room with a crystal chandelier. Over a walnut sideboard with silver candlesticks were portraits of two early nineteenth century types, a man and a woman, who looked as though they'd absorbed their Cotton Mather. The oriental scatter rugs on the polished oak floor had held their color, and my fee went up as I crossed the room.

The brown woman recited: "Mr. and Mrs. Blount will be with you in just a moment," and left. Big Michael Korda fans, the Blounts. I seated myself on a winged mahogany-trimmed Empire sofa upholstered in deep-blue and off-white stripes of silk. Not a piece of furniture to take off your shoes and curl up on. I sat like a debutante with a teacup on her knee and looked out the bay window to my right and saw the exact tree in the park under which I had met Timmy Callahan. I smiled.

"Mr. Strachey—Hello! I'm Stuart Blount, and this is Mrs. Blount."

He strode toward me from the foyer, moving like a clipper ship, an elegant hand coming out of the sleeve of a gray, chalk-striped business suit. He had a full head of wavy gray hair and a nicely chiseled face with the lines of age in the most flattering places, as if he'd picked up the design during a February golfing jaunt to the Algarve.

Mrs. Blount, a handsome, slim woman who could have been her husband's sister, wore a mauve dress of a style and cut that would not go out of fashion. Her movements had a calculatedly loose, finishing-school cockiness about them that came across as a kind of stiffness. She carried a small glass ashtray in her right hand and offered me her left. Her tanned and braceleted jingly-jangly arm raised up like a drawbridge, and she said "Hello" in a voice that once must have been musical.

I declined Mrs. Blount's offer of "refreshment"—the bank would be closing at three—and resumed my perch on the sofa. The Blounts faced me from twin Chippendale chairs with lion's-claw feet across a glass-topped coffee table. My stained desert boots with the frazzled stitching were visible through the glass.

"You come very well recommended," Stuart Blount said, nodding and trying to convince himself of something. "Jay Tarbell tells me you have quite a reputation around, ah, Albany, and Jane and I are grateful that you could rearrange your affairs and consider our son's rather problematical situation on such short notice."

I said, "Luckily a hole opened up in my schedule." I was ready to join them if they clutched their sides and shrieked with laughter.

"Well, we're very fortunate then," Blount said, feigning credulity like a man who knew what was important, "because you've certainly got your work cut out for you. The police have been searching for William for nearly a week now, Mr. Strachey, and they haven't so much as turned up a trace of the boy. However, it's my understanding that you'll have access to resources that the police are, ah, unfamiliar with, relatively speaking." He gave me a strained smile. "We're certainly hoping that you can help us out, Mr. Strachey. Can you?"

They leaned toward me just perceptibly. I said, "What is it you want me to do?"

"Why—find our son. Wasn't that clear? And bring him home to us."

Maybe there had been a misunderstanding. "Let me get this straight. Your son is William Blount—the William Blount

4

who was charged this week with second-degree murder. He's the 'missing person' we're talking about here? Or am I confused?"

Jane Blount shot her husband an impatient look and removed a Silva Thin from a gold box on the coffee table. Blount shifted in his chair and said, "Why, yes, William Blount is our son. I thought you understood that—from the media coverage. Do you think you can locate the boy?"

"I might. And then what?"

"Then what? I don't follow."

"I mean, do you want me to gather evidence that will clear your son of the charge? That's what I'm usually hired to do in these cases. I've done it."

"Oh, *we'll* handle the legal end of it," Blount said, waving the matter away. "You'll simply *find* William and bring him to Jane and me. You won't need to concern yourself with the, ah, judicial processes, Mr. Strachey. That's all being taken care of."

"How so?"

Jane Blount lit her cigarette, which dangled from one corner of her mouth, and from the other corner she spoke to me with a pained earnestness. "Jay Tarbell is helping us out—he's a dear man, do you know Jay? And hopefully this ugly business can be cleared up with a minimum of upset for all concerned. It's been such a ghastly experience for Stuart and me, and we're terribly anxious for it to be over with just as soon as possible. But Billy, naturally, must take the first step by coming home and facing up to his responsibilities."

She sounded like a mother whose son had knocked up the trashman's daughter and a settlement was in the offing. She dragged on the cigarette and blew a stream of smoke up toward a humming little vent in the ceiling, which inhaled the cloud.

I said, "I know Tarbell by reputation. If anyone in Albany can get your son out of this, he's the one. I take it you believe your son is innocent."

They looked irritated. Not injured, not offended, just irritated. "Well, we certainly *hope* so," Blount said. "My God, I'd hate to think William was even *capable* of such a thing. But let me emphasize, Mr. Strachey, that the question of William's guilt or innocence is a matter to be dealt with elsewhere. That

5

end of it would be outside your purview, as I see it. Disposition of the case would be a matter for the courts to concern themselves with, wouldn't you agree? By way of preparation for that eventuality, however, perhaps you could give us an estimate on how long it might take you to locate William."

Something was screwy here, but I didn't know what. I'd had clients in similar situations, but none so chipper and optimistic as the Blounts. I studied them for a moment, with no result. I said, "No, I can't. Two days, a week, a month—it's hard to say. I'd have an idea in a couple of days of what I'd be up against. I'd need a good bit of help from you two."

"You'll have it," Blount said. "Will you take the case?"

"You understand that once I locate your son and he agrees to come home, you and Tarbell could meet with him and then he'd have to go straight to the police. That's the law. If he didn't, I'd have to report it. There'd be no funny stuff, right? Flying down to Rio or whatever."

I doubted this was what the Blounts had in mind, though it had happened to me once before. I'd rounded up a client's embezzler-husband, who, instead of turning himself in, flashed his three hundred thou to my client and the happy couple left together on the first flight for Brazil. I'd lost my fee and barely escaped an abetting-a-felony charge and sometimes regretted I hadn't followed on the next plane.

"Mr. Strachey," Blount said, "Jay Tarbell is an *officer of the court*. He has a reputation to uphold in this community, as do Jane and I. We're hardly about to jeopardize our good names by participating in a conspiracy to circumvent justice. As I say, we are confident that some formal resolution to the matter can be arrived at that will satisfy all the interested parties. I'm afraid you'll just have to accept my word on that." He gave me a sickly smile.

"I just thank God," Jane Blount put in, "that we live in modern times."

What were they up to? Stuart Blount had a reputation around town as a high-toned wheeler-dealer—suburban real estate, shopping malls, cozy connections with the politically well placed. And while I supposed there were jurisdictions in the State of New York where you could still get a murder fixed,

6

I doubted Albany County was one of them. In the thirties, I guessed, but not in 1979. Maybe the Blounts held a genuine abiding faith in their son's innocence and were confident that, with a nudge from them here and there up the line, justice would triumph. It was a topic they didn't seem to want to go into.

I said, "Have you already done a deal with the DA, or what? I like to know what I'm getting into. I've got a license to keep."

Jane Blount's eyes flashed and she sucked furiously on her cigarette. Her husband sighed deeply. They were taking some unaccustomed abuse from me, and I guessed I knew why.

"Mr. Strachey, it's all being worked out with the appropriate authorities, *believe* me it is. What we're counting on, you see, is that a, ah, prison sentence can be avoided—that some alternative approach to William's rehabilitation can be worked out—if you get my drift."

I didn't. "Are you talking about a tour in the Peace Corps, or what? Fill me in. What's new on the correctional front?"

"I can tell you this much, Mr. Strachey. Judge Feeney has already been consulted, and he has given his blessing to the program we have in mind, as has the district attorney. Does that reassure you?"

Killer Feeney. Maybe he was going to allow the Blounts to have their son hanged at home, from the family chandelier.

I said, "If your son is innocent, isn't all this dealing a little premature?"

Blount squeezed his eyes shut for a long moment. Then, deciding I was probably worth all of this, he opened them and gazed at me wearily. "Let me explain. I'm a realist, Mr. Strachey. In my business, I have to be. I *know* what the evidence against William is. It's all been laid out for me. No, *I* don't believe that my son killed a man. William is troubled, yes, but I can't accept for a minute the notion that William would take a human life. It's just that the situation is—rather an intractable one, wouldn't you say? Jay Tarbell has gone over the evidence with me, and he's given his opinion, which is not favorable. Jane and I have been over it and over it, and we're simply doing what we think we must do."

7

"Making the best of a sorry state of affairs," Jane Blount added.

I said, "My fee is a hundred fifty dollars a day plus expenses. If you agree to that, and to giving me your full cooperation, I'll take the case."

They relaxed. "Thank you," Blount said. "Thank you, Mr. Strachey, for placing your trust in us."

I didn't trust them any farther than I could toss their walnut sideboard. But there were aspects of the case that interested me—for one, both the accused and his alleged victim were gay—and there was the additional incentive of my needing at least $2.93 to cover the check I'd written after lunch at Elmo's. I decided to risk becoming involved with these people I neither liked nor understood and then figure them out as I went along. It wasn't going to be the first time.

I said, "Tell me about your son. When did you last see him?"

I'd done it again. They looked at me as if I'd just said, "Up above the world so high/Like a tea tray in the sky." Except this time my irrelevant gibberish had them squirming in their Chippendale seats.

"We haven't seen William since before the, ah, crime," Blount finally said. "I believe it was some weeks ago—back in the latter part of the summer, if I recall precisely."

"That's not very precise."

"Billy has a lot of growing up to do," Jane Blount said. She flushed under her terrific tan.

"What happened the last time you saw Billy? Tell me; maybe that will help me begin to understand your son." And his parents.

Blount sucked in the corner of his mouth and sat looking droll. His wife gave me a full frontal of her nostrils, sighed deeply, and spoke. "On the morning of August the eighteenth, Stuart and I drove down from our cottage in Saratoga. When we arrived, Billy was here in our house with—a man."

"Uh-huh. Then what?"

"If you've read between the lines of the newspaper accounts, Mr. Strachey, you must have deduced that our son

8

has—homosexual tendencies. Billy is easily influenced, and he had spent the night on that sofa you're sitting on, Mr. Strachey, with a—a gay individual."

Tact. She went on. "Of course we had words with Billy about his behavior, and he—he simply walked out on us. Billy refused even to turn over his keys to the house, and Stuart was forced into having the locks changed. We haven't seen or heard from Billy since that day, despite our repeated messages offering to help him—as we've tried to help our son find his way on so many occasions in the past. We love Billy, you see, and we are not going to give up on him."

Tendencies. I remembered seeing Billy Blount's by-line on articles and editorials in the local gay community news bulletin a couple of years earlier—though not, I thought, recently—and I doubted he shared this assessment of his sexual makeup. Also, I tried to remember whether I'd ever run into him myself—I glanced down at the sofa, but it didn't ring a bell.

I said, "Billy was living here?"

"He has his own apartment," Stuart Blount said. "Billy has been on his own for several years now, but of course he's always been welcome here. However, you have to draw the line somewhere, am I right? I'm convinced I did the right thing."

I supposed he had, though the family dynamics here were starting to betray a certain complexity.

Jane Blount stabbed out her cigarette in the little dish in her palm. She gazed down at the butt and warbled, "Jay Tarbell tells us you may have—could we call it a "special entrée"—with Billy's circle of acquaintances, Mr. Strachey?" She looked up at me with a clammy expectancy.

"We could call it that."

Blount pulled himself forward in a herky-jerky way and spoke the words. "Jay has mentioned to us that you are a, ah, avowed homosexual, Mr. Strachey, and that you can be counted on to be familiar with the, ah, gay life-style and, ah, milieu here in Albany."

"Yes, I'm gay."

"We're broad-minded," Blount said. He assumed a facial expression that resembled the work of an early cubist. "How

9

you live your life, Mr. Strachey, is none of our business. How William lives *his* life is very *much* our business. He's our only child, you see. He has no sisters or brothers."

Or siblings. "How old is your son?" I asked. "Mid-twenties?"

"Twenty-seven."

"He sounds old enough to make his own decisions."

"Despite our disagreements with Billy," Jane Blount said serenely, "he's always considered Stuart's and my opinions important. There's always been a kind of bond."

Scanty as the evidence was so far, I figured she had something there.

"You said you had words with Billy the last time you saw him. What did he say when he left?"

"Well—in point of fact," Blount said, shifting again, "Jane and I did the actual speaking. I did get a little hot under the collar, I have to admit. Billy did not express his feelings verbally. He simply walked out the door. With his houseguest."

Who probably never even sent a thank-you note. "Is that what Billy ordinarily does when he's angry? Walks away?"

Blount took on a martyred look. "Ah, if only he would! William's silence in August was hardly characteristic of our son, Mr. Strachey. When William becomes angry, he generally makes a speech—gives us all his propaganda." Or does a desecration number on the Blounts' Phyfe sofa. "But of course we've never bought it, all the slogans and so forth. Don't get me wrong, Mr. Strachey," Blount said, giving me his Picasso face again, "we respect the activists' positions, and we do not support legal discrimination against sodomites. But for William, it isn't the thing, you see? Not the road to the fulfilling type of life that is available to our son."

If Billy Blount was not an extremely angry young man, then he had to be a turnip. "What happens when I locate Billy and he refuses to drop by and hash things over with you two? That sounds to me like a distinct possibility. Bond or no bond, he's not likely to expect a sympathetic hearing from his family. Especially given the circumstances of the crime he's accused of."

Jane Blount went for another cigarette. Her husband

10

removed a sealed business-size envelope from his inside breast pocket and handed it to me. The printed return address was for Blount and Hackett, Investment Counselors, Twin Towers, Washington Avenue, Albany. "Give Billy this," he said. "It should make a difference."

I slid the envelope into my own breast pocket and could feel it find the rip at the bottom and begin to edge down into the lining. I asked what was in the envelope.

"That is private," Jane Blount said. "Private and personal. If Billy wants to tell you about it, that's his business. I doubt that he will. You just give it to him. He'll come home." She gave me a look that said, *Understood?*

Maybe he'd come home or maybe he wouldn't, but I didn't doubt that whatever was in the envelope was going to make an impression on Billy Blount.

I asked them to fill me in on their son's whereabouts, activities, and acquaintances over the past ten years, and for half an hour they rambled around the surface of Billy's social, educational, and occupational landscape. They offered little to go on.

Billy Blount had been graduated from SUNY/Albany with a degree in political science and then had taken a series of menial jobs. Currently he worked in a record shop. He hadn't lived at home since college, though his addresses were never more than eight or ten blocks from the family abode on State Street. This latter may or may not have meant something; Albany gays tended to live within walking distance of the bars and discos on nearby Central Avenue, and Billy Blount's unbroken proximity to his parents could have been coincidental. I'd find out.

The Blounts knew no names of their son's friends. They said his social circle was, they were certain, made up of "gay individuals," and they thought I might be acquainted with some of them. This was possible; gay Albany, though populous enough, was not so vast as San Francisco.

The Blounts gave me a photograph of their son. He was good-looking in a lean-jawed sort of way, with a broad, vaguely impudent smile, shortish dark hair, deep black eyes, and the obligatory clipped British military mustache. I thought, in fact,

11

that I *had* seen him around in the bars and discos. Given my habits and his, it would have been odd if I hadn't.

They provided me with Billy's current address on Madison Avenue, and a check for one thousand dollars, which I stuffed deep in my pants pocket. I said I'd report back to them within a week but that I had a few fiscal loose ends to tie up in mid-afternoon before I began work on their case. Stuart Blount walked with me to the door, shook my hand, made a point of squeezing my shoulder as he did so, and wished me "all the best of luck."

I had the feeling I was being used by these people in a way I wasn't going to like once I figured out what it was. Outside, the cold wind felt good. I ambled down State, turned the corner away from the park, and made for the bank.

2

BACK ON CENTRAL I CHECKED MY SERVICE, WHICH HAD A ONE-word message from Brigit: "books." I flipped through my desk calendar, picked a page in mid-December, and wrote: "Brigit—books."

The *Times Union*s for the past four years were stacked on the floor next to my file cabinet, and I hefted the top unyellowed half-dozen onto my desk. Starting with the Sunday, September 30 edition, I clipped all the stories on the murder of Steven Kleckner, which had been discovered on the morning of the twenty-ninth, and which now, six days later, Stuart and Jane Blount's renegade son stood accused of having committed.

The discovery story rated two columns on page one, a photo of the deceased, and a picture of two detectives standing in front of a house. Kleckner was clean-shaven and done up in a suit jacket and tie—in what looked like a high-school-graduation photo—with a bony, angular face and a big, forced, toothy

12

smile. He had a look of acute discomfort; maybe he'd hated high school, or maybe the photographer had just said, "C'mon, son, smile like your girl friend just said she was ready to go all the way," or maybe his shirt collar was too tight. High-school photos were always hard to read. The police detectives in the other photo looked grave, and one was pointing at a doorknob. No mention was made in either the caption or the story of the significance of this gesture. I made a note to "ck sig drnb." It was possible the doorknob was simply thought by someone to have been vaguely photogenic and redolent of criminal activity.

Steven Kleckner, aged twenty-four, the main story said, had been discovered stabbed to death in his bed at 7:35 the previous morning by Albany police. The department had received an anonymous call from a man who'd said only: "He's dead—I think Steve is dead," and given the address. Police had been admitted to the basement apartment on lower Hudson Avenue by the landlady, who lived on the first floor of the rundown brick building, one of the few in the neighborhood that hadn't yet been urban-renewed.

A long kitchen knife, its blade blood-soaked, had been found on the floor beside the bed on which the victim lay. There was no sign of a struggle having taken place or of forced entry into the "inexpensively furnished apartment."

Kleckner was identified as a disc jockey at Truckey's Disco on Western Avenue who had come originally from the village of Alps in Rensselaer County. He had lived in Albany for six years and was "a bachelor." The article did not mention that Trucky's was a gay student hangout near the main SUNY campus and that Kleckner was well known and well liked among the regulars there. Twenty years earlier the headline would have been YOUTH SLAIN IN HOMO LOVENEST, but discretion to the point of uninformativeness had set in at the Hearst papers. Or maybe it was just indifference.

The article did reveal that Kleckner, who had not worked at Trucky's on the fatal early morning but had spent most of the night there dancing and drinking with friends, was last seen leaving the bar around three A.M. "with a male companion."

A small sidebar contained remarks from people who knew

Kleckner back in Alps. His basketball coach said Kleckner was "a nice kid, polite, and kind of shy" who "didn't fool with drugs and didn't date much." The manager of a Glass Lake supermarket where Kleckner once bagged groceries called him "sort of bashful" but "reliable and well brought up." Kleckner's older sister, Mrs. Damon Roach, of Dunham Hollow, spoke for the family: "He was just a mixed-up kid, and he didn't deserve a thing like this. It's too late for Steven, but maybe other boys will learn a lesson from it."

A day later, on Monday, October first, the *Times Union* said police had identified the "male companion" as William Blount, of Madison Avenue, "son of a prominent Albany financier," and were seeking his whereabouts so that he could be questioned. The same article said the medical examiner had estimated the time of Steven Kleckner's death as five-thirty A.M. and had "stated his belief the victim died instantaneously from a single puncture wound to his heart." Also, for the first time, word was out: traces of semen had been found in Kleckner's rectum. No forthright speculation was offered on how the substance had found its way there, but Billy Blount, the murder suspect, was now identified as a "one-time gay activist" who had been chairman of the Albany-Schenectady-Troy Gay Alliance Political Action Committee in the early 1970s.

Follow-up stories over the next four days offered no new hard news, except that the DA's office now considered the evidence against Blount to be "conclusive," and a warrant had been issued for his arrest. Blount was being charged with second-degree murder.

The *Times Union* had not editorialized on the crime; moral inferences, for what they'd be worth, would have to wait. The paper did print a letter to the editor from Hardy Monkman, president of the Gay League Against Unfairness in the Media, taking the paper to task for its "insulting reference to a gay citizen's body" and including a "demand for equal time." Whatever that meant. The gay movement still had strength in Albany, but occasionally one of its leaders came forth with a public utterance espousing a notion and couched in terms of such sublime daffiness that gay men and women up and down

14

the Hudson Valley cringed with embarrassment or, as might have been the case with Billy Blount, said the hell with it and dropped out.

I slipped the clippings into a file folder which I marked Blount/Kleckner, then called Albany PD and learned that the detective handling the Kleckner murder was out of his office and wouldn't return until Monday.

I drove out Central to the Colonie Center shopping mall. At Macy's I picked out a black lamb's wool sweater and slipped it on under my jacket. I wrote out a check for forty dollars, signed it in a bold hand, and laid it on the counter in front of the bored clerk. He glanced at the check as if he'd seen one before, and then he glanced at me as if he'd seen one before. He looked familiar. I said, "Kevin—Elk Street?"

"My name is Kevin, but I live in Delmar. I don't believe we've met. No—no, I'm sure we haven't."

Like hell. "Sorry," I said. "I had you mixed up with a guy I once knew who'd drawn little valentines all over his buttocks with a ball-point pen. Inside the valentines were the initials of all the men who had visited there. It must have been another Kevin. Sorry. Funny story, though, isn't it?"

"H-yeah, ha ha."

The Music Barn record shop was along the main arcade of the shopping center, across from a long brick-and-blond-wood fountain that tinkled and hissed like an old toilet tank. Bernini in the suburbs. I spoke with the Music Barn clerk and was directed to the back of the store, where I found the manager opening up a carton of Donna Summer "On The Radio" LPs.

"She is that," I said.

"Who? Beg your pardon?"

"On the radio—Donna. Driving out here, I dialed around and picked her up on three stations. 'Dim All the Lights' once and 'No More Tears' twice. My own favorites, though, are 'Bad Girls,' 'Hot Stuff,' and 'Wasted.' Donna always cheers me up."

"She's okay, I guess, but she sure as heck isn't Patti Page." This was said with a straight face, no irony intended. He was losing his hair and looked to be a little older than I was, forty, and I guessed he'd had his good times twenty years ago and wasn't living his life backwards.

15

"I'm Donald Strachey and I'm a private detective." I showed him the photostat of my license. "Billy Blount's parents want to help him, and they've hired me to locate him."

He felt around inside his beige V-neck sweater, brought out a pair of glasses with pink plastic rims, and studied the laminated card. "No kidding, a real private eye! Jeez. I'm Elvin John, pleased to meet you," he said and offered his hand. I wanted to say, Hi, Elvin, I'm Nick Jagger, but I supposed he'd heard it before. His moon face and blinky blue eyes showed confusion.

"Billy's parents are helping the police capture him? Golly, I sure don't understand *that*."

I wasn't certain I did either, but I said, "They think it's best that he turn himself in and then let a good lawyer handle it. They're probably right. Billy can't have much of a life as a fugitive."

"They don't think Billy actually *killed* that guy, do they?"

"Well—no. I take it you don't either."

Elvin John set down the stack of records and shook his head. "Nope, I don't. Billy's a messed-up guy, I suppose you could say, and he *was* kind of mad at the world. But actually *kill* somebody? I'm no expert, but—holy cow, no. I don't believe it."

"You said Billy's messed up. How so,"

He gestured, and I followed him. We went into an alcove, where John slid onto a metal stool, retrieved a cigar from behind a carton of plastic bags, and unwrapped it. "When I say messed up, I don't mean what you *think* I mean." He gave me a knowing look and fired up the cigar, which definitely was not Cuban, though still possibly communistic. Albanian, maybe. "I don't know how broad-minded you are," John said, "but I'm tolerant of minorities myself, and I wasn't talking about Billy being a homo or anything like that." He said it with a trace of smugness, a challenge to my liberal sensibilities.

I said, "Good, I'm gay myself."

His pale eyebrows shot up. "Oh yeah? Jeez, you don't look it!"

"Well, you don't look Jewish either."

"I'm not. I'm Lutheran."

"Well then, you don't look Lutheran. You look—Methodist."

"I'm half. My father's a Methodist."

"I can always spot one," I said. "There's something about the way they move."

He gave me a wary look.

I said, "In what way was Billy Blount messed up?"

"Oh, just a little bit paranoid—well, not paranoid, actually—defensive. Always ready with some lip. Always thinking you were going to criticize him."

"Were you?"

"Heck, no. Billy was always a good worker—clean, neat, polite. And always on time, even when he showed up looking a little the worse for wear, which he sometimes did on Monday mornings. I asked him once when he was looking like an old sleepyhead if he'd had a heavy date the night before, and he said yeah, the date's name was Huey and he was a real hunk. Said it just like it was a woman, except he said 'hunk.' Lord, I didn't know *what* to say."

"If it had been a woman Billy had gone out with, what would you have said?"

"Oh heck, I dunno. 'Get any?'"

The quaint observances of the straight life. I said, "What was Billy defensive about? What would set him off?"

"Oh, just the one thing, really. The first time he told me he was gay, I won't forget that. I made a crack about a swishy kid who came in—nothing derogatory, you know, just a joke—and Billy really lit into me. He said *he* was gay and he'd appreciate it if I kept my homophobic thoughts to myself. That's what he called it, 'homophobic'—I'd never heard that word before. I'm from Gloversville, and nobody back home ever uses that word. Anyway, I said I was sorry, but he thought I meant I was sorry he was gay. He started carrying on like I was some kind of Hitler and I started to get mad, but then some customers came in and we dropped it. The subject came up again every once in a while, and to tell you the truth, I was sort of interested in hearing Billy talk. He's quite a speech-maker. Of course, I didn't always agree with him. He's just too much of a radical. Golly, I don't think most people give a hoot about anybody else's sex life, do they? C'mon now, admit it."

"Some don't," I said. "But you run into a surprising number who consider homosexuals as dangerous as the Boston strangler, but not as wholesome. This can make you edgy. Has Billy been in touch at all during the past week?"

"I've got his paycheck, but he didn't pick it up. He didn't show up Monday morning, and at first I was plenty ticked off. I called his home and he wasn't there, sick or anything. And then my wife called—she'd seen the paper—and she said Billy was wanted for murder. Gee whiz, I just couldn't *believe* it!"

"And you still don't."

He flicked his cigar ash in a tuna can. "No, not hurt somebody like that. He wouldn't, as far as becoming really violent. Billy's a talker. If he got mad, he'd just make a big wordy speech."

"It runs in his family."

"'Homophobic.' Whew."

"Did any of Billy's friends ever come in? I've got to locate some of them. I need names."

"Sometimes there were people he knew, but Billy never introduced any of them. It would have been nice if he had. After all, everybody's welcome here. You know, come to think of it, the one time I saw Billy get *really* upset, I mean lose control and just go bananas, wasn't with me at all. It was when a guy came in Billy *thought* he knew, but it turned out to be somebody else. This guy was just going out the door when Billy came out of the back room and saw him and started yelling *Eddie! Eddie!* and running after the guy. The kid turned around and looked at Billy like he was some kind of weirdo, and when Billy saw it wasn't who he thought it was, he came tearing back here and started cursing and throwing stuff around like he *was* a little bit nuts. Then he sat down and started shaking like a leaf and said he was sick, so I sent him on home. Billy scared the bejesus out of me that day. I'd never seen him act like *that* before."

"When did this happen?"

"Maybe six, eight months ago."

18

"Billy thought it was someone named Eddie? That was the name he called?"

"Yeah, but when I asked him who Eddie was, he said it was none of my effing business. Except he said the word. You know the one."

"Right. But you don't recall any other names of Billy's friends, other than Huey?"

"No, they'd come in sometimes, but I never knew their names. They'd buy the disco stuff. That's what the younger ones go for, you know. I mean the, uh, middle-aged ones, too. I mean—*some* of them." Elvin John shifted on his stool and took on a confused look.

"What do the elderly ones go for?" I said. "I'll make a note of it for future reference."

His round face tightened. "It sounds to me like you're pulling my leg. In a mean kind of way. You gays are real cynical, aren't you? I've heard that."

"With role models like Oscar Wilde, what can you expect? If only Eleanor Roosevelt had come out." I handed him my business card. "If Billy gets in touch, do him a favor and contact me before you call the cops. They've been in, right?" He nodded. "Just give me a day's head start and then do what you think you have to."

"Well, um—I'll have to think about that. I don't want to get in any trouble. You know?"

"I know."

He inserted the card in a plastic sleeve in his wallet. "Say, where do you think Billy might be hiding?"

"I've no idea."

"I suppose he might be with some other homosexuals, wouldn't you say? They tend to stick together."

"Many do."

"Maybe Billy went to San Francisco."

"Could be. To seek sanctuary with the Mother Church."

Elvin John burst into laughter. "Oh, that's rich! The Mother Church! Like it was the Catholic religion, ha! ha! That really cracks me up! Is that what they call fag humor?"

"Yup."

*   *   *

I had a bowl of chowder and a grilled cheese at Friendly's, made a note to check out Huey and Eddie, then called Timmy from the pay phone. He'd just gotten in and said he had a frozen pizza in the oven, and why didn't I come over?

I said, "The homosexual gourmet at work. A sizable discretionary income, the leisure time to refine one's tastes and skills—it's a good life."

"Right, and I suppose you're calling from Elmo's—no, it's the dinner hour—Wendy's."

"Friendly's."

"You going out?"

"Around nine. Should I pick you up?"

"Yes, and I want to dance. I'm keyed up. I spent the afternoon with a roomful of Democratic county chairmen."

"How about Trucky's? You won't run into too many county chairmen out there. Only two that I know of. Anyway, I have to go there."

"Sure. You have to?"

"Business. The Blounts called. I'm on the case. To find their son."

"I knew it. I'm involved with a man with a reputation."

"They did mention that I had credentials the Pinkerton Agency couldn't necessarily come up with."

"But I thought you knew a couple of Pinkerton guys who—"

"Closet cases. Think of the business Pinkerton must be losing."

"Two, three cases a decade at least. Do you have any idea where the Blounts' son is?"

"No."

"He did it, though, right?"

"The police think so. I haven't formed an opinion. The only thing I know for sure is that it'd be hard growing up in the Blount household without thoughts of homicide at least passing through your mind."

I drove back into the city through the Friday evening commuter traffic. Billy Blount's apartment was on the third floor of a white brick Dutch colonial building on Madison near

20

New Scotland. It was almost directly across the park from his parents' house.

The front door to the building was locked. I stood in the cold and peered through the heavy glass at the mailboxes in the entryway. One said "H. Pickering." A middle-aged man in a topcoat and knit cap came up the steps and inserted a key in the door. I followed him in and said, "Excuse me, isn't this Helen Pickering's place?"

Two bushy eyebrows went up. "*Harry* Pickering. *I'm* Harry Pickering. No other Pickerings live here. What do you want?"

I said, "I'm collecting for the Steve Rubell Defense Fund. Would you care to donate?"

A look of alarm. "You'd better leave, mister."

He shoved the door shut behind me and went up the stairs, glancing back once menacingly. I went and stood at the curb. Ten minutes later a woman in a trench coat and a pretty Indian silk scarf trudged up the stone steps with a bag of groceries. I tagged along.

"This Harry Pickering's place?"

"I think so," she said.

"You should get to know him. One of the sweetest guys you'll ever meet."

She smiled and entered a first-floor apartment, and I walked to the third. Blount's name was printed on a card on the door of 3-A. I went through the lock with a lobster pick that had been a wedding gift from Brigit's cousins Brad and Bootsy, and went in.

The living room, which looked out on Madison and the park, had off-white walls that were bare except for a big poster of the 1969 gay-pride march that had a lot of raised fists and looked like an ad for Levi Strauss. There was a daybed with a faded floral print coverlet and a couple of scruffy easy chairs. A bent coat hanger had replaced the antenna on a battered old black-and-white TV set. The newer, more expensive stereo amplifier and turntable sat on a board resting on cinder blocks, the speakers on either end. The two hundred or so records lined up on the floor between more cinder blocks were mostly disco, with some baroque ensemble stuff—Corelli, Telemann, Bach. No Judy Garland. The post-Stonewall generation.

The fake walnut bookshelves contained a row of old poli-sci textbooks, some fiction paperbacks—*Catch-22; Man's Fate; One Flew Over the Cuckoo's Nest,* other good modern stuff—and a collection of current gay literature: Katz's *Gay American History; Out of the Closets and into the Streets; Loving Someone Gay;* others. There was a nongay fifteen-year-old assortment of radical opinion: Cleaver, Jackson, Sol Alinsky, various antiwar writers, and a dusty hardback copy of Fanon's *The Wretched of the Earth* with a bookmark stuck a third of the way into it. He'd tried. He also probably had some politically aware friends who'd come of age in the sixties, making them close to my age.

The small kitchen was clean and appeared to have been little used. The old Frigidaire contained only an egg carton with two eggs, a bottle of Price Chopper ketchup, a pint of plain yogurt, three bottles of Valu Pack beer, and a plastic bag with enough grass left in it for maybe one joint. Another gay gourmand for Edmund White to visit.

The bedroom, in the rear, was furnished with a mattress on a box spring; the bed was unmade. On the floor beside the bed lay a copy of the August 27 *Advocate,* a half-full popper, a telephone, and a phone book. Four first names and numbers had been handwritten on the back cover of the phone book. I copied them down: Huey, Chris, Frank, Mark. Huey again. But no Eddie.

A single bureau was cluttered on top with coins, ball-point pens, old copies of the capital-district gay guide. No personal papers of any kind, not even an unpaid bill. Albany's finest had been there.

The dresser had three drawers. The top one was filled with summer clothing: tank tops, T-shirts, shorts, jeans. The bottom drawers were nearly empty, except for one ratty crew-neck sweater with a dirty collar and a pair of new corduroys with the price tag still stapled on—wrong size, lost the receipt.

The bathroom, a high-ceilinged pit with a dim light bulb about a mile up, had two racks clotted with dirty bath towels and appeared to be missing three items: toothbrush, toothpaste, razor. When Billy Blount disappeared, he'd had his wits about him and probably knew where he was heading: to a wintery place where the population observed habits of oral hygiene and

22

good grooming. This meant that I would not be searching for Billy Blount among the Ik people, which was a start.

I switched off all the lights and was about to depart when Billy's phone rang. I picked up the receiver and said, "Blount residence." No one spoke. I was aware, though, of a presence at the other end of the line. I said, "I'm Donald Strachey and I'm trying to locate Billy Blount for his parents, who want to help him. Who's this?" No response. Then, after a time, there came a sort of choked sound, and the line went dead.

3

I DROVE OVER TO MY PLACE ON MORTON. I COULD SEE MY BREATH in the air in the front room, went to the kitchenette, set the oven at 450, and opened the door. Ten days. Hurlbut the landlord would make steam October fifteenth, the day he left annually for Fort Lauderdale. Then I could grow orchids on the windowsill and fungus on my shoes until the old man reappeared to shut off his rain forest machine on March fifteenth, the first day of Hurlbut's summer.

I set the phone on the kitchen table, propped my feet on the oven door, and phoned three people I knew who'd been involved in the early days of the gay movement in Albany. Each expressed roughly the same opinion about Billy Blount: that he was a decent, likable young man, if slightly pushy and opinionated, who had dropped out of the movement several years earlier because he found the local organizations insufficiently radical in their outlook and tactics. Each man I talked to was skeptical of the official view that Blount had killed a man, but none had any idea where Blount had gone or even who his current friends were. I'd have to find out the hard way.

I flipped on the TV for the six o'clock news. Dick Block, action man for the anchor news team, was squinting into the camera trying to puzzle out the names and places of the day's calamities. Fresh news on the Kleckner murder was not among them. I stripped to my briefs and did sit-ups while Snort Harrigan grappled disgustedly with the sports report.

I remembered the envelope the Blounts had given me for their son. I dug it out of my jacket lining and slid it into the jacket of Thelma Houston's "I'm Here Again."

I went into the bathroom, showered, and shaved. I spotted a single white hair in my mustache, probed around and got a grip on it, and yanked it out. I checked my armpits, chest, and groin. No change below the neck yet. That was when you'd know it was for real.

I went to the daybed, set the alarm for eight-thirty, pulled the old Hudson Bay blanket over me, and slept.

"Tell me about the Blounts," Timmy said. "I get the impression they aren't exactly Albert and Victoria."

We were heading down Delaware toward Lark in the Rabbit. Timmy was beside me in a Woolrich shirt over a dark blue turtleneck and faded jeans the color of his eyes. I had Disco 101 on the radio—Friday-night pump priming—and they were playing Stargard's "Wear It Out."

"They're more like the duke and duchess of Windsor," I said, "by way of Dartmouth, Sweetbriar, and the Fort Orange Club. I think they might have a few vital parts missing. They talk as if their kid might come out of all this with the Nobel Peace Prize."

"Kissinger got one."

"Yeah, but the Albany County DA's office wasn't consulted."

"I heard they were. It was part of a deal worked out with the mayor, the Swedish Academy, and a vending company in McKownville."

"Ahhh."

We swung onto Lark.

"Even so, they must be upset with all the publicity. People with old Albany names like Blount prefer their names on downtown street signs, not in the newspapers. The social pages are okay, and then eventually a seemly obituary. But the front page is bad taste, pushy. It's for the Irish and the Jews."

"This is true. The missus especially is not pleased with the gay angle getting bruited about. She thinks that part of it's all a horrid misunderstanding, anyway. She says her boy has 'tendencies.'"

"A phase he's going through."

"The craziest thing is they seem to be looking at all this as some kind of opportunity—make the best of it, the missus said. They've got a weird relationship with their son. There's a lot of tension and bad feeling over the way he lives, yet he seems to keep coming back to them when he needs them or when he wants to embarrass them. They sound like they expect this recent messiness to lead to a big, wonderful final reconciliation. Or something."

"It'll be interesting to get Billy Blount's slant on the relationship."

"It will."

I turned up Central and found a parking place a few doors past the Terminal Bar. We went in.

On weekends the Terminal was misnamed. It was a relatively quiet neighborhood drink-and-talk pub where on weeknights people often dropped in for an hour or two. But on Friday and Saturday nights the bar was where a good number of gay men started out for the evening before ending up at the big shake-your-ass-bust-an-eardrum discos on up Central. Those who hung around the Terminal until four A.M. closing were mostly the "serious drinkers," many of them alcoholics, who sometimes, in moments of clarity, referred to the bar as the Terminal Illness.

We bought fifty-cent draughts and moved through the murk beyond the pool table and the bar to the back of the room, where we knew we'd find friends. One of the five tables was empty—it was just after nine, early yet. Another table was occupied by three theological activists in the gay Happy Days Church, gazing mournfully into their beer, pitched, as they always seemed to be, in medieval gloom. Happy days, glum nights, I guessed. Some fresh-faced SUNY students sat at another table in the company of an older admirer. Timmy and I spotted a couple of the Gay Community Center crowd and went over to their table as the Rae's "A Little Lovin'" came on.

"Where've you guys been hiding yourselves? Haven't seen you since—last night." Phil Jerrold, a lanky blond with a crooked smile and what Timmy once described as "a winning squint," shoved his chair aside so we could squeeze in around the little table.

"Is it tonight?" Timmy said. "I thought it *was* still last night. When I'm in here, I get mixed up. What night is it, Calvin?"

Calvin Markham, a young black man with the aquiline features and high forehead of an Ethiopian aristocrat, said, "I really wouldn't know the answer to that. I know it's October, because my hay fever's gone. That's as close as I can get, though. Sorry. What time is it?"

I said, "Nine twenty-six. At nine twenty-seven will you become cheerful and optimistic, or have you just been told you have third-stage syphilis?"

Calvin and Phil looked at each other. They began to laugh. "Clap," Calvin said. "I've got clap. I don't have the test results yet, but I know—I *know*—that I've got clap."

"Oh," I said.

Timmy said, "Maybe it's something else. Can you get hay fever of the crotch?"

"Not after the first frost," Calvin said.

We laughed, but Calvin didn't. "I'm getting another beer." He went to the bar.

"Where'd he pick it up?" Timmy said. "The tubs?"

Phil said, "It was the first time he'd been there in six months. Like Carter said, life is unfair."

"I thought Nixon said that."

"No, it was Carter. To the welfare mothers."

"Yeah, but Ford said it first, to the COs."

Timmy said, "No, I think it was Anne Baxter to Bette Davis, and when she said it, it made Thelma Ritter wince. Hey, can I say that? Are we still allowed to make Bette Davis jokes, or have they become politically incorrect?"

"It is politically acceptable," Phil said, "if you do it once a month, but not if you do it every ten minutes. That is no longer permissible. Thank God."

"Well, these *are* new times, aren't they? I think I feel an identity crisis coming on. You know, that's how I found out I was a homosexual. When I was seventeen, I was walking through the park and an older man pulled up beside me, leaned out his car window, and whispered a Bette Davis joke in my ear. I loved it, and all of a sudden I *knew*."

Phil said, "That's the most touching coming-out story I've ever heard. Where has sophistication gone?"

"To Schenectady, I think. A man was arrested in the bus station over there last week for impersonating Monica Vitti. Don't get me wrong, I mean I *love* trendy Albany, but really, I think you have to concede that progress is a very mixed blessing."

We conceded this unenthusiastically and drank our beer. Calvin came back. The juke box was playing "Good Times" by Chic.

I asked what anyone had heard about the Kleckner killing.

"Just what's in the papers," Phil said. "The cops still haven't found the Blount guy. They sure as hell better catch up with him fast and get him locked up. A lot of people are damn nervous with a gay psychopath running around loose, me included."

I asked Phil and Calvin if they had known Billy Blount.

"I remember when he used to come to the center," Calvin said. "He was kind of snotty and always going around acting like he was better than you were. Most people weren't too crazy about him."

"A lot of repressed anger," Phil added.

"Who are Blount's friends? Do you know anybody who knows him?" They thought about this but couldn't come up with any names. I said, "I'm looking for him, too. Blount's parents have hired me to find him."

"Jesus, no kidding. You think he's in Albany?"

"I don't know. I'm just starting."

"We should have known you'd get mixed up in that one," Calvin said. "The weird people you hang around."

Timmy said, "Thank you."

"I mean his customers—clients, or whatever they're called. Who was that one you were following around last month? The one with the pet pigs?"

"He wasn't the client. His wife was the client. She thought

he had another woman he was sneaking out to meet. What he had was a small pig farm out in East Greenbush. A secret pig farm. I caught the guy in the act of feeding his pigs one night—got some nice shots with the Leica, too—and then I started feeling sorry for the guy and went over and talked to him. I asked him why he didn't just level with his wife about the secret pigs, and the poor devil began to weep. He said she'd never understand, that it would destroy his marriage. He was an assistant commissioner in the Department of Mental Health."

Phil said, "Well, consensual pig farming is one thing, but getting involuntarily stabbed to death by your trick is definitely something else. A lot of the disco bunnies are scared shitless. Especially out at Trucky's. Blount *is* the one who did it, isn't he?"

"I don't know. It looks that way. How's business at Trucky's? Are people coming back? Truckman has had his hard times."

"Wednesday night was packed," Calvin said. "It was two for one. And people aren't going to the Rat's Nest much anymore. Not with the cops still hassling them. I heard on Monday they arrested the bartender and two customers. In the *middle of the afternoon* they busted in, and there were fifteen people in the back room!"

Timmy said, "It isn't just for breakfast anymore," and we groaned obligingly.

The Rat's Nest was a new place on Western Avenue about a mile beyond Trucky's, just outside the Albany city limits in the village of Bergenfield. It was what the papers coyly called controversial and was the Albany area's first "New York style" gay bar, with black lights, crumpled Reynolds Wrap on the ceiling, and nude go-go boys on a wooden platform that looked like an executioner's scaffolding.

In the back of the Rat's Nest was a separate grope room with a bartender in a dirty jock strap and lighting that would have caused a wildcat strike by any mildly assertive local of the United Mine Workers. The advertising slogan for the Rat's Nest was "Come in and Act Disgusting," and when it opened in mid-summer, there were those who predicted the place would be laughed out of existence.

It was not. The Rat's Nest boomed for nearly a month, drawing most of its hundreds of regular customers away from Trucky's, where "acting disgusting" was much rarer, more random, and not so aggressively institutionalized.

And then it happened. The Bergenfield police force began a series of raids on the Rat's Nest, arresting employees for serving liquor to minors, which may or may not have been the case, and busting patrons on dope, drunk and disorderly, and, in a few cases, consensual sodomy charges.

The crowds fled—most of them back to Trucky's, where the death by stabbing of a popular disc jockey caused a dampening of spirits and a jittery watchfulness, but no mass move to a less tainted nighttime hangout.

A couple of the Central Avenue bars, witnessing the unexpected popularity of the New Decadence, made gestures in that direction. One disco, teetering on the edge of extinction, changed its name from Mary-Mary's to the Bung Cellar and regained its wandering clientele overnight. Another bar was less successful. The owner of the Green Room attempted a "Western" motif by hanging a child's cowboy hat on a wall sconce, but this was not enough.

We left the Terminal at ten and made our way up the avenue, hitting all the gay watering holes and discos except Myrna's, the lesbian bar—an oversight that turned out to be a mistake on my part. I'd been an investigator for nearly fifteen years: army intelligence; the Robert Morgart Agency; four years on my own. But I was still learning.

I talked to the doormen and bartenders in all the spots we hit, and while some said yes, they knew who Billy Blount was and had seen him around, none knew him except by name and none knew who his friends were. I did not speak with the disc jockeys—they were absorbed in their art, like marathon runners or poker players—but I collected their names and phone numbers so I could check them out later if no leads developed elsewhere.

We lost Phil and Calvin at the Bung Cellar, then headed out Western and hit Trucky's, the bar where the murdered DJ had worked, at two-fifteen, when the disco night was peaking. Debbie Jacob's "Don't You Want My Love" was on when we went in. The place was jam-packed and smelled of beer, Brut, fresh sweat, cigarette smoke, and poppers. The dance area at Trucky's, in the back beyond a big oval bar, had flashing colored lights on the walls, on the ceiling, under the floor. It was as if Times Square of 1948 had been turned on its side and people were dancing on the neon signs. The music, pounding out of speakers the size of Mack truck engines, was sensuous and ripe, with its Latin rhythms and funky-bluesy yells and sighs, and the dancers moved like beautiful sexual swimmers in a fantastic sea.

Timmy and I made our way through the crowds along the walls, stopping to shout into the ears of people we knew, and danced for six or eight songs. We bought draughts then, and I made arrangements to talk to the bartenders after closing at four. Timmy headed back to the dance floor with an assistant professor of physics he knew from RPI, and I went looking for Mike Truckman.

The owner of Trucky's was not hard to spot. He'd been a famous football tackle at Siena College in the early fifties, and at six-three or -four and a mostly well distributed two-ten, he still cut a formidable figure in his pre–Calvin Klein white ducks and a bulky-knit black sweater that almost concealed the beginnings of a paunch.

I found Truckman in a corner uttering sweet nothings to and massaging the neck of a notorious hustler I'd seen on the streets but rarely in the bars. He was a smooth-skinned, athletic-looking young man with a smug, sleepy look and a green-and-white football jersey with the number 69 stenciled on it. Cute. I didn't feel bad about interrupting.

I'd met Truckman on several occasions, most recently at an early summer National Gay Task Force fund-raiser for which Truckman had donated the drinks, and he remembered me. I told him what I was doing. He stared hard at me for a few seconds, then slugged down a couple of ounces of whatever was in the glass he held and signaled for me to follow him.

We made our way past the disc jockey's glassed-in booth, turned, and went into an office with a thick metal door marked Private. I shut the door behind me. Truckman had been a bureaucrat with the New York Department of Motor Vehicles before he'd opened his bar two years before, and he'd brought his tastes, or habits, of office decor with him: gunmetal gray desk, filing cabinet to match, steel shelving along the wall. The bass notes from the speakers outside the door bumped and reverberated into the little room and made the metal shelves sing.

I said, "I feel like I'm in the basement of the Reichschancellery. I hope you're not going to offer me a cyanide tablet."

The crack was ill-timed, and Truckman did not laugh. He sat behind his desk, made further use of his half-full glass of what smelled like bourbon, and I hoisted myself onto a stack of Molson's crates.

"Whadda you wanna know?" Truckman said in a boozy-gravelly voice. "I'm cooperating with everybody on this thing, but I don't know what the hell else I can tell you. Christ, this fucking thing is just dragging on and on. Christ, I dunno. What am I sposed to do? Christ, I dunno. It's just a tragedy, that's what it is, just a fucking terrible, terrible tragedy."

He was drunk, and it had changed his personality from the one I knew. I remembered Truckman as a serious man, and sometimes agitated, but never morose and confused. I doubted that he'd made a habit of this. People who ran successful bars stayed sober. He brought a dirty white handkerchief out of his back pocket and mopped the sweat from his forehead and neck. He had a big, craggy face with a wide, expressive mouth and would have been matinee-idol handsome if it hadn't been for his eyes, which were cold gray and ringed with puffs of ashen flesh.

I said, "I'm sorry, Mike. I'm sure this is rough. Were you and Steve Kleckner close?"

"Whaddya *mean,* 'close'?" A sour, indignant look. "*Sure,* we were close, that's no secret. Christ, Steve looked *up* to me, you know? What I'm saying is, Steve *respected* me for how I was so up front about being gay and how I always did so much for the movement—one hell of a lot more than the other bar owners did, the assholes. Steve thought I had—Christ, you know—*principles.*"

He grimaced. A rick of milkweed-color hair stuck out over one ear, and I wanted to pass him my comb.

I said, "I didn't know Steve. What was he like?"

He squeezed his eyes shut with his free hand. "A nice kid," Truckman said, shaking his head. "Oh, such a nice sweet kid Steve was. But—naive. *God,* was that kid naive! Steve was naive, but he was learning, though, right? Steve was young, but he was catching on. We all have ideals, right? But you've gotta be tough in the way you go about it. A means to an end, right?"

He was beginning to slur his words. I said, "Right."

More bourbon.

I said, "Mike, you're drunk."

He shook his head. "Nah, I'm drinking but I'm not drunk. Anyways, Floyd's out there, the doorman. Floyd can run the place if I feel like taking a drink. Floyd can do it, right?"

I nodded. I asked him why anyone would want to hurt Steve Kleckner.

He rolled his eyes at some imaginary companion off to my right. "Christ, how would *I* know the answer to that? You'll have to ask the sonovabitch who did it, right? If the goddamn cops ever catch up with the little shit."

"You mean Billy Blount?"

"Hey, the Blount guy did it, dinnee? I thought *everybody* knew *that*—the kid Steve left with here that night. With here. Here with."

"Did you know Blount?"

"Nah, but I saw it happen—saw Steve and that little shit turn on to each other. I mean, don't get me wrong, right? I was glad to see it, honest to Christ, I was. I was glad to see Steve being so *up* for a change. Christ, moping around here the way he was, I just wanted to pick Steve up and shake him."

"How come he'd been down?"

Truckman emptied his glass and brought a new bottle of Jim Beam from his desk drawer. He kicked the drawer shut and filled his glass as well as a second one. He said, "Join me."

"I've got a stein of your fifty-cent horse piss outside. Thanks, I'll stick with that. Why had Steve been depressed?"

"Dunno. Maybe his rose-colored glasses fell off." He drank.

For an instant I wondered if Kleckner had actually worn rose-colored glasses, like Gloria Steinem's. It wouldn't have been unprecedented at Trucky's.

32

I said, "Had he talked about it?"

"Nope, unh-unh." He poured the drink for me that I'd declined.

"Had you ever seen Steve with Blount before?"

"Not that I remember. The cops asked me that. Fucking cops."

"Why 'fucking'?"

"Oh, you know, Don. *You* should know. Cops."

"Have they been hassling you?"

"Nothing to speak of. Drink up."

"Vigorish?"

"Nah. They fucking hadn't better try."

"What did you tell the cops about that night?"

"What all I knew, why shouldn't I? That Steve and the Blount kid danced, and horsed around, and left about an hour before closing. Shit, Steve could of done a lot better than that kid, a fucking *lot* better. And *now* look what happened! It's just a tragedy, that's what it is, a fucking terrible, terrible tra-guh-dee."

His eyes were wet, and he tugged out the hankie and wiped his face. Then, more bourbon. He said, "Don, you're not drinking."

I sipped. "Do you ever wish you'd stayed with the state, Mike? You had a nice neat, clean life down there."

He snorted messily. "Hah, that's all *you* know! At the department it was everything *but* murder. Hell, no! I'm doing what I wanna do, Don. And no way—*no way*—am I gonna lose it, right? You wouldn't. No way, baby."

I said, "Business looks good."

"Yeah. S'good." He gazed down morosely at his drink.

"I want to talk to your bartender after closing."

"S'up to them. Floyd'll be locking up. I'm cuttin' out at four."

"Heavy date?"

"H-yeah. Real heavy."

"The cute number in the witty jersey?"

"Nah," Truckman said. "Not him. He's for later." He shut his eyes and laughed bleakly at some private joke.

"Well, I suppose you could do worse."

"Oh, I *do-ooo* do worse." He gulped down the rest of his drink. "I sho nuff do. Hey. Don. How 'bout a drink?"

I guessed Truckman knew more about Steve Kleckner's recent life than he'd told me, but he was in no condition to be reasoned with, or pressured, or led. After Truckman's office the stench of smoke, poppers, and hot sweat outside it was a field of golden daffodils. I found Timmy at the bar talking—shouting— to a sandy-haired man of about thirty in a plaid flannel shirt.

Timmy leaned up to my ear and yelled, "I've got one!"

"One what?"

"One friend of Billy Blount's. Don, this is Mark Deslonde. Mark, Don Strachey."

He had soft brown eyes, a fuzzy full beard, neatly trimmed, and a tilt to his head that was angled counter to the slant of his broad smile. I didn't know whether he practiced this in front of a mirror, but it was devastating, and if Timmy hadn't been there it would have had its effect on me. Not that it didn't, a little.

I said, "Can we go somewhere?"

He smiled again and said okay and slid off his stool, and as we turned toward the door, Timmy cupped his hand over my ear and said into it, "You can do *me* a favor one of these days."

I said, "See you around—Tommy, wasn't it? I've really enjoyed myself and I hope we run into each other again sometime." I kissed him on the forehead. He laughed lightly.

Deslonde and I went out and sat in the Rabbit. The air was frosty, and a cold, luminescent half-moon hung over the motel up the road and across Western from Trucky's parking lot.

"You're friend is nice," Deslonde said, still grinning. "Is he your lover?"

"Sort of," I said. What the hell was I doing? "Well, yes. He is. We don't live together."

"That's smart. It makes discretion possible. I lived with my ex-lover for three and a half years. It was great for the first two. Until one of us started fooling around once in a while, and because we were living together, this was noticed. Nothing heavy, right? Just the occasional recreational indiscretion. But

34

Nate was Jewish enough, or insecure enough, to believe in monogamy, and that was the beginning of the end."

I said, "Do you have regrets?"

"Sure."

"Timmy says you're a friend of Billy Blount's."

"Yes, I know Billy. Your lover—whom you don't live with—says you're a detective. But not a cop, right?"

"Right. Private."

"Then you'd have a license."

I stretched out and dug my wallet out of my hip pocket. He studied the laminated card, and I put it back.

Deslonde said, "Smoke?"

"Love it."

He took a joint from his shirt pocket and lit it. We passed it back and forth while we talked.

"I'm working for Billy's parents," I said, determined to concentrate on something other than Deslonde's face. "They want to help him."

"I'm sure they do," Deslonde said evenly. I couldn't tell if he was being sarcastic.

"How do you know Billy?"

"My old roommate and Billy were involved for a couple of months, before Dennis freaked out and took off for Maine. Billy and I kept running into each other in the bathroom in the morning, and one day I gave him a lift out to Colonie. I work at Sears."

"Sportswear?"

"Automotive supplies."

Strachey, you ass. "Right," I said. "Billy works at the, ah, Music Barn."

"I live right up the street from Billy on Madison, and he started riding out to Colonie with me regularly. Sometimes we went out together, or with other people, out here or to the Bung Cellar. We got to be pretty good friends after a while. Billy's really one of the more stimulating people I know and quite enjoyable to be around. In fact, I've become very fond of Billy over the past few years. There's nothing sexual in the relationship; it just didn't work out that way. Billy and I talked about that once. We both found each other attractive, but sometimes the chemistry just isn't there, right? And then other times it is." He looked at me and grinned.

"Yeah," I said. "Funny how that works." I could feel the damn thing stirring. I said, "Where do you think Billy might be?"

"I have no idea."

"Do you think he's innocent?"

"Yes. Of course he is."

"How can you be that certain?"

"Because I know that Billy hasn't got a violent bone in his body."

"Uh-huh." I shifted, tried unsuccessfully to cross my legs. "I've gotten the impression that Billy is rather an angry young man. How does he let it out?"

Deslonde laughed. "Yeah, Billy is not one of the more relaxed people I know. What he does with all that indignation is he runs off at the mouth a lot. He can bend your ear for days on end about the world's four billion homophobes. I'm a realist myself—I told him maybe he ought to shop around for another planet."

"Maybe he's the realist. We seem to be stuck on this one."

He rolled down the window and flipped the roach onto Trucky's gravel drive. He exhaled and said, "For some of us the realistic thing is to find a way to eat and pay the rent. Try coming out as a radical faggot when you spend thirty-eight hours a week at Sears Automotive Center. I don't mean to sound melodramatic, but I thought you'd understand that. Or are you independently wealthy?"

He looked at me with his beautiful skewed smile again, but this time there was a hardness in his eyes. I wanted to do something to show him how I really felt about him. I shifted position again.

"I know what you're saying," I said. "There's neurotic secretiveness, and then there's discretion. I am not opposed to discretion. I've even been known, from time to time, to indulge in it myself."

What had I said? He'd been watching me, and now suddenly he burst out laughing, a big robust ha! ha! ha! ha! He gave my thigh a quick squeeze and then, still smiling, lit another joint.

36

I said, "About Billy Blount—remember him? Billy Blount?"

"Oh, right. Billy Blount. Let's talk about Billy some more." He grinned and passed me the joint. Our fingers touched.

"What about, uh, Billy's parents? How was his relationship with them?"

"They must be a pair," Deslonde said. "I've never met them, but Billy talked about them sometimes, and they sounded like real horrors. Tight-assed old family types. He wasn't crazy about them, and Billy was frustrated with the way they hated his being gay. But I wouldn't say they really preyed on his mind much. He just stayed clear of them, and that made life easier."

"They said he brought a trick to their house last month."

He shook his head and laughed once. "Oh, boy, what a screw-up. I'd asked to use Billy's apartment that night—my straight cousin was job hunting in Albany and staying in mine, and I had a friend I was going to sleep with coming up from Kingston—so Billy said I could have his place and he'd take his chances in the park. It was one of those gorgeous hot nights, and you knew everybody'd be out. So he meets this hunk from Lake George, see, and he's really turned onto this guy, but they've got no place to go. It was dumb—Billy knew it—but they went to the Blounts' place, which was right across the street. His parents weren't supposed to be back from Saratoga until Labor Day, and—well, you know the rest. Bingo."

"No, actually I don't. I was wondering what they managed to accomplish in the way of sexual bliss on that mahogany museum piece?"

He looked uncomprehending. "Come again?"

"They spent the night on Mrs. Blount's antique sofa. Or so I've been told."

"That's crap," Deslonde said. "They spent the night in Billy's old room. They were downstairs smoking and about to leave when the Blounts busted in with guns blazing. They were pissed, and Billy really was embarrassed. I don't think he's seen them since."

"So his relationship with his parents was strained and unhappy. But there was nothing about the relationship that struck you as—a little weird?"

"Weird? No. Awhile back—a long time ago, it must have

been—the Blounts did something that still makes Billy furious when he thinks about it, something that hurt him a lot. But he never told me what it was. It was something so painful he couldn't even make himself talk about it. But since I've known him he hasn't been bothered by them very much. It's as if they hardly exist."

Another new perspective. Why was I surprised? It was nearly always like this, *Rashomon* with a cast of sixteen.

I said, "I've got to find him and talk to him. He hasn't been in touch with you?"

"No, I wish he would. I'd like to help him."

"Who are his other friends? Somebody might know something. Has he ever mentioned out-of-town friends?"

"Here in Albany there's a guy named Frank Zimka who Billy sees once in a while. We've all gone out together a few times. He lives off Central—Robin or Lexington, I think. Sort of a weird guy, actually; he deals dope, and I get the idea he hustles. I could never figure out what Billy saw in him, and when I tried to find out, Billy didn't want to go into it. He just said something like, 'Oh, Frank can be fun sometimes.' Except if Frank was ever a barrel of laughs or whatever it is he has to offer, it definitely was not in my presence.

"Then there's a black guy over in Arbor Hill Billy sleeps with once in a while. I met him a couple of times, too, and they seemed to have a nice *simpático* relationship. Nothing very intense, but nice. His name is Huey something-or-other. He's a construction worker or something and he's into martial arts. I think it's Orange Street he lives on.

"Out of town, I don't know. Billy had some radical gay friends once who live on the West Coast now, I think, and he might be in touch with them. When he quit the movement in Albany—the guys here are too wishy-washy for Billy the revolutionary—he talked about moving out to California, but by then his friends' organization, whatever it was, had fallen apart, so he didn't go. I don't know what their names are out there."

Frank and Huey were two of the first names written on the back cover of Billy Blount's phone book. Along with Deslonde's and one other.

"Did he ever mention somebody by the name of Chris?"

"No," Deslonde said, trying to remember. "I don't think so. Who's he?"

"I don't know. A name Billy wrote on his phone book. And a number."

"Call him up. He might be helpful. Or cute. And discreet." He chuckled.

"I will," I said, shifting again. "What about an Eddie? This would be someone out of Billy's past he'd be excited about running into again."

Deslonde shrugged and shook his head. "Unh-unh. Never heard of him. No Eddie."

"You mentioned your old roommate. Dennis, was it?"

"Dennis Kerskie."

"How long ago did he leave Albany?"

"More than two years ago—almost three. Dennis went off to the forest in Maine to live off berries and write his memoirs."

"Was he an older man?"

"Twenty-two, I think. He and Billy were a hot item for about two months until one day Dennis suddenly decided to purify his body and give up french fries, Albany tap water, and sex. He'd read a leaflet somebody handed him in the Price Chopper parking lot, and his and Billy's relationship deteriorated very rapidly. Dennis left town about two weeks later, and I don't think Billy ever heard from him again. I know I didn't."

It was ten to four and people were starting to drift out of Trucky's and head for their cars.

"Just a couple of other things. Were you with Billy the night he met Steve Kleckner?"

"For a while, I was. I gave him a lift out here, but then he got this heavy thing going with the Kleckner guy, and when I was ready to leave around one, Billy said to go ahead, he had a ride. I told all this to the police. Should I have?"

"It happened. I'm sure they got the same story from other people, so don't sweat it. How was Billy acting that night? Unusual in any way?"

"No, I wouldn't say so. He looked like he was having a good time. Actually, so was I. I'd met this tall number named Phil and went home with him. Real nice. Somebody I wouldn't mind running into again."

"Blond, with a squint?"

"That's Phil. Do you know him?"

"He's at the Bung Cellar tonight. He'll probably end up in the park. Another fresh-air freak."

Deslonde looked at his watch, then did his head-smile thing. "Maybe this night won't be a total wipeout after all."

I gave him a quick, tight smile. "Right. It's early." I hiked out my wallet again and gave him my card. "Do Billy a favor and call me if you hear anything, okay?"

"Business cards. That's a new twist." He did it again.

"I do this for a living."

"I'll bet you do."

He got out of the car, then leaned back in through the open door. He smiled and said, "See you around, Don. Meantime, don't do anything discreet."

"I'll check it out with you before I do," I said. "You're the expert."

He laughed. We shook hands, and he shut the car door. He walked toward the other side of the parking lot. He looked back once and grinned. I watched him go and sat for a minute concentrating my mind on a bowl of Cream of Wheat. Then I went inside.

Timmy was just coming off the dance floor. "Where did you go to talk? The Ramada Inn? Mark has a way about him, doesn't he?"

I said, "He was helpful. How did you find him?"

"He found me. I was asking around about who might know Billy Blount when Mark walked up to me and said, 'I don't know where you came from, but I love you.'"

"He didn't."

"You're right, it was different. I was standing by the DJ's booth, and he very shyly edged up and asked if I'd like to dance. I acquiesced."

"You raise acquiescence to a high art."

"*I* do?"

"One of us does. Whichever."

The music stopped. The thirty or forty people left in the place began drifting toward the front door. Fluorescent lights came on, turning all our faces a hideous gray. People walked faster. Mike Truckman moved unsteadily toward the cash register, removed a wad of bills from under the tray, stuffed it into his jacket pocket, and exited with the crowd.

I talked with the bartenders while they gathered up glasses and ashtrays and empty bottles. They added little to what I knew. On the night before Steve Kleckner was found dead, Blount and Kleckner had danced and drunk together, seemed to everyone to have hit it off famously, then left Trucky's around three. The bartenders noticed all of this because Steve Kleckner had been depressed and preoccupied the previous two weeks—Kleckner had refused to tell anyone why—and with Billy Blount, he had snapped out of that. No one had seen them together before.

None of the bartenders knew Blount except by face and first name, but they all knew Kleckner. None could think of anyone who particularly disliked Steve Kleckner, who invariably was described as happy-go-lucky and a real nice guy. Not helpful. I did learn, however, that the person who knew Kleckner best was an ex-roommate named Stanley Loggins, who lived with his lover on Ontario Street—and that Steve Kleckner had once had an affair with Mike Truckman.

4

I WAS UP BY TEN. TIMMY SNORED LIKE A MASTODON WHILE I RAN four eggs and a pint of orange juice through the blender. I showered, found some of my clothes among Timmy's clean laundry, left a note, and drove over to Ontario Street. My job was to find Billy Blount, but it wasn't going to hurt if I learned more about the sort of man he'd been attracted to. In fact, I guessed there were even better reasons for looking into Steve Kleckner's life, but I didn't know yet what they were.

Stanley Loggins, in green chinos and a lavender T-shirt, was pixielike, with bright pink eyes and buck teeth. His lover, Angelo, was big and beer-bellied and had hands like hair-covered coal shovels. They sat side by side on an old brown sofa with antimacassars marching up and down its back and arms, a Woolworth's Mary-with-a-bleeding-heart hung on the wall above. Angelo eyed me suspiciously and swigged from a quart bottle of Price Chopper creme soda while Stanley told me about Steve Kleckner.

"Yeah, we roomed together for two years," Loggins said, his girlish voice cracking like an adolescent's. "Until I met Angelo, and then Steve moved down to Hudson Avenue. Jesus, if I hadn't met Angelo, maybe Steven would still be here in this place—*alive!*" His little eyes bugged out.

Angelo said, *"Fuck* that shit!"

"Angelo, I wasn't *accusing* you, for chrissakes, now come *off* it!"

"Daaaaa!"

I said, "Tell me about Steve."

"Oh, he was such a nice boy, *rea-l-l-ly* nice. Very into music and all. Music was his way of life—like Patti LaBelle, ya know? I just can't *believe* it that Steven is—that he doesn't even *exist* anymore. Last week he was here, and this week he's just—*gone.* I never knew anybody who died before. Except my stepfather, and he was such an *asshole.*" Angelo looked away in disgust.

"Were you and Steve good friends?"

"Oh, yeah, Steven and I were very tight. I mean, we lived together and went out and all. Till I met this ol' *grump* here. Mister stay-at-home. But Steven and I still kept in touch, gabbed on the phone and all. Steven usually called on Monday and we'd yackety-yack about the weekend. He'd tell me all the dirt that went on and all, who's doing who. God, I can't *believe* he's never going to call again, I just can't *believe* it. Gives me the creeps. *Iggghhh!*" He shivered.

"Who were Steve's other friends?"

"Oh, the jocks, I guess. He hung around mostly with the jocks. Steven was very into music, ya know?"

"I know. What about Billy Blount? Do you have any reason to believe he and Steve had known each other before the night Steve died?"

Loggins looked away. "No. Steven always told me about all his hot tricks. No. He would of said." He glared back at me as if

I were somehow responsible for what had happened to his friend. "Ya know, I don't even know who this Blount asshole *is!*"

"Right. I've yet to meet Blount myself. What about Steve's love life? Did he ever have a lover?"

Loggins screwed up his face. "Sa-a-yyy—can I ask you something personal?"

"Sure."

"Are you gay?"

Angelo watched me, ready to pounce if I didn't come up with the right answer. Except I wasn't sure what the right answer was. I said, "I wouldn't have been run out of Blooms-bury Square."

Angelo's lips moved as he repeated this to himself.

Loggins tittered and said, "Well, personally I've never been to San Francisco, but I get your message."

I said, "Who were the men in Steve Kleckner's life that he talked about?"

"How much time have you got, about a *day?*" He tittered again. "No, I'm just kidding. Really. Steven played around some, like we all do—I mean *used* to do." He squeezed Angelo's thigh; Angelo smirked lewdly. "Steven never got into anything heavy, though. Not like *Angelo* and I. He went mostly for one-nighters, ya know? No hassles and all. Except that gets *so-o-o* tired after a while, right, Angie?" Angelo belched theatrically. Loggins said, "Do you have a lover, Donald?"

"Yes, I do. His name is Timmy."

"Well, I hope he's like Angelo."

"Thank you. What about Mike Truckman? I heard he and Steve were involved at one time."

"Yeah, Steven and Mike were getting it on for a while, right after Steven started working out there. But that was *ages* ago. Two years ago, it must have been. It didn't work out. Mike was too old for Steven. I kept *telling* him that. Steven liked to have a good time, dance and go out and all, but Mike's idea of partying was to sit home and get sloshed and then grope around and fall asleep. The pits, Steven said. And Mike was *so-o-o* jealous. Steven couldn't even look *cross-eyed* at another guy without Mike having a conniption fit. Steve broke it off finally,

43

but they stayed tight, even what with Mike boozing it up more and more and starting to fool around with whores. Really *sleazy* lays, Steven said they were. Even still, Steven really loved Mike, I think. But more like a father. He looked up to him and all. *Used* to, anyway."

"Used to?"

"Yeah. It was sad. Something bad happened. A bummer."

"What was it?"

"I don't know. Steven wouldn't tell me. Just that it was something *incredibly* tacky that Mike did. About three weeks ago. It really got Steven down, whatever it was."

"Steve didn't say anything about what it was? Nothing at all?"

"Steven said he'd tell me about it sometime, and I know he would've, but—but—oh, God!—poor *Steven!*" It had caught up with him. He shuddered once, lowered his head, and began to tremble.

Angelo pulled Loggins against his chest, looked at me, and said, *"Fuck* this shit!"

I waited until Loggins had recovered and gulped down some of the creme soda Angelo shoved at him. I said, "Just one last thing. What about Steve's family? Was he in touch with them?"

"No—" He snuffled. "They were on the outs." Angelo pulled a Valle's Steak House napkin from his back pocket, and Loggins blew his nose in it. "Steven's folks live over in some hick place in Rensselaer. Last Christmas Steven told his sister he was gay, and she told his mom, and his mom asked him if it was true, and Steven said yes, and you know what Steven's mom said? She started screaming and she says, 'Oh, *please,* Steven, *please* don't have an operation! *Please* don't have an operation!' And then his dad came home and threw him out. He had to thumb back to Albany, and it took him *three rides* to get back here. He never did figure out what his mom meant by don't get an operation. Sex change, I guess. Who the fuck knows."

Angelo said, "He shouldna told his sister. Bitch! Never tell a woman *nothin'!*"

44

"Oh, Angelo, you're such a sexist asshole! Quit being such a fucking pig, would you *pu-leez!"*

"*Daaaaa!"*

At one I put four Price Chopper frozen waffles in Timmy's toaster oven. He handed me his old Boy Scout hatchet and said he'd pass. I said, "*Fuck* this shit," and ate an apple. Timmy said he'd do dinner at seven and had to spend the afternoon at the laundromat.

I drove over to Morton. Summer was back, and the air was hazy and sweet. High mackerel clouds swam across the sky over the South Mall, recently renamed the Nelson A. Rockefeller Empire State Plaza in memory of the man who had caused the great granite bureaucratic space station on the Hudson to happen. Back at the apartment the heat, inexplicably, was on. Hurlbut must have forgotten his golf bag and come back. I opened all the windows.

I checked my service—no calls—then dialed the number for Chris. There was no answer. Frank didn't answer either, but I reached Billy Blount's other friend, Huey, and told him I was looking for Billy. He said he doubted he could help but that I could drop by around three. His voice sounded familiar.

I did sit-ups and push-ups, jogged around Lincoln Park for half an hour, then showered, put on jeans and a sweat shirt, and drove back up Delaware. Huey lived on Orange Street, between Central and Clinton, in one of Albany's two mainly black neighborhoods. As I climbed the front-porch stairs of the small frame house with its three or four tiny apartments, I knew I'd been there before.

"I *thought* I rec-a-nized that sexy voice," he said. "How you been, baby?" A smile spread across his shiny dark face, and his eyes were bright with sly pleasure. He had on a vermilion tank top and cutoff shorts and was barefooted. He'd told me during the night I'd spent with him a year or so back that his tight, neat, muscular body was "the finest in Albany." He'd said it with delighted satisfaction and no trace of embarrassment, and for all I knew, which was a good bit, he might have been right.

In Huey's living room I sat on the old, worn, boxy couch

45

with little strands of silver running through the black uphol-stery. I said, "Your voice sounded familiar, too, except I could have sworn the voice belonged to a guy I once knew named Philip Green."

He threw his head back and laughed. "Did I call myself that? Yea-hhh, well. You know how it is, baby."

I knew. "I'd hoped I'd run into you again," I said loudly.

He turned down the volume on Disco 101—M's "Pop Music" was on—and sat on the chair that matched the couch. He smoothed out a fresh white bandage that was wrapped around his exceedingly well developed upper arm and said, "That would have been sweet. We sure had a real good time, as I remember, Ronald."

"Donald."

Laughing, he leaned over and squeezed my ankle. "Can I get chu somethin' to drink? A Coke or a glass of wine or somethin'—*Dahn*-ald?"

"You can. A Coke."

He went into the kitchenette. There was no evidence that anyone other than Huey was staying in the apartment. I could see into the small, windowless bedroom. The bed was made. The clothes piled atop the old dresser beside it looked like garments Huey could get away with wearing, but not Billy Blount.

"Too bad this ain't a social visit, Donald." He handed me a Coke in a Holiday Inn glass. "Even if you *are* a cop." He sat down and looked at me.

I said, "I'm a private detective," and showed him my license.

"No shit." He examined the card carefully. "How you become one of these dudes? Take a test?" He handed it back.

"You have to have three years' experience as a police, army, or agency investigator, pass an exam, and hock the family jewels to get licensed and bonded."

"Must be in-ter-estin'. You *been* a cop?" His smile was strained.

"Army intelligence."

"Ooooo, a spy! That sexy."

"That was a while ago. Now I'm on my own and I'm looking for Billy Blount."

46

"Yeah. You said." He lit a Marlboro. "How come you lookin' round my place, Donald? I don't truck wit no desss-per-ah-does."

"Your name was written on Billy's phone book."

"Yeah. Sergeant Bowman come around, too. Asshole come out here a hell of a lot quicker than the cops who come last night. Took them suckers half an hour to show up after I called, and meanwhile I'm bleedin' like a stuck pig. Some sumbitch busted in here to rip me off, and when I caught him, he cut me. See that?" He raised the bandaged arm. "Eight stitches! Guess I was lucky, though. Coulda been ninety-two. This is what you call your high-crime neighborhood, Donald."

"It was a burglar who cut you?"

"Yeah, I know about the routine. First the dude calls to see if I'm home. This one called *twice* last night. I answer the phone and there's no one sayin' anything and he hangs up. Checkin' to see if I'm home, which I am, with a friend I run into earlier over at the Terminal. Then around two in the mornin' my friend leaves and I guess this dude's watchin' the house, see, and thinks it's *me* goin' out, and he comes in that winda there. I was just goin' to sleep and I hear this fucker and I get up and I'm gonna jam his nose right up into his brain, see—I do martial arts, right?—except the guy's got a knife and he cuts me and it's so dark he's back out the winda—head first, I think—before I can kick his balls up his ass. There'd a been lights on, they'd of carried that dude outa here on a stretcher. Anyways, I think he ain't comin' back. Not if he don't want his neck busted off."

"Did you get any kind of look at him?"

"Too dark. Average-size guy, and I'm pretty sure white with light hair. But I doubt I'd rec-a-nize him on the street. Guess I better get the lock fixed on that winda. Been meanin' to for six months."

"Yeah, you should. Look, I might be way off base, but—how do you know this was a burglar?"

A bewildered look. "I don't get chu, Donald."

"Well—it's like this. You know that Steve Kleckner was stabbed in his apartment in the middle of the night just a week ago. The people who know him don't think Billy Blount

47

committed the murder, and it's possible—do you see what I'm saying?"

He blinked, and I could see the icy tremor run through him. He said, "Nah. Nah, no way. That bad stuff go on all the time around here, Donald. Shee-it. Nah. I don't believe it was the freak who done that murder. This was just some shit-ass dude after my stereo. I didn't even *know* that Kleckner boy. Had nothin' to do wif his friends or anything."

"But you know Billy Blount. The, uh, intruder—he didn't look like Billy, did he?"

He gave me a cold, hard look and said, "No. Billy I'd know. I know Billy."

"Sure. You would. And you're right; there's probably no connection. But you'll get that lock fixed, right?"

"Sure, Donald. If it'll put your mind at ease." He grinned. "Wouldn't want chu to worry about ol' Huey unless you was gonna be here to worry 'bout me in person and we could cheer us *bofe* up. Ain't that right, baby?"

"Just get the lock fixed," I said, ambivalence swelling like a doughy lump in my lower abdomen. "Knowing that you're safe will cheer me up enough for now."

He chuckled.

I said, "Fill me in on Sergeant Bowman's visit. What did you tell him?"

His eyes narrowed, and I could see the perspiration forming on his forehead. "I told him, 'Yassuh, no suh, yassuh, no suh.'" He laughed quietly. "Motherfucker called me some nasty names." He dragged deeply on his cigarette.

I said, "I'll meet Bowman on Monday. He sounds like a treat. I take it Billy hasn't been in touch."

"Unh-unh. I wisht he did. I could help him out."

"How?"

"Hide him out wif some friends of mine."

I said, "It's obvious you're among the many who don't think Billy did it—killed Steve Kleckner."

He contained his impatience with my belaboring what was plainly absurd to him. "No. Not do a thing like that. Not Billy. Now, what else do you want to know, Donald. Just don't ask me no more questions that might make me mad. Okay, baby?"

"Then tell me what you know about Billy. If he didn't do it,

48

I want to help get him out of this. But I'm going to have to find him first."

Huey slouched in his chair and fingered the bandage on his arm. "Billy's a sweet man, that's what. One of the sweetest men I've had the pleasure to meet around Albany. Present company excepted." He leered pleasantly. "We've had some very enjoyable times together, Billy and me."

"Did you go out together much?"

"Sometimes we'd go dancin'. At the Bung Cellar, or Trucky's if we could get a ride. Mostly we'd just hang around his place, or he'd come over here. Just listenin' to music, and smokin', and lovin'—that's what we bofe liked mostly. A sweet, nice man."

"When did you last see Billy?"

"'Bout a week before the thing happened. Spent the night right there on that couch you're sittin' on. He gets up Sunday mornin', says so long, and that's the last I seen him. I was about to call him when I seen on TV what'd happened."

Billy Blount the sofa fetishist. "Is this a hide-a-bed?"

"Yeah, folds out. Billy couldn't stand my bedroom. No windows. Freaked him out. Made him all antsy. I figgered maybe he'd done time wunst, but when I axed him he said unh-unh. Wouldn't of figgered, anyways. Billy went to college. I done ten months at Albany County Jail myself—told Billy about it and it made him mopey. Made *me* mopey, too, baby! I was seventeen. Breakin' and enterin'. And I'll tell you, Donald, I ain't gone back in. Them places fulla booty bandits! Me, I like to pick and choose. I'da choosed Billy any day. A sweet man, Billy."

I asked him where he and Billy had met.

He chuckled. "Where did you and *me* meet, my man?"

The great outdoors. "Who are his other friends in Albany? Anybody he might go to or get in touch with?"

He looked a little hurt with the idea Blount might have closer, more relied-upon friends. He shrugged. "Maybe some guy name-uh Mark who rode us out to Trucky's coupla times. White dude wif whiskers. And Frank somebody. I never seen that one—I think Billy mostly just bought dope from him. Got some for me wunst when my dealer was busted.

"And then there was this chick, I think, too. We run into

49

this chick up at McDonald's on Central one night, and Billy goes out to the parkin' lot for about an hour, it seemed like. I seen 'em outside in her little V-dubya buggy. I got pissed and tired of waitin' and went out and stood, and then Billy come along. Says she's the finest woman he knows and if things was different he'd marry her. How about *that,* huh?"

"What was her name? Do you remember?"

"He didn't say. Just called her his lifeboat, or lifesaver, or somethin'. Billy's a trip. I'da never figgered he went for women, but you never know. I've even been known to indulge myself every now and again, though naturally I try to keep it under control. How about yourself, Donald?" He grinned.

I said, "These days, half the human race is enough for me. Though, I have a lover now."

"Ahh, that's nice, Donald. Truly. I had a lover wunst. Melvin. He was my true, true love. We was together for five bee-*yoo*-tee-ful years. Lotta good times—till the Lord called Melvin away."

"Oh, no. He died?"

"Shee-it, no. Become a preacher. Took *Jesus* as his lover. And I just couldn't compete with *that* man, baby! Melvin's out in Buffalo now savin' black folks' souls. Oh, he still pays me a visit from tahm-tew-tahm. Just on very *special* o-*kay*-zhuns." He laughed and shook his head at something that went beyond Melvin.

I said, "What about Chris? Did Billy ever mention a guy named Chris?"

Huey lit another Marlboro. "No. That one don't ring a bell. Who's Chris?"

"I don't know yet. The name was written on Billy's phone book. How about Eddie? This would be someone Billy knew once that he'd be happy about running into again."

He shook his head. "No. No Eddie I can think of. Don't know who that would be. Billy had folks, of course. That's who you workin' for, right?"

"Yes."

"They wasn't close. It's good they helpin' the boy now he needs a helpin' hand. I'm glad."

"Did Billy ever talk about them?"

"Nothin' much. 'Cept they carried on like the wrath o' the Lord about him bein' a ho-mo-*sex*-ual."

50

"We all have parents. Mine don't know. They've let it be known they'd rather not."

He dragged on his cigarette and blew the smoke out slowly. "My folks don't much mind—or don't let on, anyways. I got a gay uncle who's a big shot at Grace Baptist down home in Philly. My brothers is straight. They don't hassle me. I been lucky, I guess." He looked at me and smiled. "Say, get chu another Coke? Some wine? A smoke?"

It would have been nice to linger with Huey—for about forty-eight hours. Disco 101 was playing Earth, Wind and Fire's "The Way of the World."

I said, "No. Thanks. I'm working. Another time."

He said, "Mmm-*hmmm*. Another time. You got it, baby."

I gave him my business card. "Call me if you hear anything, right? And get that lock fixed."

"You're on. You find Billy and bring him back, hear? You want to get in touch, I'm at Burgess Machine Shop—I'm a welder—and nights you'll find me out and around."

I got up to leave.

"Huey, one more question. Tell me if it's too personal. Ready? Here it comes. What's your last name?"

His face lit up, and he came over and hugged me. "Brownlee. Hubert Brownlee. Think you can remember it?"

I said, "Until I get to the car. Then I'll write it down."

We kissed for a minute or two, and then I maneuvered my way down the stairs like a drunk, made it to the Rabbit, got out my pad, and wrote: "Huey Redmond." But it didn't look right.

5

I REACHED FRANK ZIMKA FROM A PAY PHONE ON CENTRAL. I explained who I was and what I wanted, and he said, "I can't talk to you," and hung up.

I tried Chris again. No answer.

Frank Zimka's address was in the phone book, so I drove over to his place on Lexington.

Zimka's name was taped to the mailbox of the basement apartment in an old brown shingled building. To get to it you had to crouch down and lower yourself into a concrete well under the wooden front steps. I knocked on the door glass, which rattled in its frame. The chipped porcelain doorknob hung from a string coming out of the spindle hole.

The door was slightly cockeyed—or the building around it was—and when Zimka opened it, it scraped across the threshold in jerks.

"Yes?"

His young body was slim and well proportioned in wrinkled khakis and a once-white T-shirt, and he looked at me suspiciously out of a haggard, peculiarly aged face. His eyes and curly hair were of an indeterminate color, as if something had caused the hue to weaken and fade out. The bone structure of his face was that of a classically handsome young man, but the lines of age were already set, and there was a shadowy tightness around his eyes. He looked like the result of some crazy secret Russian experiment in which a forty-five-year-old head had been grafted to the body of a man twenty years younger.

I said, "I'm Donald Strachey. If you're a true friend of Billy Blount, you'll want to talk to me. I don't believe he's guilty, and I'm going to help him get out of this." It was the first time I'd said this out loud, and when I said it, it sounded right.

Zimka gave me a blinking, blank-eyed look, as if I'd interrupted a restless sleep. "Billy's out of town. I don't know where he is." He started to scrape the door shut, then thought of something. "Billy's not in jail, is he?"

"He hasn't been found. I hope to find him soon. Can I come in?"

He blinked some more and gazed down at the leaves and debris at our feet. Finally he said, "I'm crashing, but suit yourself."

He turned and went inside, and I followed, dragging the door shut behind us. Mark Deslonde had told me that Zimka dealt dope but not that he used it. Though it figured. I'd get what I could.

We entered a low-ceilinged living room with a gas space heater on a dirty linoleum floor, an old green couch, a discount-store molded-plastic chair with chrome legs, and a lamp with a shiny ceramic panther base on an end table. A tin ashtray was full of white filtered butts. I could see a small kitchen through a doorway, and the place stank mildly of garbage. Through another doorway I could make out an unmade double bed under a dim red light bulb.

Zimka sat on the plastic chair and lit a Kent with a butane lighter. I sat on the couch. I said, "You mentioned that Billy's out of town. How do you know? Has he been in touch?"

He dragged deeply on the cigarette, as if it might contain nourishment. His dazed look came back. "Who did you say you were? Tell me again."

I got out the card. "I'm a private detective, and Billy's parents have hired me to find him. I'm not a cop, and don't judge me by what you might think of the Blounts. I've met some of Billy's friends, and I think I share their opinion that he's innocent. Do you?"

He brought his heel up to the edge of the seat and hugged his leg. He lay his cheek against his knee and said quietly, "I wouldn't care what Billy did."

"I can see that you're very fond of him."

He tensed. "Maybe I am. You really would not understand."

"Would it help if I told you that I'm gay, too?"

"A gay—detective?"

He looked at me as if I'd told him I were a homosexual table lamp.

"I'm sure there are others. I've met two. Generally they don't announce it. It's been changing a little, but law enforcement is not one of the nation's bastions of enlightened social thought."

"That's funny," he said mirthlessly. "A fag real detective. I knew some of the TV detectives were gay." He mentioned a famous television sleuth who had once passed through Albany and caused a sensation at the Bung Cellar when it was still Mary-Mary's. "But he's just an actor," Zimka said glumly, "not a real detective. Actually, I probably should have done that myself. Been an actor. I'm a pretty good one—Billy could tell you about that." A hurt, bitter look.

"It sounds like a complicated relationship you have with Billy. Complicated and very close."

He sat motionless for a long time, blinking and breathing heavily. Then, his voice breaking, just barely audible, he said: "I love him."

He pressed his forehead hard against his knee and shut his eyes tightly. The hand with the cigarette was up next to his ear, and I watched it, afraid his hair might catch fire. The smoke curled up through a shaft of dusty sunlight coming in through a window with plastic sheeting over it.

I said, "Are you and Billy lovers?"

He looked up at me with wet, angry eyes. "That's not what I said. I said *I* love *him*."

"Right. I get your meaning. That's hard."

He said, "Yes. It is." He got up and stubbed out the cigarette in the dish full of butts. "You want a white? I could use one."

"How about a beer? It's hot again."

He went to the kitchen and came back with a Schlitz for me, a glass of water and a white pill for himself. A church key was on the end table, and he opened the bottle.

"This is a treat," I said.

He sat on the plastic chair, popped the white, and washed it down. Then he lit another cigarette.

"You know where he is," I said. "Don't you?"

He closed his eyes and shook his head. "No. I don't know where Billy is. I wish I did. Maybe I'd go there. Though I guess I wouldn't."

"But you know he's not in Albany."

"Billy's somewhere a long way from here. I know that. I lent him the money."

"The morning it happened?"

"Early in the morning. He came over here." He gave me a hard, questioning look. "You know, I don't even know you, do I? How do I know I can trust you?"

"You don't know. It's a risk you're taking. You strike me as someone who takes risks."

He laughed sourly. "Yeah. I do. Look—if—if I tell you what I know—will you give Billy something from me when you find him?"

"Sure."

"You promise?"

"I promise."

"And you won't tell the police?"

"I will not."

He sighed. "Okay," he said, working up to it, shifting, putting his feet on the floor. "Okay." He sucked on the cigarette. "This is what happened. As far as I *know,* this is what happened. I don't know *all* of what happened, right?"

He waited.

"Right," I said. "Just what you know."

"Okay. Okay, then. Well—around six that morning Billy came and banged on my door. I almost didn't wake up—I'd had a busy night." He gave me a look, and I acknowledged it. "Anyway, I let him in, and I could tell he was nervous and scared. He said—he said somebody had stabbed the guy he went home with—some new guy he met out at Trucky's—and the guy was dead. That he'd felt his pulse and he was sure the guy was dead."

"Billy saw the stabbing?"

"No. He didn't say that. But I guess he didn't see it, because he didn't know who had done it."

"A threesome. Maybe they'd picked up a third guy on the way to Kleckner's place."

"Billy didn't mention that. I don't think he would've, anyway. Billy's pretty straight in a lot of ways."

"How could he not see it happen if he was there?"

"Well, he must've—I don't know. Maybe he'd gone out."

"At five in the morning? And then come back?"

"You don't believe me."

"I believe you. What else did he say? Try to remember his words."

"He just said, 'Steve is dead, the poor guy is dead, and they're going to think I did it.' He said, 'They're going to try to lock me up.' He said that about a hundred times, I think. 'Shit, they're gonna lock me up and throw away the key! They're

55

gonna zap me good!' Billy was really freaking out, and by that time I was starting to feel pretty freaky, too."

"Had Billy been locked up before?"

"I think so. I don't know. He would never talk about it. Whatever it was."

"So he came here and said these things. What happened then?"

"He wanted me to lend him money."

"What for?"

"Well, for *plane fare,* what *else?*" A sharp, hyped-up tone now—the dexie had reached his bloodstream.

"Did you lend it?"

"Of course."

"How much?"

"All I had. Almost two-forty."

"Two hundred forty dollars? You keep a good bit of cash around."

"I deal. Grass, some hash, pills. And I hustle." He waited for me to react; I didn't.

"Where was Billy planning on flying to?"

"He wouldn't tell me. He said he had friends who he knew would help him, but they wouldn't want anybody to know where they were."

"What else did he say about them? These friends."

"That's all."

"What happened next?"

"I drove Billy to New York. He asked me to."

"New York City?"

"La Guardia. He was afraid he might see somebody he knew at the Albany airport. We stopped over at his place first and he brought a suitcase."

"What kind of car do you have? Describe it." I thought I believed him, but any kind of verification of his story wasn't going to hurt.

"I don't have a car. A guy I know lets me use his sometimes."

"At that time of day?"

"If I ask, this guy helps me out. He likes me. Do you?"

"Sure. I like you. Who's the owner of the car?"

56

Zimka rolled his big, drugged eyes. "You've heard of him. But I'm sure he'd *prefer* I didn't mention his *name*." He giggled.

"So you picked up the car."

"I called my friend first and then I walked over and got the car—this guy's place is right over by the park on Willett—and then we picked up Billy's suitcase and drove out to the Thruway."

"What did you talk about during the ride down?"

"Us. We talked about us."

"You and Billy."

"Yeah. Me and Billy. I told him how I felt about him. For the first time I told him how much he meant to me."

"Was he surprised?"

"Shit, no. He knew. Nobody could experience what I've experienced with Billy and the other person not know. There's sex, and then there is—mak-ing *lov-v-v-ve*." He impersonated Marlene Dietrich.

"In my experience it's not always that clear-cut," I said. "Are you saying that in bed you were making love and Billy was just getting it off?"

He grinned inanely. "I'm not going to tell you about that. It's humiliating. It's none of your business. When are you leaving?"

"Soon. How long have you known Billy, Frank?"

"Three years. Three years next month. November fourteenth." His cigarette had burned itself out; an inch of ash fell onto his pant leg and lay there. "I met him over at the Terminal one night," Zimka said. *"He* cruised *me*. And I really thought that night that he liked me. That he liked *me*."

"But he really—didn't?"

"It's too complicated. I'm not going to talk about this anymore. Not to you. You're about to leave. It's too bad it'll never work with Billy and me. Really too bad. He's been great for me. Billy opened up a lot of positive things inside me I never knew were there. It's too bad. I can be a really *fabulous* person. Are you leaving now?"

"I'm sure you can be. I'll leave soon. What happened in New York?"

"New York?"

"At the airport. La Guardia."

"I dropped him off."

"What time?"

"Nine. Or nine-fifteen."

"You didn't go in with him?"

"He wouldn't let me. He said he'd send me the money, he thanked me, he gave me a little brotherly kiss. And then he—*took off!*" He imitated an airplane.

"You drove back to Albany then?"

"No."

"No?"

"Fucking Billy took every cent I had! I had no money for gas or tolls coming back." He giggled. "So what I *did* was, I stopped in Scarsdale and called a guy I knew. Scared the royal blue shit out of him, too. He met me at a gas station and says, 'Nice to see you, Frank,' tosses me fifty, and took off in his BMW like I'm diseased. He's one of my admirers. He likes me."

Every life tells a story. "How old are you, Frank?"

"How old do you think?"

"Twenty-four."

"Twenty-six. My face looks fifty."

"I would have said thirty, or thirty-five. Still, maybe you should be looking into a somewhat more restful line of work."

"I'm a chemist," he said. "I graduated RPI *cum laude.*"

"Why don't you work as a chemist, then? Or at something else in the sciences, or whatever, that you might be good at? Why not try it—maybe just something part-time to start out?"

His eyes were like baby spotlights now. He said, "I think I'll get a job as the president of MIT!" He laughed idiotically.

I drank my beer. I asked Zimka whether he'd had any odd phone calls recently in which the caller didn't speak but just listened, or whether anyone had tried within the past week to break into his apartment. He looked at me as if I'd asked him if his hair were on fire, then giggled. I asked him if he knew who Chris was, and he summoned up the clarity of mind to say no. I asked him if he knew who Eddie was, and this caused another fit of uncontrolled hilarity. Finally I asked Zimka if the police had been in touch—his number was written on Billy Blount's phone book. He said yes, but he'd told them he was the Queen of the Netherlands and they hadn't returned.

I thanked him, gave him my card, and asked him to get in touch with me if he heard from Billy Blount or if the money Billy had borrowed was returned in any manner. He asked me to stop by on Monday to pick up something he said he'd have for Billy, and I said I would.

I shook his hand and left. He may or may not have noticed my going.

6

AT TIMMY'S I CHECKED MY SERVICE WHILE HE MADE MASHED potatoes to go with the roast chicken. He used a real masher, and I admired his domestic skills. At my place I boiled the potatoes, put them in a Price Chopper freezer bag, and beat them with a hammer wrapped in a towel.

There were two messages, one from a former client who owed me three hundred dollars. He said, "The check is in the mail." The other message was from Brigit: "Books will be found on front lawn after noon Sunday."

I asked, "What's the weather forecast?"

"Showers or drizzle later tonight," Timmy said. "It's supposed to clear late tomorrow and get cold again."

"Crap."

Brigit's new husband and his four daughters were moving into our old place in Latham, and they needed the room where I had my books stored. The Rabbit wasn't going to do the job, and Timmy drove a little Chevy Vega.

I said, "Brigit means business about the books. We'll either have to make six trips or rent a U-haul."

"We?"

"Would you help me move the books, please?"

"Yes."

"She says noon tomorrow, then she chucks them out. She's a sweetheart."

"Right, you've been so busy for the past month." He dropped a brick of frozen peas into a saucepan.

I said, "The heart has its reasons."

"For not picking up a load of books?"

"Don't confuse the issue. Brigit hasn't been nice."

"It's a diabolical retribution—books."

"One does what one can."

"It's the final break. That's why you've been putting it off. This is really the end and you won't face it." He took the chicken out of the oven and set it on the trivet on the table.

"Not true. The final break was three years ago. In a courtroom with portraits of two Livingstons, a Clinton, and a Fish." I began hacking away at the chicken with a bread knife. Timmy winced.

"Why don't you let me do that? You carve the mashed potatoes." I went looking for a serving spoon. "The *final* final break," Timmy said, "will come when Brigit smiles warmly and shakes your hand and says, 'Heck, Don, at least we had seven wonderful years. I understand and sympathize and there'll be no hard feelings on my part.' That's the final break you're waiting for, except it's not going to happen."

"I can't find a spoon."

"Middle drawer."

"How come I keep getting mixed up with people who devote their lives to explaining me to me? Brigit did that. It's a powerful force to constantly contend with."

"Nature abhors a vacuum."

"Like the poet said, fuck you. Anyway, I make my way in the world. I understand enough of what's going on. I do all right."

"That you do."

"You don't make it easier."

"Of course I do."

I said, "You're right. You do. Let's eat."

*   *   *

60

Over dinner I told Timmy about my two visits with Billy Blount's friends and what I'd found out about Blount. "It turns out he's not so morbidly attached to the duke and duchess as I thought he was. That's just how they see it—or want others to see it. In fact, he seems reasonably stable and in control of his life. And sufficiently resourceful that he knew just where to go when trouble happened. He went somewhere you can fly to for two hundred forty bucks."

"That could be just about anywhere these days. You can get to London for under a hundred and fifty."

"Not from La Guardia. That'd be JFK. I've got to find somebody who can check passenger manifests. Deslonde says Blount once had friends on the West Coast. He could be out there."

"Maybe he flew under another name. It's easy."

"Could be. He was thinking."

"The cops could check. Are you going to tell them?"

"Later. In due course. Are there more rolls?"

"In the oven."

"The people who know Blount best speak well of him. Everybody says he's likable and fun to be around, though a bit verbose and dogmatic. But he's got no real hangups that get to people, and certainly no violent streak. He does have some private grief he keeps inside—an irrational, or possibly entirely rational, fear of being shut in or locked up. Something that happened to him once. Huey and Mark and Frank Zimka all mentioned it. I'll have to check that out with the Blounts. It would explain his panic to get away, even if he hadn't committed the murder."

"Or even if he had."

"Yeah. There's that."

"He didn't tell Zimka *anything* about how it happened?"

"Not much. Either that, or Zimka is holding something back—or even making the whole story up. This is possible; Zimka's brain couldn't have survived its owner's life unscathed. Zimka may lie as naturally as he blinks. Anyway, for what it's worth, Blount was there, Zimka said, but he didn't actually *see* the stabbing or the person who did it."

"He was in the bathroom. Had to piss."

"How long does that take?"

"Or brush his teeth."

"When you used to trick, did you carry a toothbrush?"

"That was too long ago. I don't remember. How about you?" He looked up at me from his plate and then down again.

"And another thing is, I can't figure out Blount's connection with Zimka. His other friends, so far, are nice wholesome folks. Like Deslonde, for instance."

"Right," Timmy said. "Like Mark."

"I liked Huey and Mark and saw what Blount saw in them. Zimka, on the other hand, is badly screwed up—not entirely lacking in the decenter instincts, but he's a slave to some unholy habits, and when he's down off his pills, his outlook on human life is decidedly gloomy. Why did Blount hang around a guy like that? There's a side to Billy Blount I don't understand yet."

"Money. You said the guy had ready cash. Blount used him."

"For what? Blount had no expensive habits. None that I know of." I looked at my empty plate.

"Coffee?"

"Yeah, I guess. And the knife attack on Huey what's-his-name last night. It probably doesn't have anything to do with Blount or the Kleckner killing, but still—have you ever heard of a white burglar operating in Arbor Hill?"

"That might be a first."

"Mm. It might."

"So. What's next?"

"There's a guy by the name of Chris I have to check out. And there's a woman Blount evidently was close to. Huey saw them together once."

"Ahh, a mystery woman. In an evening gown and black cape? Maybe it was Megan Marshak."

"In a VW bug. That's all I know about her. This one might slip through my ordinarily ubiquitous dragnet."

"Oh, I doubt that. You know, you're going to an awful lot of trouble to find Billy Blount, when the fact is, everybody who knows him well is convinced he's not a killer. If Blount didn't do it, shouldn't you be giving some thought to who did?"

"I'm doing that."

"Ideas?"

"None worth mentioning. Not yet."

Timmy got up and started clearing the table. "What are we doing tonight? Working or playing?"

"Let's make the regular stops and see what turns up."

When we left the Terminal at nine forty-five, a light rain was falling. I went back in and called U-Haul on the pay phone and reserved a van for eleven-thirty the next morning. Then I called Brigit and told her to expect us around eleven fifty-nine.

We made our way up Central, paying the usual Saturday-night calls, and drove out to Trucky's just after midnight.

It was another good crowd. A sign by the door said five percent of the take that night was being donated to the Albany-Schenectady-Troy Gay Alliance, and a good number of the local gay pols and organizers were on hand, self-consciously clutching their draughts and trying to blend in with the looser, more blasé types who were always readier to roll with whatever life shoved at them.

When we went in, Bonnie Pointer's "Heaven Must Have Sent You" was on, and whenever she growled "Sex-x-xyyy," the younger, less inhibited dancers yelped and shouted. I wondered what Norman Podhoretz would have made of it.

Truckman himself was at the door, tipsy and unkempt in green work pants and an old gray sweat shirt. He pulled me aside and asked me if I'd found Blount. I said not yet, that it might take awhile.

"Well, you keep at it," Truckman said, looking grim and nervous, "because the goddamn cops aren't going to do a thing."

"You mean because the victim was gay?"

"You've been around, Don. You know."

"Times have changed a little—"

"What?" He leaned closer in order to hear. The DJ segued from Bonnie Pointer into Nightlife Unlimited's "Disco Choo-choo."

63

"I said *times are changing*—partly because of guys like you, Mike. And anyway, as far as anyone knows, this is the first gay murder in Albany. Its novelty must have piqued a certain amount of curiosity among our jaded constabulary."

"Have you been in touch with the cops?" He leaned even closer to hear my answer to this, and I could smell the bourbon on his breath.

"Monday—I'll be seeing Sergeant Bowman on Monday. Do you know him? He's the one in charge."

"No." He shook his head. "Not that one."

"The thing is," I said, "even when I find Blount—I'm not so sure he's the one who did it."

Timmy came from the bar, handed me a draught, and stood listening.

Truckman glared at me, swayed boozily, and said, "Oh, he did it, the little asshole! And you just better catch up with the little sonovabitch before he does it again. The *cops* aren't gonna do it. You can't trust the fucking cops."

I nodded. "Yeah. I suppose you're right."

Truckman looked at me a moment longer. Behind the cold gray of his eyes there was anger, and hurt and, I thought, a kind of pleading. Then, abruptly, he turned and went back to the door to resume his lookout for minors, riffraff, and straight couples from Delmar in search of wickedness.

We started for the dance floor.

Timmy said, "I think you're right. Mike knows more about this than he's telling."

"He acts that way. Though guilty appearances are often deceiving. I do know he's been less than forthcoming on the subject of his relationship with Steve Kleckner."

"Should I say it?"

"Yes."

"I hate to."

"Say it."

"Where was Mike that night?"

"Here."

"Till when?"

"Four, at least."

"And what time did the—thing happen?"

"The killing. It was a killing. It happened around five-thirty."

"You could look into that."

"I could."

We passed some people we knew from the Gay Alliance and stopped to talk—shout. Taka Boom's "Night Dancin'" came on. The guys from the alliance told us some friends of theirs had arrived at Trucky's from the Rat's Nest and reported that it had just been raided again by the Bergenfield police. This time it was violations of the building code. Jim Nordstrum, the owner, had lost his temper and started screaming about the US Constitution. It hadn't helped. They'd gotten him for disturbing the peace. The alliance was considering joining Nordstrum in a court case—though with a certain reluctance owing to the bad press the alliance would get by affiliating itself with an establishment of the Rat's Nest's rather too special ambiance.

Timmy, a sometime Catholic who was pretty consistently repelled by the darker side of gay life—just being homosexual was decadent enough for his Irish sensibilities—nevertheless volunteered to help set up a legal defense fund if the alliance chose to go ahead. The pols said the organization was divided over the matter but would decide soon. Timmy said he'd stay in touch.

We made it back to the dance floor and danced for eight or ten songs, then decided to break after Michael Jackson's "Don't Stop Till You Get Enough." For the moment we'd had enough.

Back at the bar I said, "When I was twenty-five, one of the things I wanted most in life was to go to bed with Paul McCartney, who was around twenty-one. Now I'm forty, and one of the things I want most in life is to go to bed with Michael Jackson, who's around twenty-one. What does this mean?"

Timmy said, "There won't always be youth, but there will always be youths."

We drank our beer. The DJ was playing Peter Brown's "Crank It Up."

"Hi there, big guy, you come here often?" A deep voice from behind me. Apprehensive, I turned. Phil Jerrold was laughing silently. Mark Deslonde was with him.

"Thanks," Deslonde said, doing his smile-and-tilted-head thing. "He was where you said he'd be last night."

I said, "Donald Strachey—Private Investigations—Discreet Introductions."

"Actually, we'd met," Phil said, smiling a little goofily.

Timmy said, "Maybe you'll run into each other again sometime. And each of you certainly hopes so."

They both grinned, Phil with his squint, Deslonde with his whiskers and angles. Timmy was right; they were looking very couple-y.

Timmy, in the two-and-a-half years I'd known him, had threatened at least once a month to compose a song that started: "I fell in love—in Washington Park/With a man who'd remarked on the weather," but he'd never gotten around to finishing it. I knew the moment was once again upon us.

Timmy said, "I'm going to write a song someday that starts . . ."

I sang along, and Phil, who'd heard it too, joined in.

"The trouble is," Timmy said then, "nothing apt rhymes with weather."

Phil said, "Feather."

I suggested, "Tether."

Deslonde said, "How about 'sweatshirt'?"

We looked at him. We all laughed together, except for Deslonde, who looked embarrassed and said, "I majored in business."

Later, as we were about to leave, Deslonde asked me whether I'd made any progress in locating Billy Blount. Phil and Timmy went back to the dance floor for one last spasm, and Deslonde and I stepped out into the cool quiet under Trucky's portico.

I said, "No, but I've got a couple of ideas. Do you know about a woman in Billy's life? Someone he might be fairly close to?"

"He never mentioned any," Deslonde said. "If there is one, it'd probably be platonic. Billy told me he knew he was gay when he was sixteen, and that he's never had any sexual interest in women at all. He said a shrink his parents once sent

66

him to kept talking about his 'confused sexual identity,' but Billy said it was the *shrink* who was confused, that the guy couldn't understand plain English."

"Our mental-health establishment at work," I said. "Mob rule under the guise of science."

"I went to a sane one once. He was okay. Pretty cool, in fact, and smart. Where did you hear about the woman?"

"From Huey what's-his-name. He's seen them together."

"What about Frank Zimka? Did he know anything? Creepy, isn't he?"

"Frank has his problems. But, yes, he was helpful."

"He must have talked to Billy not long before it happened. He was out here that night."

"Here? Zimka was out here the night of the murder?"

"I saw him in the parking lot around one when Phil and I were leaving—that was the night Phil and I met." The head thing again. I loved it. "Zimka was sitting in the car parked beside mine," Deslonde said, "with the window rolled up. I figured he had the air conditioner on; it was a hot night. I said 'Hi, Frank,' and he just stared at me like he was spaced out. Which he probably was—I think he frequently uses his own product. Although he did look quite a bit less wasted that night than he usually does. He didn't tell you he was out here?"

What Zimka had told me was, when Billy arrived at six A.M., Zimka was asleep and had had "a busy night." That was all.

I said, "He was vague about it."

"Yeah, he would be."

"Was he alone in the car?"

"He was. Maybe he was waiting for someone."

"Describe what you remember about the car."

"Seventy-nine Olds Toronado. Gold finish, new white sidewalls. I'm not sure whether it was a standard or diesel V8. I didn't look under the hood."

"You know cars."

"Sears Automotive Center wouldn't have it any other way."

Timmy and Phil came out. Phil and Mark Deslonde soon left, and I told Timmy I'd just be a minute. I approached Mike Truckman, then changed my mind—I'd try to catch him sober on Monday—and went to the bar. I asked each of the bartenders if he knew Frank Zimka, and when I described Zimka, each said he knew who Zimka was. I then asked whether anyone had seen Zimka with either Billy Blount or Steve Kleckner on the night of the murder, and each said no, he didn't think Zimka had even been in Trucky's that night.

At three-fifteen Timmy and I drove back to his place through a cool drizzle, made love with a furious intensity that was reminiscent of the night after the night we first met, and set the alarm for ten.

7

OUT OF THE HOUSE, THROUGH THE BREEZEWAY, INTO THE garage where the rental van with the fickle transmission was parked, we hauled books—me, Timmy, Brigit, the new hubby, the four daughters. Hugh Bigelow was a big, friendly sheepdog of a man who had been a widower for a year and did something in an office for the State of New York. Timmy said he thought he'd seen Bigelow in the elevator of his building at the Mall. The daughters, aged three through eight, were chubby, round-eyed and earnest, and they worked with an unchildlike, methodical determination as they moved the residue of me out of their new home.

When we'd nearly finished, Brigit beckoned me into the kitchen and said, "Thank you for doing this." She'd had her hair cut short and looked like Delphine Seyrig in a blond wig.

"Ultimatums work with me," I said. "I can be successfully menaced."

"I wouldn't know about that," she snapped. "I never gave you an ultimatum."

Christ, she'd pulled me aside to pick a fight. Or had I done it?

68

I said, "I guess you're just too forebearing for your own good." I grinned and tried to sound lighthearted, jocular.

"It was because I'm kind. And naive."

"Could I have some of that coffee?"

She poured a cup. I sat at the Formica counter. She stood.

"Would you really have tossed the books out in the rain? It may freeze tonight. Booksickles."

She tried to keep from smiling. She succeeded. "How are you doing?" she said.

"Well. Quite well. I like my life."

"Good. I like mine. For a long time I didn't."

I slurped at the coffee, trying to keep it from burning my lips. "He seems like a nice guy," I said. "Hugh."

"He is. You'd like him." She poured herself some coffee. "He's sweet, and funny."

"He's a bureaucrat, right?"

"Hugh's an inspector for the Public Service Commission." She eased onto the stool across from me. "Hugh really enjoys his work and he thinks its terribly important. Which it is, of course. Hugh doesn't become excessively wrapped up in his job, though. He's extremely easygoing."

"He seems to be. You must be devoted to him—he doesn't exactly come unencumbered."

"Oh, I *love* the girls. Well, *most* of the time." Now she smiled a bit. "It's a big adjustment to make. But I'm doing it."

"Will you keep teaching?"

"I think so. There's a baby-sitter the girls are used to. I'm not sure yet."

"Are you planning on having any of your own?"

Timmy staggered past the doorway balancing three boxes of books one atop the other. Brigit glanced at him as he went by and said to me, "I don't know yet. Are you?"

She knew it was a dumb thing to say, and she flushed as she said it. But she'd pulled the old trigger. She had not liked being a victim of my self-deception, and during the last years of our marriage, the malicious humor that was part of what had drawn us together in the first place had hardened into cruelty on both our parts. I hadn't liked being a victim of my self-deception either, and I often took it out on Brigit, who dished it right back. And now here we were, in character to the awful end.

I sipped my coffee and said, "There's an equality, a symmetry about Timmy's and my sexual relationship. It has balance. In seven years you never fucked me once."

She tightened like a fist. "Yes. And you must have fucked me twelve or fifteen times." She smiled, tight-lipped, the flesh around her lower jaw quivering.

Sex. It isn't everything in a relationship. But it's plenty.

Hugh Bigelow came into the kitchen panting. "Whew. Jesus. Whew. Done." He tried to mop his forehead with the sleeve of his Orlon windbreaker, but it just smeared the droplets around.

"Thanks for all your help, Hugh," I said. "That was twenty-two years' worth of books. Dinesen to Didion to Don Clark."

"Whew—oh—anytime, anytime."

Brigit and I glanced at each other quickly, then looked back at Hugh's big, nodding, wet face.

Timmy came in, and Hugh asked us to stay for peanut-butter-and-Fluff sandwiches. We thanked him but said we'd made other plans.

In the garage I said, "Good-bye, Brigit," and she said, "Good-bye, Don," like two stockbrokers who had just ended a business lunch. My impulse was to shake hands, but I knew mine were trembling.

Through a steady rain we drove out to the Gateway Diner on Central and had bacon and eggs. We didn't say much. I knew what Timmy was thinking but was too sensitive, and canny, to say out loud.

I said, "I suppose this would be a good time for me to move over to your place, now that we've got that van. Except the goddamn thing is full of books."

Timmy, ever the rational man, winning another war over his Irish soul, looked at me and said nothing.

We put half the books in my apartment—the stacked boxes took up an entire wall—and carried the other half down to the storage alcove in the basement of Timmy's building.

We showered together at his place, and one thing led to another.

At six we showered again, separately, and while Timmy made coffee, I dialed the number for Chris.

"Hello?" A woman's voice. Young, pleasant, a bit tentative.

"May I speak with Chris, please?"

"Oh—Chris isn't in just now. May I take a message?"

Discretion was indicated. "Yes, would you please have him call Donald Strachey at this number?" I gave my service number. "When do you expect him?"

A pause. "Who *is* this?" A real edge to the voice now.

"Uh—Donald Strachey. Chris may not recognize the name, but if you'll just tell him that I—"

The receiver was slammed down.

"What did I say?"

Timmy set a mug of coffee beside me. "What happened?"

"A woman—she hung up. It was something I said."

"It was something you are. Somebody's wife hung up on me once, too."

I decided to do what I'd planned on doing on Monday and should have done the day before. I said, "I'll be back in twenty minutes. I'm going over to the office. How about putting this brownish wet stuff you gave me back in the pot?"

"Will you want food?"

"Nothing much. Eggs or whatever."

"We had eggs for lunch."

"Then whatever."

I drove over to Central through a slicing cold wind under low, black, flying clouds. In the office I got out my directory of Albany phone numbers listed numerically. There it was. The Chris number was listed beside the name of *Christine* Porterfield. Of course.

I copied down the address on Lancaster Street and called Timmy.

"Chris is a woman. The woman I spoke with got pissed off when I referred to Chris as 'he.' They're lesbians. It was as if a strange woman called you up and said, 'Is Don there, when will *she* be in?' I want to go over there now and apologize—and probably learn something about Billy Blount. How about you going along? It should help if she knows I'm gay."

"Should I suck your cock while we're there?"

"A knowing glance or two should do it. I'll pick you up."

71

"I've got two frozen meat pies in the oven."

"Take them out and set them under a warm radiator. You'll hardly notice the difference it makes."

We pulled in behind a dark green VW Beetle in front of Chris Porterfield's Lancaster Street address. I wrote down the bug's license number.

The old Greek Renaissance town house looked warm and serene with its crusty yellow brick and brown shutters. The young maples growing from neat squares of earth at the edge of the sidewalk still held most of their dead leaves, some of which exploded into the gusts of wind as we walked up the steps. The brass lamps on either side of the front door had flickering flame-shaped light bulbs. Early American Niagara Mohawk Electric.

I pressed the button and could hear the bing-bong inside.

"Maybe the woman you spoke to was Christine's mother," Timmy said. "Or her grandmother."

"Too young."

"Or her daughter."

"No. It all fits. Chris is the woman-friend Huey Brownlee saw Billy Blount with, and the woman of delicate sensibilities who answered the phone is Chris's lover. You'll see."

"You once told me that it's only in novels that things all fit. Real life tends toward implausibility."

"Not always. Which is exactly my point."

"That's quite a logical progression. You should run for the State Assembly."

Two brown eyes appeared in the little window in the door. The door opened the three inches its lock chain would allow.

The middle third of a face said, "Yes?"

"I'm Donald Strachey, I'm a private detective, and I want to apologize for my call a while ago. I only had Chris's first name, and since I knew only that someone named Chris was a friend of Billy Blount's, I assumed it was a man. That was unintelligent and presumptuous of me. Are you a friend of Chris's?"

She stared out at me as if I were selling aluminum siding. She said, "I don't know what you're talking about. Did you say you're a detective?" Her voice was flutey and pretty and apprehensive, and her face was dark and smooth, with maybe some Mayan in it.

"I'm private." I hiked out my card and held it up to the crack. "This is my associate, Timothy Callahan." Timmy edged into range and showed his Irish teeth. "I've been hired by someone to help Billy Blount. But I've got to find him first. Could we talk?"

She hesitated. We didn't look the way detectives were supposed to look. I had on jeans, a flannel shirt, and a down vest. Timmy, who wore a Brooks Brothers suit to his job at the State Senate Minority Leader's office during the week, looked as if he'd just stepped off a B-29 after a run to Bremerhaven.

"I—well, I don't know. Chris isn't here. She's out."

"You look familiar," I said. "Have I seen you in Myrna's? I drop in there sometimes with friends from the alliance."

I could sense Timmy looking at me and raising his eyebrows questioningly, as if to say, "Now?"

The woman smiled tentatively. "Yes, I've been to Myrna's. But—you don't look much like a detective."

"My Robert Hall suit's at the cleaners. And I've never been big on the Raymond Chandler sort of private-eye high drag."

She thought about this. She looked as if she were trying to remember if her instructions covered this unusual set of circumstances. I guessed they hadn't and we'd thrown her off balance.

Finally she said, "All right. I can talk to you, but just for a minute. That's all. Chris isn't here." She fiddled with the chain, and the door opened.

We sat in a cheerful room lined with white wooden shelves holding clumps of old, handsomely bound books alternating with bright, graceful figurines and pottery from Central America. The wine-colored velvet chairs were deep and soft, and the stereo receiver was tuned to public radio, which had on Purcell's "Dido." The woman, thirtyish, and definitely from south of the border, wore olive slacks and a cowl-collared orange turtleneck with a red stone hanging from a silver chain. Her expression was one of vulnerable distraction—the look of a woman who had recently received a crank phone call and now the crank had arrived at her door. She told us her name was Margarita Mayes and that she was Chris Porterfield's "room-mate."

"Do you know Billy, too?" I asked.

"I've met him," she said, then quickly added, "but I haven't seen him recently. Not since—oh, August, I think. I have no idea where you could find him."

I looked for evidence of a male presence in the house but saw none. Frank Zimka had told me Billy Blount had flown to another city, but I now knew Zimka had been less than forthcoming about one matter and could as easily have been untruthful about others.

I said, "Are Chris and Billy good friends? I've gotten the impression they're close."

She looked at me quizzically. "They're very close, yes. But how did you know about Chris? Their relationship is—special. They've never mixed with each other's friends, and they've sort of saved each other up as a kind of, oh—refuge." She tensed, regretting she'd used the word.

"A friend of Billy's saw them together once in Chris's VW," I said, "though the friend didn't know at the time it was Chris. And Chris's first name and number were written on Billy's phone book. That's what led me here."

"I know," she said, looking worried. "That's where the police got it."

"They've been here?"

"Last week. Chris wasn't here. I said she was on a business trip. We own Here 'n' There 'n' Everywhere Travel. I told them she was in Mexico setting up Christmas tours."

"They could check on that with Mexican immigration." She winced. "I'll try to find out if they have. Chris is with Billy, isn't she?"

She said nothing.

I said, "Are they in Albany?"

She sat motionless, barely breathing. The apprehension in her dark eyes made Timmy uncomfortable. He picked up a copy of *Travel and Leisure* from an end table, peered at the cover, then set it down again. Finally she said, "I think you'd better speak with Chris."

"I'd like to."

"But what's your interest in this? Your connection. You said you wanted to help Billy. Why? Chris will want to know."

"His parents hired me to locate him. But my interest goes beyond that. Billy has been charged with murder, and I think

74

he's probably innocent. Also, Billy is someone whose difficulties in life are ones for which I hold a special sympathy."

She looked at me, then at Timmy, then back at me. "I hope you don't mind my asking, but—are you gay?"

I glanced at Timmy and caught him looking at me sappily. I said, "Yes, Timmy and I are lovers." He started to move toward me, and I thought, Oh Christ, but he swung around and just shifted position in his chair.

Margarita Mayes caught this and smiled. Timmy said, "He's very straitlaced."

"Good," she said. "So am I. I think I'd better have Chris get in touch with you. She'll call you. Why don't you give me your number again."

I handed her my business card. "Please have her call as soon as she can. There's a certain urgency in all this, as you can imagine. Have Chris and Billy been friends for a long time?"

"Oh, yes. Ages."

"College?"

"No. I mean, they met around that time. But at another place."

"A mental institution?"

She blanched. Timmy stiffened and gave me an indignant look.

"You'd better talk to Chris," Margarita Mayes said. She stood up. "I don't know what she wants you to know and what she doesn't want you to know." She looked put out and resentful at having been left with a lot of useless, incomplete instructions. "I'll ask her to call you, and then you two can work it out. I don't even know if Chris would want me to be talking to you like this."

"If I could see her, it would be easier."

"She'll call you." She moved toward the open door. "Or I'll call you." She was panicking. I'd pushed too hard.

I said, "Impress on her the fact that if Billy is going to come through this, he'll need a skilled, full-time friend working on his behalf—to clear him, and to find out who the real killer is. The police are harried, overworked, underpaid, generally not too smart, and they can't be relied on to do that. I can be. But I'm going to need Billy's help, and first Chris's."

She nodded, played with the cowl on her pretty sweater.

"All right. Thank you. We'll be in touch soon." She walked quickly to the front door, and we followed.

"Sorry again about the rude phone call," I said. "It was just a dumb misunderstanding on my part."

"Oh, that's all right. I was mixed up, too. I'm half-afraid to pick up the phone these days. I've been getting crank calls since yesterday morning, so I've been uptight about the phone ringing."

"You have?"

"Someone calls and then just listens, doesn't say anything. I can hear the person breathing. But it'll stop soon, I'm sure. You'd better go now. Chris will be in touch."

I said, "Do you have a burglar alarm in this house?"

"Yes, as a matter fact we do. Chris set it off accidentally once, and it makes a horrible racket. Why do you ask that?"

"Well, it's just that—that's an MO burglars sometimes use. They'll call to see if you're home, and if you're not home, they may try to bust in and clean you out before you get back. No one's tried to break in recently, though, right?"

"No. But of course I've been home every night."

"Right. And you're sure the alarm is working?"

"Yes, that little red light by the door there goes on when it's activated. I set it every night."

"Good idea."

"I like your Ken Edwards Tonala," Timmy said. "I can see why you wouldn't want those stolen. There are some lovely things here."

"Yes," she said, "It's not the Ken Edwards stuff, though, it's Armando Galvan."

"Oh. Right. Did you bring them back from Mexico yourself?"

"Yes. We did. Good night now. Chris will be calling you soon, okay?"

The cold wind was rushing in the open door.

We drove down Lancaster, then swung right on Dove. "What was that 'mental institution' crap? I thought you'd lost her with that one."

"I guessed. Blount's difficult, painful secret. I knew he'd

76

been locked up and hated it, but where? He'd told Huey Green—Brownlee—that it hadn't been jail or reform school. Which wouldn't have been the Blount family's style, anyway. A little nuttiness, though, would not have been out of character among the Blounts. And Margarita didn't deny it. She seemed to confirm it."

"Or maybe he'd been locked in a room a lot as a kid or something. That would have left scars."

"No. I've hit on something else. For what it's worth."

"Is all this necessary? All this probing around in Blount's psyche and his past? It seems like there should be an easier way. It's not pleasant."

"I don't know. I'm finding out what I can. Then I'll see where it points. A murder charge is not pleasant. Nor a murder."

We turned onto Madison. Timmy said, "Maybe it points to Mexico."

"Unlikely. He could get into the country easily enough with just a voter's card or some other proof of citizenship. But there'd be a record of his entry, and I think he'd have thought of that. My guess is, he's in this country. Wherever."

"If Blount *was* in a mental institution, I wonder what particular variety of mental problem he had?"

"I was wondering that, too."

"Margarita was showing the strain of it all. I felt bad for her. And the crazy phone calls can't be making it easier."

"Yeah, everybody seems to be getting them these days. Somebody called Blount's apartment while I was there Friday evening and hung up after a few seconds, and Huey Brownlee got two of the same kind of calls several hours before somebody came through his window with a knife early Saturday morning."

"So—it's the full moon. Or something."

"Yeah. Or something."

8

ON MONDAY MORNING I WENT TO THE OFFICE AND CHECKED MY
service—no calls—and my mail—no check from my "check is in
the mail" former client. I made an appointment to meet the
Blounts at one, then phoned Margarita Mayes to find out if
she'd had a safe, uneventful night. Irritated, she told me she
had, and that Chris *would* be in touch. I explained that
patience was not one of my two or three virtues, rung off, then
drove down to police headquarters on Arch Street in the Old
South End.

Division Two headquarters looked like an Edward Hopper
painting of an American police station in the twenties, plain
and solemn in the sunlight, with tall windows set in a heavy
brick facade and a sign hanging out over the street corner that
said POLICE. It sat back to back with and was connected to the
newer Albany Police Court building on lower Morton, presum-
ably to facilitate the speedy dispensation of justice or its South
End equivalent.

I was directed to a second-floor office, where I found
Detective Sergeant Ned Bowman typing out forms on an old
Smith-Corona. He had on a black sport coat and brown slacks,
and his face, which had the usual human features placed here
and there on it, was roughly the color of the institutional green
walls around him.

Bowman lost no time in showing me his winning personality. "Yeah, I've heard of you," he said after I'd introduced
myself. "You're the pouf."

"What ever happened to 'pervert'?" I said. "I always liked
that one better. It had a nice lubricious ring to it. 'Faggot,' too, I
was comfortable with. The word had a defiant edge that I liked.
'Fairy' wasn't bad—it made us seem weak, which was mislead-
ing, but also a bit magical, which was wrong, too, but still okay.
'Pouf,' on the other hand, I never went for. It made us sound as
if we were about to disappear. Which we aren't."

"Don't count on it," he said. "What do you want?"

"Billy Blount."

"So do I. He killed a man."

"Maybe not. There are other possibilities."

"Sit down."

I did.

"Who hired you? Who thinks I'm not capable of delivering Blount?"

"His parents. They thought I'd have access to places and people you wouldn't."

"They would be wrong. I know quite a few of your people."

"Hustlers, drag queens, and bar owners. Your gay horizons are limited."

"You mean there are *more* of you? I'll be goddamned."

"Don't you read banners? We are everywhere."

"Not here. Not yet."

"Don't count on it."

He leaned back in his swivel chair and peered at me. "So. You've got Blount waiting outside in a taxi. Found him under your bed. Or in it."

"He's not in Albany. I'm reasonably certain."

"And where would you be reasonably certain he is?"

"I don't know yet. I want to deal."

"I won't need that. But talk to me."

I said, "I'll bring him in, and then you and the DA go easy on him until I locate the guilty party. Just don't rush it."

The lumps and openings on his face rearranged themselves randomly. A feeble smile. "There seems to be this opinion rampant in certain quarters that Billy Blount is nothing worse than a wayward lad who could stand a good talking to. Get sent to his room with no supper."

"The DA?"

"My own opinion is that he's a fucking screwball who stabbed a man to death. I've got evidence, and it's going to court. If, after he's found guilty, somebody wants to toodle Blount on out to Attica in a limousine with a full bar, I won't object. Just so the little creep gets locked away from society for the rest of his natural life. That's my opinion. That's my intention."

"Your evidence is circumstantial. Why do you call him a screwball?"

"He's taken a human life. Even the life of a queer has worth in God's eyes. See? I'm a liberal."

"I hope you'll come and speak at the next Gay Alliance meeting. You can increase the number of your already-countless gay friends. What evidence have you got that Jay Tarbell won't have a jury guffawing over? Blount was seen leaving Trucky's with Kleckner a few hours before it happened. That's it. Anything could have happened in that time."

"We've got this." He opened a drawer and held up a reel of tape. "'He's dead—I think Steve is dead.' It's Blount's voice."

"Who identified it?"

"The Blounts, Mister and missus."

"Swell, good for them. So many people don't want to get involved these days."

"And when we have Blount, we'll get a voice print and nail it down."

"The newspapers say you have the weapon. Were there prints?"

"There were."

"Blount's?"

He frowned, looked at his reel of tape.

"Ah. So. Whose were they?"

"We don't know." He put the tape back in the drawer, slammed it shut. "They're not on record."

"Diabolical devil, that Blount. He wore somebody else's hands that night."

"What the fuck. He held the knife in a towel, in a handkerchief. Who knows."

"That sounds awkward. Maybe he brought his mittens along."

"Screw you, faggot. Whoops—pardon if I got you hot."

Oi. "And the doorknob. When you got your picture in the paper, you were pointing at Kleckner's doorknob. A meaningless photogenic gesture, right?"

He laughed.

"You've got no case," I said. "And sooner or later you're going to have to admit it. Better now than when Jay Tarbell goes to work on you in Judge Feeney's courtroom. Also, there's the matter of another psycho out there who could kill again. Why wait?"

80

He sat for a moment looking thoughtful and a little bewildered. Then: "Tarbell won't be a problem. Not much, anyway. He's already been talking to the DA about a deal. That's not Jay's style, and I don't get it. Though if Jay assumes his client's guilty, who am I to argue?"

The fine hand of the deranged Blounts again. I said, "What sort of deal?"

"Put him in a psycho ward instead of the slammer. I get the impression Feeney's in on it. My guess is, they've already got some country club all picked out. Personally, I won't go for it. Not that my opinion's been asked."

An idea came to me that froze my innards. I didn't say it out loud. Bowman might not have disapproved.

I said, "It'll be useful to get Billy Blount's perceptions of these events. That's what I'm after."

"We agree on something."

"You've paid a call on Blount's friend Huey Brownlee. I take it you're aware somebody came through his window Saturday morning and went after him with a knife."

"I saw the report. A burglary attempt."

"It was the second knifing of a gay male in a week's time. There could be a connection."

"Sure, and there could be a connection between Watergate and the French and Indian wars. Relax, Strachey. Those people in that neighborhood slice each other up at the drop of a welfare check. I know. I've seen it. This was some junkie after your fag pal's twelve-hundred-dollar sound system. Believe me."

"You're quite the keen social observer, Sergeant."

"Thank you."

"You've also been to see Margarita Mayes."

"The lez."

"You found her roommate's name on Blount's phone book."

"Her girl friend. Did we leave that phone book behind in Blount's apartment? How slovenly."

"And an eighth of an ounce of grass in the fridge."

"Blount's refrigerator was boring. His homicidal proclivities are not. Who let you into that apartment?"

I fed him his line. "The lock fairy."

"That figures."

"Is Chris Porterfield in Mexico?"

He looked at me. "I can't tell you that."

"I'll tell you what I know," I lied. "We'll trade."

He said, "You go first."

"All right. The morning of the killing, Blount borrowed money from someone for plane fare."

"How much?"

"A good bit."

"Who from?"

"I'll hold that for a while."

"Don't. You'll be committing a felony."

I said, "Maybe Chris Porterfield."

"Unh-unh."

"You don't know that."

He looked at me sullenly, regrouping the topography on the front of his head again. "At the time of the crime, you might as well know, Christine Porterfield was in Cuernavaca, Mexico. She entered Mexico on September twenty-sixth." He held up a telex printout. "I received this Friday at two o'clock. It took my federal colleagues three days—*three days*—to establish that simple fact."

"And she's still there?"

"Now you tell *me* something, you know so goddamn much about this. Which airport did Blount use? Not Albany. We checked that. Where'd he fly out of?"

"La Guardia."

"What time?"

"Around nine."

"A.M.?"

"A.M. The same day. Is Porterfield still in Mexico?"

"She departed Cuernavaca October second."

"Three days after the murder."

"Correct. She flew back to Albany by way of JFK."

"She's here now?"

"No."

"Where then?"

"First this. How did Blount get to La Guardia? Not by bus. Not by train. How?"

I said, "He was driven."

"Who by? The person who lent him the money?"

"Yes."

"Aiding a fugitive, abetting a felony, accessory to murder. I may have to lock you up, Strachey." He reached for his phone.

"Idle threats. Anyway, with me loose I'll continue to add to your non-too-encyclopedic knowledge of this case. And in one week I'll have Kleckner's killer." This was a bit fanciful. "Well, maybe two."

He put the receiver down. "Add to my knowledge right now, Strachey. I think I can stand you for another ten minutes. Well, maybe five."

"If I'm not mistaken, it's your turn. Where is Chris Porterfield?"

He said, "I don't know."

"You know that her roommate lied about Chris's still being in Mexico. Why don't you bring her down here and work her over with a rubber hose?"

He looked at me stonily. "I may yet. That's not a bad idea."

"But you won't really have to, because you know that. . . ." I cocked my head and waited.

"Because," he said, "I happen to know that on October fourth, two days after she returned to Albany from Mexico, Chris Porterfield flew to Cheyenne, Wyoming, and rented a Hertz car for a thirty-day period, the car to be returned at Cheyenne airport, and that the car has not yet been turned back in. So, Strachey, you are now in possession of privileged official information. It's your turn."

"Ask away."

"Who lent Blount the money and took him to La Guardia?"

I knew I'd come to regret this. I said, "Alfred Douglas. Sometimes known as Bowsie. Or Al."

"Who's he?"

"A hustler. Hangs out at the Greyhound station. I don't know where he lives, but your undercover guys could ask around down there at two or three in the morning."

He wrote the name down. "A hustler who owns a car?"

"He borrowed it from an uncle."

"Uncle?"

"A client. Trick."

"How much did he lend Blount?"

"Two hundred forty dollars."

"Jesus, I'm in the wrong line of work."

"I doubt it. Your Cheyenne colleagues are on the lookout for the Hertz car, I take it."

"They are. What else do you know?"

"You've got it all."

"You're lying."

I stood up, clenched my teeth like Bogart, and said, "All right, copper, I've had about all the abuse I'm going to take from you!"

He looked up at me with his plate of potatoes and said, "No, you haven't."

9

BACK AT THE OFFICE I PHONED MARGARITA MAYES AT HERE 'N' There 'n' Everywhere Travel and told her that the Cheyenne, Wyoming, police were looking for Chris Porterfield. She thanked me and said she would relay this useful information.

Next I called a New York Telephone Company employee I'd met a few years earlier at the Terminal bar who'd helped me out from time to time. He called back half an hour later with a list of long-distance calls made over the past month from Chris Porterfield and Margarita Mayes's home phone and from Here 'n' There 'n' Everywhere Travel. The lists were long, but nowhere was there included a call to Cheyenne, Wyoming. The closest was a call from the travel agency to a number in St. Louis, which didn't look useful, though I'd check it out. My friend at the phone company mentioned in passing that a Sergeant Bowman of the Albany Police Department had requested the same information a week earlier.

At noon I walked up Central and had a leisurely lunch at Elmo's. I paid cash, and Elmo said, "Have a nice day."

Under a hard, bright autumn sky, I headed over toward the

park and arrived at the Blounts' on State Street just after one. The maid let me in, and I waited on the much-talked-about sofa while the Blounts went over their lines offstage.

At one-ten they rolled down the foyer stairway and into the salon like a couple of presenters on the Academy Awards show, Stuart Blount with his elegant long arm, Jane Blount with her ashtray.

"We didn't expect to see you so soon," Blount said, "but we're absolutely delighted."

"Absolutely," Jane Blount said. "Would you care for some tea? Something stronger?"

I said no thank you, and we all sat down, the Blounts looking almost cheerfully expectant.

"I haven't found Billy," I told them, "but I've got some ideas. For now I've got more questions than answers."

Their disappointment showed, and Jane Blount lit a Silva Thin. "How much longer do you think it will be?" she asked. "We're all really terribly anxious to have this business taken care of. Believe me, it's taken its toll on both of us."

"Jane, I'm sure Mr. Strachey is moving ahead on this as rapidly as anyone possibly can," Blount said, giving me a man-to-man, don't-mind-her, women-will-be-women look. "What more can we tell you, Mr. Strachey? What else would you like to know about our son that might assist you?"

I said, "Did Billy once spend some time in a mental institution?"

They froze. They looked at each other. They looked at me. "Why do you ask?" Blount said. "That was nearly ten years ago. What bearing does that have on the present situation?"

"That is a private family matter," Jane Blount said. "It is, I'm afraid, *strictly* between Stuart and me." She blew smoke up to the ceiling vent. "I'm sure you can appreciate how difficult such an unpleasant state of affairs can be for a family like ours."

I did not tell them what I suspected. I said, "Any past mental illness of Billy's might not be entirely irrelevant to the, ah, present, ah, problematical situation." After this was over I'd need deprogramming. "The thing is, if Billy has a history of sudden, unexpected, violent behavior—"

They picked up the bait. "No, no, that wasn't it," Blount rushed to assure me. "Not at all. You mustn't get the wrong idea."

"As we explained on Friday," Jane Blount said in a voice I supposed she had honed over the years on the maid, "Billy was *not* a violent boy. He was contentious and impossible at times, of course. But invariably he kept his temper. Billy got that from Stuart's side of the family, I suppose. We Hardemans are more—passionate by nature. Though of course not excessively demonstrative."

Stuart Blount winked at me.

I said, "What was the nature of Billy's illness? Once I know I can relax about it and drop the subject."

"Mr. Strachey," Jane Blount said, her passionate nature asserting itself, "I be-*lieve* we hired you simply to—"

"No, no—Jane, Jane. Let me put Mr. Strachey's mind at ease. There'll be no harm in that that I can see." She sighed heavily and stubbed out her cigarette. "Billy's problem," Blount said, "was a problem of—social adjustment. He was in no way a menace to society. Only to himself. Just—himself."

He looked at me evenly, waiting. He knew that I knew. Jane Blount glowered at the chandelier.

"And was the social-adjustment problem ironed out?" I asked.

Blount said icily, "I think you know the answer to that, Mr. Strachey. Now then. What can we tell you that will help you locate our son and bring him back to us? That's what we're here for, isn't it?"

I said, "Who is Chris Porterfield?"

They both looked at the walls and thought about this. "The name sounds familiar," Blount said. "But—I can't place it."

"Is he a friend of Billy's?" Jane Blount asked.

I said yes, that was what I'd heard. "An old friend," I said.

"Perhaps from Billy's Elwell School days," Blount said.

"No, Stuart. I would very much doubt that. Billy has never kept in touch with his schoolmates. Understandable as that may be in Billy's case, it is a pity, in a way. Those ties can be so important in later life."

"Or from Albany State—SUNY," Blount said.

"For what *that* would be worth." She lit another cigarette.

Blount said, "Is this Chris someone Billy might have gone to for help?"

I told them yes, and that I was making progress in locating Chris Porterfield. Then I said: "I spoke with Sergeant Bowman, the police detective. He tells me you two identified Billy's voice on the tape of the phone call notifying the police of the killing."

She squirmed inwardly, but he let it show. "What would have been the point of lying?" Blount said. "Someone else who knew Billy would have identified him at some point in time in the course of events. And, in point of fact, the only significance of the tape is that it demonstrates that Billy reported a crime."

Father Recommends Son For Citizenship Award. "You're sure it's Billy's voice?"

"We are certain," Jane Blount snapped. "We know the voice of our son. Now what else do you want from us?"

"Another five hundred dollars," I said. "I expect to have to do some traveling."

They gave me the check and all but shoved me out the door.

I walked across State Street and into the park. The weather was warming up again—fickle October—and I lay down on the grass under the high white sky. The ground was damp and cold. I got up and sat on a bench. I wanted a cigarette. I'd quit soon after I met Timmy, when it had suddenly occurred to me that I wanted to live for a long, long time. I just chucked them out one night, and Timmy had put up with my cruelty for the week it took to get unhooked. Now I wanted one, for the calming narcotic·effect they'd always had on me. I guessed what I was feeling was the Blount Effect. I thought, half a joint would be nice. And I knew who'd have one—the man I was planning to call on next.

I walked back to Central and down to my bank and bought five hundred dollars' worth of traveler's checks with the money the Blounts had just used to purchase my speedy departure. I made my way back up to Lexington then and rattled Frank Zimka's front door. After a time it opened.

He looked at me and blinked himself awake. "Oh. Hi. C'mon in." He was shirtless and barefooted in stained red bikini briefs. His old man's face was unshaven and looked unfocused from the inside out.

In his state of relative undress, the contrast between Zimka's ravaged face and his slim, smooth swimmer's body was even more striking. And the clinging briefs made clear how he'd been able to stay in business as a prostitute. I'd seen them cruising the park in their Buicks and Chryslers, the men who must have been Zimka's johns—middle-aged, closeted, probably married with grown children; sad, desperate men locked into choices they'd made back in the days when, for some men, there didn't seem to be any. And less interested in a pretty face than in what Frank Zimka had to offer—Zimka, the meat man. Though why Billy Blount? What did Zimka have that could interest him? That I couldn't figure out.

Down in the depths of his apartment, Zimka said, "Smoke?" He dragged on a half-gone joint.

"Maybe I'll just take some along. A bag?"

He got a bag from the refrigerator, and I dropped it into my jacket pocket and on into the lining. I supposed he accepted traveler's checks, if not Master Charge, but I had ten dollars cash and gave him that.

I said, "No whites today? For you, I mean. Not that you're not better off without them."

"It's early," he said. "Sit down. I've got something."

While Zimka went into his bedroom, I sat on the couch and read two panels of the sci-fi comic book open on the end table. Zimka came back and handed me a dirty envelope sealed with Scotch tape. "Billy" was written across the front. The "i" was dotted with a little heart.

"You won't lose this, will you?"

"I won't." I shoved the envelope down with the grass.

"Did you find Billy yet?"

"No. But I'm close. I think."

He sat on the plastic chair and brought his knee up for a hug. The head of his cock peeked out one leg of his briefs and he absently tucked it back in.

"Where do you think Billy is?" he said. "God, I miss him."

"He's out West."

"In Hollywood?"

88

"Not that far west. I'm not sure. I'll know soon. Frank, I want you to clear something up for me."

"You do? What?"

"Describe the car you used to drive Billy to La Guardia."

"Describe it?"

"The make, the color."

He squeezed his eyes shut as if to rummage around inside his head for some usable brain cells. Finally he opened his eyes and said, "It's a green car. An Impala, I think. Impala—isn't that a car?"

"It is."

"Why do you want to know that? Did somebody see us? I mean, I don't want to get somebody in trouble—the guy I borrowed the car from."

"I don't think that'll be a problem. Do you know anyone who owns a new gold-colored Olds Toronado?"

He shut his eyes again. After a moment they opened, blinking. "I'm sorry, but I really don't think so. I might have been in one once. It's hard to say. I've been in a lot of cars."

It seemed possible he simply did not remember that the Olds was an Olds, or even that it was a motorized vehicle. Sorting out the particulars of his nights couldn't have been easy for him.

I said, "The night of the killing. Where did you spend it?"

He fidgeted. "Here," he said. "In there." He gestured toward the bedroom. "I told you that before, didn't I? I thought I did. Who's been asking about me?"

"Were you alone?"

"No. Who is it who wants to know about that?"

"For now, I do. Were you here around one?"

"I *said* I was here all that night. A guy—somebody had called around eleven-thirty, and came over at twelve—I think. Yeah, that's what happened. I remember because somebody else had just left when this guy called. He was a priest, the first guy, and he always left before twelve. In for a quick pop, then back to the rectory. I was kind of wiped out after him, but the second guy was somebody who's always been pretty nice to me, so when he called I said, sure, what the fuck, c'mon over. I smoked some while I waited, and then he came, this friendly old fucked-up guy, and he stayed till—about two, I guess. Then I fell asleep till Billy showed up at six. It was one of those nights."

I said, "You were seen sitting in a gold-colored Olds in the parking lot at Trucky's around one. How did that happen?"

His head jerked back and he gave me a mean look. "Hey, what is this? Is somebody trying to fuck me over or what? Who said that? Somebody has me mixed up with somebody else. Whoever said that about me—that's wrong." He muttered something else under his breath and reached for a Kent.

I said, "What's the friendly old fucked-up guy's name? Maybe he can help put my mind at ease. This will stay between the three of us. Or maybe you could get us together."

He lit the cigarette and ingested its nutrients. "No-o-o-o way." He exhaled. "Forget *that*."

"Look," I said, "you know me a little by now. Am I discreet, or am I discreet?"

He shook his head. "Nnn-nnn. That's a no-no. Why don't you tell *me* something? Who was it who says he saw me at Trucky's? A cop?" He gave me a look of deep, wounded bitterness which, since Billy Blount's departure, seemed to be Zimka's one remaining nondrug-induced emotion.

I said, "No. Someone who knows you. Someone whose car was parked next to the Olds. He looked right at you and spoke, and you looked back. Remember, now? A friend of Billy's?"

He frowned at his cigarette and slowly shook his head. Then, as if he were about to remember something, he squeezed his eyes shut and said, "Well, maybe I—no. It must have been another night I was out there. Or maybe I was stoned. I don't think so, though. It's hard to remember. My mind does weird things sometimes."

"Do you know Mike Truckman?"

"Sure. Why? Who wants to know? Everybody knows Mike."

"Is Mike one of your johns?"

"Look, I *said* certain things are confidential."

"Did you meet Mike that night?"

"Goddamnit-to-shit, I *told* you I was with these two other guys! Now, who is it that's telling these lies about me? Did *Mike* say that?"

90

"No. Give me the names of the priest and the fucked-up old guy, and then maybe we can clear this up, and I'll drop it."

"No. Oh, no. I *can't* do that. Hey—shit—am I going to get in trouble?"

"I don't know."

"Oh, God. That's all I need. Cops. I'm so fucked up. So *fucking* fucked up."

He selected a pill from the eight whites lying openly on the end table and placed it on his tongue.

10

FRANK ZIMKA WAS SUCH A BLUR OF A HUMAN BEING THAT IT WAS hard to form an opinion about the veracity of any statement he made. He could have been telling the truth, or lying, or, most likely, some of each. Or his brain could have been so addled by drugs, or by his grief over himself, that *he* no longer knew for sure what was true in his life and what wasn't, and cared about which was which only intermittently. I'd run into that before.

I went back to the office and phoned Mark Deslonde at Sears Automotive Center. I asked him if he was certain it was Zimka he'd seen in Trucky's parking lot that night, and he said *almost* certain—at least it had never occurred to him that the man he greeted in the Olds Toronado had *not* been Zimka.

I asked Deslonde not to mention any of this to anyone, and he said he wouldn't. He said if Timmy and I went out Wednesday night, maybe he'd see us. He told me he'd be with Phil, and as he said it, I could see him doing his angled-grin-and-head thing. I said, yes, I hoped we'd run into him, which was the truth, and hung up.

I called my service and was told a Chris had phoned me and said she would call back. She had left no number. I told the service I'd be at home, then drove over to Morton. I stuffed the bag of grass into the Major Gray's chutney jar in the refrigerator and slipped the letter from Frank Zimka to Billy Blount into the jacket of Thelma Houston's "I'm Here Again" alongside Blount's letter from his parents. I thought about steaming that one open, but decided to wait and see if it came to that.

After half an hour of sit-ups, push-ups, and jogging in place, I set the phone on the bathroom floor and showered. While I shaved I spotted another gray hair in my mustache. I lectured myself on the special rewards of going gentle into that good night, left the gray hair, and got into my jeans and sport shirt. Then I had second thoughts, went back to the mirror, and ripped the little fucker out. There was just the one, which would have looked damned silly all by itself, an affectation.

At six Timmy let himself in with his own key. He had French bread and salad makings and suggested I "do a quiche." I laughed and opened the freezer door. I caught sight of a Mama Cadenza's frozen lasagna embedded in the Arctic wastes of my freezer compartment, found a screwdriver, and pried the aluminum tray full of hard orange stuff out of its cardboard container, which was stuck in there for good.

While we waited for the lasagna to heat up, Timmy listened to the Haydn Quartet in G Major in the stereo headset and I watched Dick Block eye his cue cards suspiciously and recite the little snatches of Albany news written on them. The Kleckner murder was not mentioned, but two sentences were devoted to the Saturday-night raid by Bergenfield police on the Rat's Nest, "a controversial bar patronized predominantly by members of the gay community."

We ate the orange and yellow food and waited for Chris Porterfield to call. She did not. At eight Calvin Markham and a SUNY friend stopped in, and we played hearts until around ten, when they left for a quick foray to the Terminal before heading home. Timmy decided to stay over, and we got out the Scrabble. At a quarter to twelve, with the score nearly tied, he went out with "pomelo," a kind of grapefruit, so he said. I looked it up. "A kind of grapefruit."

We went to bed. I'd always loved the sight of Timmy's milk-white skin under the blueish glow of the streetlight outside my front window, and I was sitting there running my fingers over all the different parts of him as he lay uncovered beside me when at exactly five before midnight the phone rang.

"Hello. Don Strachey."

"This is Christine Porterfield. I'd like to know who you are and exactly what your game is." A strong, confident voice.

I said, "I'm a private detective hired by Billy Blount's parents to get him out of this thing. Their idea of what getting him out of this *means* may be different from mine, or yours, or Billy's. I'm interested in hearing Billy's and I'd like to talk to him. I have this idea you could help me with that."

"Mr. Strachey, what if I told you that Billy doesn't need any help. That he's safe, and happy, and he's starting to make a new life for himself. You know that Billy and I understand each other—we're very close, and you've found that out. So why don't you just take my word for it that he's all right, and tell the Blounts not to worry. Will you do that?"

"I'm glad he's okay," I said, "because I keep hearing nice things about him, and I don't think he deserves any more grief. But it can't last, and I think you know that. Billy's too young to spend his life looking over his shoulder. The police have already traced you to Cheyenne, and if you're with him, it's only a matter of time before you stumble. That will be disastrous for both of you."

A hesitation. Then: "Look—thank you for telling Margarita about the Cheyenne police. We appreciated that. But we're not really in Cheyenne, and we're with people who know how to help us—how to help Billy. They're not amateurs at this, and they know what they're doing. Actually, I'm coming to Albany in a week or so—Billy is getting the support he needs from other people here. Maybe we can get together and I can reassure you. Though I'm afraid there really isn't much more I'll be able to tell you. I'm sorry."

"There's another thing," I said. "And I hope you'll give this a lot of thought. Billy did not commit a murder—we both believe that." In fact, I wasn't a hundred percent certain of this, but I was nearly there. "But someone *did* kill Steve Kleckner," I said, "and the odds are that he's still in Albany. If he took a life once, he could do it again. He may, in fact, be the man who attacked a friend of Billy's Saturday morning and wounded him. Only Billy knows exactly what happened the night of the Kleckner murder, and he has a responsibility to someone—maybe someone he knows—to help identify the killer before he kills again. If I could just *talk* with Billy about that night—for now that's all I'll ask."

Silence. Then: "Just a minute. Can you hold on for just one minute?" She sounded irritated, frustrated.

"I'll wait."

The receiver was set down with a clunk. I could hear a TV set on near the phone somewhere. The PBS Paul Robeson special ended, and Monty Python came on. That'd be Pacific Time, or Mountain. I'd check. Two minutes went by.

She came back. "I'm very sorry—I *do* understand what you're saying, but—I just can't help you, Mr. Strachey. You said a friend of Billy's has been wounded. Could you tell me who that was?"

"Huey Brownlee. The attack might or might not have had anything to do with the Kleckner killing, but if the attacker *is* the same man, I've got to talk with Billy fast to figure out what that connection might be. See what I'm saying? Anyway, tell Billy that Brownlee wasn't badly hurt. He's okay."

"Oh, thank God for that. You see—well, the fact is, Billy did not actually *see* who stabbed Steven Kleckner, and he has no idea who could have done it. So how could he possibly help you? Please—try to understand—"

"You mean Billy wasn't there at the time? He'd gone out, or what?"

"He was—taking a shower."

"Taking a shower."

"Billy is quite fastidious in some ways."

That made sense. I wondered if he also carried an ashtray around with him.

I said, "And no one else was there when he—went into the bathroom?"

"No."

"Nor when he came out?"

"No. He says he thought he was going crazy. He couldn't understand how it had happened. The other man, Steven, had fallen asleep, and when Billy came out of the shower, at first he thought the man was still asleep. And then he saw the blood all over the man. He felt the man's pulse, even though he said he could see that the poor man was dead. Then Billy panicked and ran away. He did notify the police, but he knew everyone would think he had done it, and Billy was absolutely *terrified* of being put in prison. Billy does not like to be locked up unjustly. It happened to him once before."

"I know," I said. "I'm sorry. Would you mind telling me where and when that happened?"

A pause. "Why do you want to know that?"

"Just checking all the angles," I lied. "Maybe Billy made an enemy there—some real psycho who'd track him down later and set him up as a murder suspect."

This sounded flaky, but it was the best I could come up with on no notice. In fact another much more logical notion was beginning to shape itself.

She said, "Mr. Strachey, I don't want to tell you how to run your business, but that sounds a bit off the wall to me. This happened *ten years ago*. I know about it because I was there. And believe me, Billy's only enemies were the lunatics in charge of the place. From what Margarita told me about you, I'd expect you to understand that."

They both must have been around sixteen when they'd gone in, under the age of consent. "Did your parents have you committed, too?" I asked. "For reasons of 'poor social adjustment'?"

She said, "Yes. On account of our homosexuality. Our 'sickness.'"

I'd heard stories like Chris's and Billy's and had read of such atrocities in the gay literature. Before Stonewall it was not all that uncommon and is still today not entirely unheard of. But I'd never known anyone it had happened to, and it amazed me that two people could come through it with their minds as cleansed of rage as Chris Porterfield's and Billy Blount's apparently were. *If* they were. I had yet to meet either Billy or Chris face to face.

I said, "What was the name of the place? I'd like to find out if it's still operating with the same medieval outlook."

I could have asked her directly what I had in mind, but I might have lost her—and driven her and Billy from the city where I now suspected they were hiding.

She said, "Sewickley Oaks. In New Baltimore. I doubt that it's changed."

"How long were you there?" I asked.

"Long enough," she said. "More than a year."

"Were you and Billy released at the same time?"

She hesitated, "Oh—yes. We were."

That was it. I had it. I'd find them.

"Look," she said, "I really can't talk to you anymore. I hope I've helped you somewhat, and Billy and I *do* want the murderer to be found. I know, it's horrible that someone like that is still there in Albany loose somewhere. It's just that—Billy understands so little of what happened. Even now he's quite confused about it. Do you understand what I'm saying?"

I said, "Yes and no. It'd still be better if I could sit down with Billy. For an hour, that's all."

"I—I'm sorry, Mr. Strachey. Good luck to you. I mean that. Maybe I'll see you in Albany."

"You realize the Albany police will be looking for you when you come back. You'll meet Sergeant Bowman, a man with his quirks of manner and viewpoint. You won't like him."

"I realize that."

"What will you tell him?"

"I'll lie. I've learned how to do that. Good-bye, Mr. Strachey."

She hung up.

Timmy had been up on one elbow listening to my end of the conversation. He said, "So?"

I slumped into the easy chair near the daybed where Timmy lay and recounted what Chris Porterfield had told me. Then I told him what I thought I'd learned.

"So, maybe you know now where Blount and Porterfield are," he said. "But not who the killer is. Get moving, Strachey."

I said, "I'll take what I can get when I can get it. Like Blanche said, 'Tomorrow is another day.'"

"Scarlett said that. Blanche said—something else."

"'Here's looking at you, kid'?"

"Close enough. I'm tired. I'm going to sleep."

"I'll join you."

11

IN THE MORNING I WENT TO THE ALBANY PUBLIC LIBRARY AND dug out the *Times Union*s for the late fall of 1970, a little over a year after Billy Blount and Chris Porterfield would have been committed to Sewickley Oaks. What I was looking for, or thought I was looking for, was not in the index, and I had to slide the microfilm around for thirty or forty issues until I found the short article in the Tuesday, November 24, edition.

ALBANY DUO ESCAPES MENTAL FACILITY

New Baltimore—Two teenage inmates at Sewickley Oaks, an exclusive private mental institution on Ridge Road, escaped from the medium-security section of the establishment late Sunday night. William Blount, 18, and Christine Porterfield, 18, whose families live in Albany, fled a residential building through a heating tunnel and are believed to have been driven away by unknown persons who apparently aided the two in other aspects of the escape.

According to the local police, a chain securing a door to the tunnel had been cut through from the tunnel side. Officials say the escape appeared to have been carefully planned and executed.

Blount and Porterfield were discovered missing Monday morning when they failed to show up for breakfast, and a search was undertaken. Later, an area resident told police he had been driving on Ridge Road just past midnight Sunday and saw five young people emerge from nearby woods and enter an older model Plymouth station wagon. Two of the five were bearded and "looked like hippies," the witness said.

Dr. Nelson Thurston, Sewickley Oaks administrator, described the escapees as "mentally troubled" but not dangerous.

State police are assisting in the search for the two.

I made notes on the article, then drove over to Billy Blount's apartment building on Madison. I wanted to check something I should have checked before. I waited around on the front stoop until the sidewalk was clear, then felt my way through the lock. I still had my lobster pick in hand when I arrived at the door to Blount's third-floor apartment, but I didn't need it. The door had been jimmied open, crudely, messily, as if with a crowbar.

I stepped inside and listened. There was no sound except that of the traffic down on Madison. I checked the rooms and found them as I'd left them on Friday.

I knelt by the low bookshelves and pulled out the hardback copy of Fanon's *The Wretched of the Earth*. Inside the front cover was a hand-written inscription: "Billy—This will explain some things—From your friend, Kurt Zinsser—December 15, 1970." I copied the words onto my pad.

Back in Blount's bedroom, I sat on the edge of his mattress and tried the phone. It was still connected and probably had another week or two before New York Telephone would be galvanized into frenzied plug-pulling by the unpaid bill. I dialed the Albany Police Department, and while I waited to be put through to Sergeant Bowman, I noticed it: Billy Blount's phone book was not where I had found it on Friday, and left it, beside the telephone.

"Bowman!" He made his own name sound like an accusation.

"Don Strachey. I want to report a breaking-and-entering."

"You'd better watch your step with me, Strachey! I warned you once and I'm warning you again. Now, what do you want?"

"Billy Blount's apartment has been broken into. With a wrecking ball, I think. His phone book with his friends' numbers written on it is missing. I'm there now."

"You think I'm a goddamned idiot. You're covering for yourself. *You* did it. You're lying."

"Wrong. I'm tidier than this. I'm a bachelor, remember? Obsessively neat." I wished Timmy were there to hoot with merriment over that one. "This is definitely the work of a sloppy amateur, except all he walked off with was Blount's phone book. I think that's interesting, don't you?"

"Yes. I do."

"And puzzling."

"That, too."

"I thought you'd want to know, and to check it out around here. See how helpful I'm being? Before this is over, Ned, I'm going to earn your respect and devotion." He made a strangling sound. "Anyway, what's happening down there on your end of things?"

"Listen, Strachey, I wanted to talk to you about that—about 'my end of things.'" The sarcasm was like gelignite. "This Al Douglas you sent me chasing after—Bowsie. None of the Greyhound perverts ever heard of the guy."

"Did I say Greyhound? I meant Trailways. It's the Trailways station where Al hangs out. Jesus, I'm sorry. Really."

A silence. "Strachey—are you jerking me around? You oughtn't to do that. You want names of people who've tried, I'll provide references. They'll tell you. Don't do it. Tell me you're not fucking me up the ass." He made a gagging sound and muttered something else.

"Consider yourself told," I said. "With you, Ned, I'm straight." My palms were sweating. I held out my free hand to see how steady it was. Not too. I said, "What'd you get from the airlines at La Guardia? Anything?"

"Nah. Blount either used a phony name or didn't fly out of there at all. I hope, for your sake, Strachey, it was the first. You're on trial in this town, you know."

Maybe he just talked like a South End Torquemada and when push came to shove, he'd reveal a heart and mind worthy of Learned Hand. But I supposed he wouldn't. I said, "I'll be in touch, Sergeant. Have a nice day." I hung up.

I searched the apartment to make the sure the phone book hadn't simply been moved to another spot. It hadn't. It was gone.

Back at the phone, I made a credit-card call to California. It was just eight-thirty Pacific Time, so I tried the home number of the party I wanted. I'd known Harvey Geddes since army-intelligence days, and we'd stayed in touch through his coming out and into his years as a fund-raiser and organizer at the Los Angeles Gay Community Services Center in West Hollywood.

"Hello?"

"Harvey—Don Strachey."

"Don, what a surprise! I was just leaving for the center. This is great! Are you in LA?"

"I wouldn't mind if I were. I'm in Albany up to my brain pan in a murder case."

"Too bad. I'd love to see you. Who's your client?"

"The parents of the accused. Except I doubt he did it. He's skipped, and I've got to locate him and find out what he knows. That's why I'm calling."

"Is he gay?"

"He is."

"Do you think he's out here?"

"Somewhere out that way, yes. Harv, do you remember the FFF?"

"Sure. Forces of Free Faggotry. They were active eight or ten years ago. They predated us at the center by a year or so, I think. They were even pre-Stonewall when they got started. They've been defunct for several years, though. They were considered too radical even for the hell-raisers who got this place going—Kight and Kilhefner and that bunch."

"Yeah, that's what I remember reading about them. They worked underground, right? Went around snatching gays out of mental hospitals they'd been forced into and then hiding them out. They worked on contract, as I recall, with friends of the people who were locked up."

"You got it," Geddes said. "That was the FFF. J. Edgar Hoover had them on a list of thirty-three degenerate organizations that he carried in his wallet."

"I don't know yet who would have arranged it, but I'm pretty sure the FFF performed its service for my clients' son once, in the late fall of seventy. A lesbian friend of his was brought out, too."

"Yeah," he said, "it would have been around that time. That sounds right. Maybe the parents made the contract. Your clients."

"Hardly. They're the ones who put him in. For 'problems of social adjustment.'"

"One of those."

"One of those."

100

"The hospital probably used electroshock therapy," Geddes said. "Blast the demons out. It used to happen a lot. It still does. More than you'd think."

"You really think they'd have done that? To a couple of kids?"

"I'd say so. Check with the guy when you find him. I'd put money on it."

"Harv, does the name Kurt Zinsser ring a bell with you?"

"He was one of them," Geddes said, "an FFF founder. The group split up, I heard, in seventy-five or -six when a couple of them got busted up in Oregon, and then there were the usual hassles over theology and tactics. Some of them are still out here in Santa Monica and Venice. Zinsser, the last I knew, was back in his hometown, Denver."

Of course—Mountain Time, not far from Cheyenne. I said, "Can you get me an address and phone number?"

"I'll try."

"Call me."

"Will do. Hey, Don, how's it going for you back there? Are you ready to make the move yet? You know, we've got men out here, too."

"Oh—I don't know, Harv. It's my masochistic streak."

"You into that? Well, if that's your bag, Don, who am I? Anyway, we've got that, too."

"No, I meant staying in Albany. No, that's wrong, too. I like it here. Albany's not exactly London or Vancouver, but I like my friends here. And a lover—I have a lover. I didn't tell you that?"

"The last time we talked you'd just gotten your divorce from Bambi."

"Brigit."

"Right. That was—?"

"Three years ago."

"God, was it really? We grow old, we grow old, we shall wear our Levis rolled. I hit the big four-oh this year, Don. They're moving us right along, aren't they?"

"Yeah, me too, Harv. I'm forty now. Last night I found the first gray hair in my mustache."

"Pluck it out?"

"Nah, I would have felt ridiculous. Hey, listen, give me a call on Zinsser, will you? I've gotta get moving."

"It was great talking to you, Don. Glad to hear about the man in your life. Peace to you both. I'll be in touch on Zinsser. Give me a day or so."

"I'll appreciate it."

"Glad to do it. See you, brother."

"Right, Harv."

I made another credit-card call, to New Baltimore, fifteen miles down the Hudson from Albany.

"Good morning, Sewickley Oaks."

"The administrator's office, please."

"One moment."

Click-click.

"Dr. Thurston's office."

"Yes, this is Attorney Tarbell, and I'm calling for Stuart Blount. Mr. Blount wishes to know whether Dr. Thurston is fully prepared for the admission of Mr. Blount's son, William—particularly in regard to strengthened security. Mr. Blount is especially anxious that there be no unfortunate recurrence of the nineteen-seventy situation. And Judge Feeney, of course, shares that view."

"Well, I—Dr. Thurston has stepped out, but as far as I know, he's done everything he and Mr. Blount and the judge talked about last week. The judge was quite insistent regarding the maximum-security aspect, and Dr. Thurston, I know, has been making arrangements. Has young William been located?"

"Not just yet. But he will be soon, hopefully."

"Should I have Dr. Thurston call you?"

"Thank you, no. Mr. Blount will be in touch. In a week or so, I should think."

"All right, then. Thank you for calling, Mr. Tarbell."

"Thank you for answering when I did. Have a nice day."

"Thank you. Good-bye."

"Bye now."

I hung up and said it out loud: *Asshole Blounts!* Hardy Monkman had once lectured me against the pejorative use of the word "asshole." It was counterrevolutionary; it mimicked homophobes. But, as I'd tried to explain to Hardy, there were assholes and there were *assholes*. The Blounts were *assholes*.

I phoned Stuart Blount's office and told his secretary I'd need another two thousand dollars within forty-eight hours. She put me on hold, then came back and said she would mail the check to my office that afternoon. I said, "Have a nice day."

I drove over to my apartment and retrieved the Blounts' letter to their son from the jacket of "I'm Here Again." I wanted to rip it open, but I didn't. I carefully steamed the flap loose, then unfolded the typed note. It said:

Dear Billy:
    You must come and talk with your mother and me. We can help you, plus we have good news for you. We know where Eddie is, and perhaps we can arrange to put you two in touch.
                                        Your father,
                                        (Signed) Stuart Blount

Eddie again. The guy whose lookalike had once gone into the Music Barn and sent Billy Blount into a tailspin. Who the hell was this Eddie?

12

I DROVE OUT WESTERN. DISCO 101 WAS PLAYING THE VILLAGE People's "Sleazy." I switched over to WGY and wound down with some Tommy Dorsey—way down, too far. Public radio had on a Villa-Lobos guitar piece, and I stayed with it on the drive out to Trucky's.

Truckman put out a light buffet every day from twelve to two—for $1.95 you could fill up on water-soaked starches and poisoned cold cuts. It was popular and drew a mainly straight crowd from SUNY and from the State Office Campus.

I ate macaroni salad and salami with yellow mustard on a

103

day-old bun. I looked for Mike Truckman but didn't see him around. The dance floor was roped off and the juke box was playing something of the Bee Gees'. I went back to the disc jockey's booth and saw a DJ I'd met a few times at parties. He was inside, sorting through records and listening to something on his headset. I opened the door and went in.

Niles Jameson was a small, skinny black man with a full Afro and a big nimbus of black fuzz all around his placid, delicate face. He wore black pants and a black T-shirt and looked like a dark balloon on a dark string. He glanced my way as I came in and shoved the headset off one ear as he went on examining a stack of new records.

"Hi. I forget your name." He had a big, resonant voice, like a radio DJ's.

"Don Strachey. We've met at Orrin Bell's. I was there the night the guy from Tulsa went through Orrin's waterbed with his spurs."

He looked at me and smiled. "Niagara Falls."

"The people downstairs thought so."

"Wet."

He flipped a record off the turntable and, using the palms of his hands like fingers, popped it into its jacket. "You're the detective, right? Superfly."

"Something like that." I looked at the records he was going through. "What's new that's good?"

"The Pablo Cruise is nice. And an Isley Brothers that's gonna knock your socks off." He put another record on and moved his body to the sound in his ear.

I always felt like Barbara Walters in these situations. I said, "Is disco going to last?"

He said, "Is dancing?" He was young. But I nodded knowingly.

I said, "Have you taken Steve Kleckner's place?"

"Some nights," he said. "I free-lance."

"Where abouts?"

"Parties, college dances, a straight club in Watervliet. Whoever'll hire me."

"You knew Kleckner, didn't you?"

He changed records. "Yeah. I knew Steve. He set me up

104

with Truckman. The DJs all help each other out, mostly. There's a couple of turkeys, but not too many. Steve was a good man. I liked Steve."

"I heard he was depressed about something the couple of weeks before he was killed. Do you have any idea why that might have been?"

He flipped the record on the turntable over with his palms and set the needle back on it. "Nope. I don't."

"I don't think Billy Blount killed him," I said. "I'm trying to find out who did. Steve was popular, I know. But it looks as if somebody didn't like him. Who didn't?"

He pushed the headset down around his neck and looked at me now. "I know the Blount dude's friends all think he's innocent," Jameson said. "And maybe that's so. But if Blount didn't do it, I can't help you out, brother. I wish I could. People liked Steve, and we all miss the hell out of him. I mean, yeah, Steve was a little bit loose and sometimes he probably went home with people he shouldn't have. And shit, maybe he ran into somebody once, some crazy fuck who wasn't playing with a full deck, somebody who couldn't stand anybody gay being as cool and together as Steve was—I've met that type—or maybe somebody who didn't dig the records he played, or didn't like the way he kissed. Shit, I've met a few weird people. They're around. But not *that* weird." He gazed down at the spinning turntable and shook his head in disgust.

Through the big window overlooking the empty dance floor, I saw Mike Truckman come in a side door and head up towards the bar.

I said to Jameson, "Were you here the night it happened?"

"I was over doing a party in Schenectady." He pulled the headset over one ear again and moved the turntable arm to the second cut of the record that was on. "I heard the next night when I came in. From the cleaning lady. She was having the jimjam fits. Carried on like the crazy bitch she is."

"You mean Harold?"

He nodded. "You know Harold?"

"I've seen her—him—her around."

"A trip, isn't she?"

Harold was the sometime drag queen who cleaned up after

closing each night at Trucky's. She had the look of a forties movie queen and the meanest, foulest mouth in Albany County. Her shrill anger, as she pointed out to anyone who would listen, resulted from the twist of fate that had made her a cleaning lady instead of a star. She claimed that if she had been born in 1926 instead of 1956, her life would have been very different. And it might have been. With peace of mind, or enough Valium in her, Harold could have been some other studio's answer to Rita Hayworth, or at least Virginia Mayo.

Jameson said, "I'd seen Harold freak out before, but nothing like that day. I mean, it really got to her. Fact, she said she'd seen it coming. She knew something bad was coming down with Steve. She started screaming and throwing things around, and finally Mike had to hustle her out of here. Mike was sauced up even more than usual, and we were all down, and Harold was just making it worse."

"Mike has a bad drinking problem, doesn't he?"

"Yeah, especially since summer it's gotten worse. It's a shame. Mike's a good man. Floyd the doorman is pretty much running the place now."

"Does Mike have blackouts? When he can't remember where he's been and what he's done?"

"Could be. I wouldn't know about that."

"What's Harold the cleaning lady's last name?"

"Snyder."

"Where does she live?"

"Pine Hill somewhere. Floyd's not here, but Mike could tell you, if you catch him sober. You gonna visit Harold?" He raised his eyebrows and grinned.

"I think so," I said.

"You watch out now. That bitch is man-crazy. Came in here one night after closing and wanted to do me on that stool over there."

"I'll be careful," I said. "We'll chat through her keyhole."

"Yeah, well, don't get too close or she'll do you right through the keyhole." He started to change the record, then looked back at me. "No offense."

I said, "I'm reasonably secure."

"I'll bet you are."

Games. I liked them once in a while, though not so much just after lunch.

I left Jameson and went looking for Mike Truckman. I found him in his office going through invoices and looking as if the papers in front of him were atrocity reports from Amnesty International. Alongside the papers were a glass and bottle.

"Don, hey Don, nice to see you. How you making out with the Blount kid? Have a drink."

I slid up onto the Molson's crates. "I've got some ideas," I said. "Another week or so and I think I'll have him back here."

"Oh, yeah? Where's he at?"

"West of Utica."

"Syracuse?"

"Farther. Meanwhile I still don't think Blount did it. I'm working on who did. Any more ideas since I saw you last?"

He stuck his lips out and slowly shook his head. The puffed flesh around his eyes was the color of dirty snow, and his hair stuck out in yellow-white clumps. One hand lay on his telephone, as if he might need to grasp it for leverage or support. The telephone gave half a ring before the hand snatched it up.

"Trucky's—Well, hello, a friend of yours is here right this minute!" He looked at me and mouthed Timmy's name. "Sure thing, Tim, I'll tell him—mm-hmmm—mm-hmmm—Right—Oh, yes—Swell—Oh sure, oh sure, as always—A hundred. No, *two* hundred. Who do I make it out to?—Sure thing, Tim, I'll send the check along with Don here—Right—Okay, kid, see ya, then."

He hung up. "Your pal Timothy says to tell you he'll be at the alliance meeting tonight. They're setting up a legal-defense fund for the people arrested at the Rat's Nest. Nordstrum is handling his own suit, but the alliance is going to help the customers who were busted—for 'buggery' or whatever the fuck it was. Here—." He scrawled out a check. "Things are tight right now, but not so tight I can't help fight a fucking-over like this one. As always." He raised a glass and saluted.

I folded the check and put it in my wallet. "Did Timmy mention whether the other bar owners are helping out?"

"He didn't say. He probably called me first so he could let those other tight-asses know I gave. For what that'll be worth.

You and I know, Don, don't we? They're only out for themselves. Even the gay bastards—*especially* the gay owners. They're so goddamn chintzy they won't part with a nickel unless they can figure a way to get a dime back on it. I don't know whether they see the movement as competition or what. But they're killing themselves. It'll all come back on them."

"I doubt that," I said. "Eighty percent of the homosexuals in this country would patronize Anita Bryant's place if she had a hot dance floor and sold drinks two-for-one on Friday night. Ten years ago ninety percent would have, but there's still enough indifference around to feed any amount of greed. It's changing a little, but we're still a minority. Face it, Mike."

He nodded. "I have. I know. *Do* I know."

"You're a rare one, though, Mike, and there are people who appreciate it. You'd better know that, too. You're a—a credit to your sexual orientation."

He tried to laugh, but it wasn't in him. I felt for him and didn't want to bring up what I knew I had to. I said, "Mike—this is hard, but—I'm sort of going through a process of elimination. I'm hard-headed and thorough, you must have heard that, and I've got a thing about making lists and crossing things off. Or, to put it in the more positive light that's appropriate in your case, I'm trying to establish alibis for the night of the murder for all the people Steve Kleckner knew best. I know you and Steve had an affair once and that you were—well, sort of jealous of Steve's other men." He froze. I said, "For the sake of my obsessive neatness, then, just tell me where you went that night after you left here at four."

He stared at me through his alcoholic haze, stricken, and for an instant I thought he was going to cry. My inclination was to keep rambling on in the same convoluted vein, but I knew it would only come out worse. Not that it mattered. His hurt altered into anger, and he said—croaked the words out, "I wouldn't have believed it! After *everything I've done*—"

That irritated me. "Mike," I said, "that's beside the point—in a thing like this. Just rattle it off and that'll be the end of it. Really—"

"Fuck you, Strachey!"

"Look, Mike, you know I'm discreet to the point of—"

"I said *fuck you,* Strachey!"

"Mike, if you were with someone underaged, or whatever the hell it might have been—"

He looked at me with ferocious scorn and—I was sure of it—with fear.

"Okay," I said. "It's okay, Mike. Look—we'll talk again. After you've given some thought to what I'm trying to do. One request, though. I want to talk to Harold the cleaning lady. Could you give me her address?"

He didn't move. "You've hurt me deeply, Don. Please leave." Tears ran down his cheeks.

"Yeah. Okay." I stood up. "One last thing, Mike. Do you know anyone who owns a late-model gold-colored Olds Toronado?"

I watched his expression, but it didn't change. He just sat there, the tears rolling down his face and dripping onto his invoices.

I asked him if he'd been with Frank Zimka that night. He flinched when I said the name, but still he didn't move.

I said, "Okay, friend," and left him.

I got Harold the cleaning lady's address from one of the bartenders and drove back down Western into town. I kept the radio off, and I wanted a cigarette.

13

I STOPPED FOR GAS AND REACHED HAROLD SNYDER FROM A PAY phone. I explained who I was and what I wanted, and he said, "Fuck off, dear," and hung up.

I drove over to his place on South Lake Avenue. I went in a side entrance of the old frame house and knocked on the second-floor door that had Snyder's name painted on it with what looked like shiny red nail polish.

The door opened and a movie star stood there in a filmy negligee and boxer shorts.

I said, "I'm Donald Strachey. I'm persistent."

"Did I tell you to fuck off, or did I tell you to fuck *off? Hey?*"

She stamped her foot and made an indignant flouncy movement with her shoulders and hips. I'd always found effeminate men unappealing, but once when I'd made a crack to Brigit about "that faggy guy over there," she'd replied, "Faggy is as faggy does." Which missed the point by a mile but still left an impression on me. I tried to become more tolerant.

"If you're interested in having Steve Kleckner's killer caught," I said, "you'll want to talk to me. And what happened to Steve could happen to someone else if the killer isn't found. Another gorgeous man lowered forever into the cold, cold ground. Help me make that not happen."

She looked interestedly at my face for a moment, and then at my crotch, and then at my face again. "What *are* you, anyway, doll-face? You're mu-u-uch too cute to be an Albany cop, but you *did* say you were a detective. You said that on the phone. Explain yourself, luv."

"I'm a private detective." I showed her the card. I half-closed one eye like Bogey and said out of the side of my mouth, "I work alone, sweet-haht."

She gave me what I took to be a Lauren Bacall look. "Well, you do look a *little* like Robert Mitchum. You should have mentioned that when you called, hon, it might have made a difference. Even if you didn't, it *might* not be too late for us." She gave me a sultry look with no apparent humorous intent, though it still appeared to have been learned from Carol Burnett.

I said, "You got a cold beer? It's warming up again."

"H-well! I just don't know if I should have a man in my apartment who's drinking. Who knows *what* might happen?"

"I wasn't going to drink it, I just wanted to hold it in my left armpit. I'm naturally hot-blooded."

I thought: "A smile played about her sensuous slash of mouth." A smile played about her sensuous slash of mouth. She said, "Do-o-o come in."

I went in and she shut the door. I sat on the divan across

110

from a plaster model of an Academy Award Oscar painted gold. She brought an open bottle of Valu Pack beer from the kitchen and seated herself beside me.

I said, "I hear you cared a lot about Steve Kleckner." I took a swig of beer.

She reached over and felt my cock through my khakis. The damn fool thing stiffened.

She said, "I could go for you, Donald."

I said, "The day after Steve was killed, you told people out at Trucky's you'd known something bad was going to happen to him. How did you know that?"

"Let's not talk about that," she said, and her mouth went wetly over my ear.

"No, let's. It's, uh—important."

She continued to massage me, and I found myself shifting so she could get a better grip on it. A spot appeared on my damn cream-colored pants. I said, "Do you know—anyone who—who owns an—an Olds—"

"Oooo, Donnie—it's like a *Molson's bottle!*"

"Look, Harold—"

"Sondra."

"—Sondra. Look—I have an appointment in half an hour. If we could just *talk,* now, then maybe another time—"

"Gaw-w-w-d, you're fan*tas*tic! I've seen you around, Donnie, at Trucky's and here and there, but I never dreamed you'd go for a woman like me. I figured you were like all the other pansies in this candy-ass town—that you liked *men,* and you were just another faggot. There are so *many* of them these days. It can get so very lonely for a woman like me. With so few *real* men around." She was working at my belt buckle.

"Look," I lied, "I really *do* have an appointment at three." Our hands fought over the belt buckle. "What about—tonight? Are you busy tonight?"

"Now, baby, *now!* You *know* you want me!"

She was panting and squirming against me. Underneath it all, she was slim and hard and muscular—male. She was getting to me fast. I yanked myself free and stood up. She fell back against the arm of the couch, the erection in her shorts poking up through the front of the negligee.

She looked at me contemptuously and snorted, "You're queer, aren't you?"

I said, "The thing is, it can't happen for us just now, Sondra. That's the truth. Not this afternoon. But don't despair—I'm bisexual."

She made a little-girl look. "Tonight then, baby? You said tonight. I heard you say tonight."

"Yes," I said. "Tonight."

"What time?"

"Eight. Around eight." I'd figure a way out.

She sat up, crossed her legs, and lit a pale green Gauloise. "All right then, Donald. I've learned to be patient. I know that men have their male things they must do. Holding sales conferences, splitting wood, jerking each other off in the shower—all that pigshit. While we women sit around watching the soaps and causing static on the police radios with our defective vibrators. But it's okay. We will survive. I can wait for the ERA. I can even wait until eight o'clock tonight—for you. Hunk." She blew me a kiss.

I remained standing and said, "Tonight's social, but now's business. Look, you really have to answer a few questions for me, Sondra. Like, why had Steve been so depressed, and whether or not Mike Truckman had anything to do with it. Don't you understand why I have to know these things?"

She let herself relax—or tense up—into being Harold Snyder just a bit, and said, "Yes. I do. But I don't believe there's any connection between Steve getting killed and anything else that happened. I really don't, Donnie."

"Between *what* else that happened and Steve getting killed?"

She sat with her back stiff, the hand with the cigarette resting on the crossed knee, like Gloria Graham in *The Big Heat*. She said, "That part did have something to do with Mike. What Steve was freaked out about, I mean. Steve saw something. I saw it, too, darling. But, that's—there was no connection. No, I don't think so." She grimaced, remembering it.

I said, "I'm as eager as anyone in Albany to show that Mike had nothing to do with the killing. You can help me do that by telling me what you know. It'll be between us, Sondra. Just something to clear the air. If that's what needs to be done."

"No," she said, shaking her head, "if a woman isn't *loyal*, then what is she?" She gave me a Greer Garson look. God.

I said, "A life was taken. Another life could be taken. The life of a man."

"I'm sorry," she said. "I'm terribly sorry. You have your job to do, Donald. I understand. Now you must try to understand me. And you will in time. But—does this mean—?" She sat poised.

I wasn't about to get roughed up by this one. "No," I said. "I'll be here. How could I not? Eight o'clock, then."

She stood and walked over to me. One arm came up around the back of my neck, like Grace Kelly's arm around Cary Grant's neck in *To Catch A Thief.*

"Till tonight, then, darling."

"Till tonight."

Our tonsils met.

As I headed down Washington Avenue, I ran the standard list through my mind:

1. It's been a long day, and I'm worn out. I'm really very sorry.
2. I drank too much tonight, it'll never work.
3. I think I've got clap.
4. I'm too nervous—this is only my second time.
5. Oh, God, I just can't do this to my lover!
6. I'm into scat, what are you into?

At seven-thirty I'd phone Harold, pick from the list at random, ask for a rain check, and that would be that. Except I *did* have to have a talk with Harold. Maybe what she knew about Mike Truckman was unconnected to the Kleckner killing, but I was beginning to have a sickening feeling about Truckman's involvement in all of this, and I had to find out everything I could, as fast as I could. Maybe I'd look Harold up out at Trucky's and we could talk in a public place. Sure. I'd work it that way. Wednesday night. I relaxed.

I found the landlady for Steve Kleckner's Hudson Avenue apartment in her own first-floor-front quarters. She was a plump, middle-aged woman with blue eyes, a pretty mouth, and a small white goatee. I introduced myself as Lieutenant Ronald Firbank, an associate of Sergeant Bowman's, and she agreed to let me into Kleckner's basement apartment. She said his rent had been paid through the end of the week and that she was waiting for his relatives from Rensselaer County to pick up his belongings so she could clean the place up before the new tenant arrived on Monday. The apartment, she said, was as it had been on the night of the murder, "except for what those other policemens took away."

The woman led me outside the turn-of-the-century three-story brick building and into a narrow alleyway just off the street. We went down three cement steps into an alcove, and she unlocked the old wooden door with a skeleton key. A second door, leading from a bare passageway into the apartment itself, was opened with a key fitting into a newer Yale lock. She said, "I'm not gone in there no more till I hafta," and left me alone.

The living room had an old greenish rug over the concrete floor, a thirties-style brown velveteen overstuffed couch, two easy chairs, a black and white Philco TV resting on a vinyl-covered hassock, a large expensive Technics sound system on a wooden table, and about a thousand records, all disco, on big metal shelves against a wall. The room had been fairly recently painted a pale mauve. Dim light came from two windows that began at ground level halfway up the wall facing the alleyway.

A doorway to the right led into a tiny, windowless kitchen. The refrigerator contained a can of V-8 and a half-dozen eggs, nothing more. I checked the counter drawers and found some five-and-dime silverware. The one sharp knife was an ivory-colored, plastic-handled paring knife.

I went through a second doorway at the back of the living room and entered the small bedroom. A double bed sat in the corner, its veneer headboard against the rear wall, its left side next to a wall with a ground-level window. The bedding had been removed and I could see the big dark blotch on the mattress. I crawled onto the bed, raised the yellowing window shade, and lifted the sash; its weights clanged down inside their casing and the sash went up easily. I breathed in the fresh air from the alleyway. I groped around between the bed and the wall and pulled up the adjustable window screen that probably would have been in use on the night of the killing.

Access to the bathroom was through a door on the bedroom's right wall. I looked inside, then went back to the living room, took Anita Ward's "Ring My Bell" from the record shelves and placed it on the turntable. I waited for the amplifier to warm up, then played the record at high volume. A second set of speakers fed the sound into the bedroom.

I went back to the bathroom, closed the door securely, turned on the shower in the metal stall, and stuck my head inside. I stayed out of the direct line of spray but still got a wet face from the ricochet. I listened. I could hear an occasional bass note and, just barely, a distant thump-thump-thump. But I had to work at it. Mass carnage could have taken place in the bedroom outside and I might or might not have heard it.

I shut off the shower, dried my face with a towel on the rack by the little sink, then went out to stop the music.

The landlady was standing in the doorway. "That stuff gives me a headache," she said. "The new guy, I gottim from the deaf school. I figger, they can't hear, they won't play no loud music. I hadda do it, see. That stuff gives me a headache."

Back at the office, I called Ned Bowman. I said, "You've got the murder weapon. What kind of a knife was it? The papers just said 'kitchen.'"

"First you tell me what you're doing, Strachey. Account for your activities for the past six hours. Then I might bend the rules a bit and reveal official police information. Remember, I said *might*."

"Jesus, you know what gay life is like, Ned. It's constantly a lot of raunchy stuff you really wouldn't want to hear about. Like, I spent the earlier part of the afternoon getting fondled by a drag queen who thinks she's Rita Hayworth. That kind of craziness. You want to hear more?"

"Strachey, your credibility with me is just about *zilch!* I'm seriously thinking of cutting you off. Or maybe arranging for you to have a wee licensing problem. How would you go for that?"

I said, "St. Louis."

"Tell me more."

"So far, that's all I know. Check St. Louis. St. Louis, Missouri."

A dribble of sweat ran down my ribs. I'd checked the St. Louis number on Chris Porterfield's business phone bill and reached another travel agency.

"I'll check it out," he said. "I'll have to alert the St. Louis department to watch for the Hertz car from Wyoming. It'll take time."

Right, it would. I said, "The knife, then. Please describe it."

He said, "A carving knife. Wooden haft. Long, thin, stainless-steel blade. Fourteen inches end to end. Sheffield."

"That sounds expensive. Kleckner's other kitchenware is junk. Do you think Blount carried a carving knife with him that night? In a violin case?"

A pause. "I concede that there exist certain questions relating to the alledged murder weapon. All that'll be cleared up once I've had the opportunity to chat with William Blount. Of that, Strachey, I am certain."

"I don't think Blount would have had a knife like that either," I said. "One of the disadvantages of being young and gay, Ned, is that you don't get any wedding presents. People with Sheffield cutlery are well off, or married, or both. Also, you still haven't explained how someone else's prints were on the knife, not Blount's. You're heading the wrong way, Ned, admit it."

"I'll admit no such thing. In fact, if you want to know the truth of it—not that truth is anything you'd care that much about—the truth of it is, I'm now working out a theory that Blount had an accomplice—the guy who busted into Blount's apartment and made off with his phone book."

"Guy?"

"We went out to Blount's place and found a witness to the break-in you reported. A woman on the first floor let somebody in the front door behind her around eleven o'clock Friday night and a bit later heard the door get busted in. Ten minutes after that she sees the guy out her window getting into a gold-colored car. Ring a bell with you?"

Friday night. The night I'd been in Blount's apartment around seven, answered the phone, and heard the caller wait and then hang up. I said, "A gold-colored car? Nope, haven't run across that one. How come the woman didn't report the break-in?"

116

"She—well, she did."

"Let me guess—"

"Fuck you, Strachey."

I said, "A patrolman checked it out, wrote it up on some forms, and you weren't told. Right?"

"I retire in six years, two months, and twenty-six days. In the big picture that's not a long time. It'll pass. Time flies when you're having fun."

"Describe the man—the lock smasher."

"It's blurry. Twenties, light hair, light blue sweater. Carried a gym bag of some kind, probably with the tools in it. Big, new gold-colored car. Keep an eye out among your fag friends, will you?"

It could very well have been Zimka, though he struck me less as a gym-bag type than a paper-bag type. I said, "I'll be on the lookout. He's probably one of us. The light blue sweater is a code. It means he's into ice cubes."

"*Ice cubes?* Kee-rist!"

"You don't want to hear it, Ned. It's pretty kinky. Real Krafft-Ebing."

"*Kinky,* you call it! You people draw some pretty fine distinctions."

"It's a way of life," I said. "Just another way of life." He muttered something. "I'll be in touch, Ned. You too, okay?"

"Sure, I will."

He hung up, still muttering.

I called PBS in New York, got the name of its Denver affiliate, KRNA, Channel Six, then phoned out there and asked what programs the station had run on Monday night. I was told the Paul Robeson special had been on from eight to ten, local time, and at ten o'clock Monty Python came on. That would have been midnight, eastern time. Just right.

I phoned American Airlines in Albany and made a reservation for a 9:50 A.M. flight on Thursday, changing at O'Hare for a Continental flight to Denver.

I looked up Huey Brownlee's place of employment in my notes, then called Burgess's Machine Shop. The woman who answered put me on hold; a male voice came on the line, then I listened to five minutes of roaring and grinding sounds before Huey answered.

117

"Donald, my man, how's it shakin'?"

"Huey, I've got a funny question."

"You want a funny answer to it or a *see-ree*-yus answer, baby?"

"It's serious. I haven't found Billy Blount yet, but I'm getting close to him, and meanwhile I'm trying to verify something. Did Billy always take a shower after sex?"

He laughed. "At first, I kinda took it personal. I never knowed anybody to do that—except for this married dude from Selkirk who used to drop by wunst and a while. Damn Billy'd spend ten minutes in there washin' me off him, even when he slept over. I kidded him, and he said it was just a habit he always had, so I gave it no mind after a while. Why you want to know that?"

"Because Billy told someone that he was in Steve Kleckner's shower at the time of the killing. It makes sense."

"I'd believe that. Spic 'n' Span Billy."

"Thanks, Huey, you've helped me a lot. Hey, one thing—did you get that window lock fixed?"

"Sposed to be fixed today, Donald. Landlady said she'd see to it."

"And you haven't gotten any more weird phone calls?"

"I wouldn't know, baby. I ain't been home the last coupla nights. Don't ask me where I was, 'cause I ain't sure I could tell ya. Rotterdam, it might of been. Anyways, I'll be back home tonight—if you'd like to drop by for coffee."

I could see him leering wholesomely. "Well, to tell you the truth—a small part of it, anyway—I've got to work tonight. Look, now, you be careful. And let me know if you get any more of those crazy phone calls. Somebody who might be mixed up in the Kleckner killing has got hold of Billy's phone book with your number on it, and someone else whose name is on the book has been getting crank calls, too."

"Don't worry about ol' Huey, Donald. Asshole come after me again and he gonna be carried outta my place in one of them puke-green trash bags."

"Right. Just—be loose."

"Always, sweetheart. All-*ways*."

I called Timmy's office and caught him just about to leave for the day.

118

"I'm not going to be at the alliance meeting tonight," I said, "but I've got Truckman's check. And tomorrow I'll have another one for the fund. From an anonymous donor."

"Great; we're going for four thousand. How're you doing? Are you working tonight?"

I'd made a decision without knowing I'd made it. I said, "Tonight I'm going to do something immoral."

"Oh? Immoral by what standards?"

As a teenager, he'd considered becoming a Jesuit. I knew why. "Immoral by just about anybody's standards," I said. "Believe me."

"Then don't do it."

"I've already decided."

"That's sound thinking. Charles Manson should have used that one. 'But, your honor, we'd already decided.'"

I said, "Don't make it worse."

"Ahh, now I'm an accomplice. Will it be fun, *our* immorality tonight?"

"I'm going to hang up now, Timmy."

"Don, the predestinationist. My mother once warned me about getting mixed up with Presbyterians. See you around, lover."

"Yeah, bye."

I wondered if there was a patron saint for the sarcastic.

14

I EXERCISED, JOGGED AROUND LINCOLN PARK FOR HALF AN hour, showered, dressed, and had a bagel and a cup of plain yogurt while I read the *Times Union*. I went over my notes on the case and added to them. I left the apartment at five after eight under a starry autumn sky, aiming to arrive at Harold Snyder's apartment fifteen minutes late for the sake of dramatic tension. Not that his life lacked it.

"Donnie! Donnie, Donnie, *Donnie!*"

She had on a sheer negligee with a leopard-spot design and panties to match. In the afternoon she'd worn a cheap, wavy orange wig, but now I witnessed her own hair, honey-colored and longish, a smooth whorl combed down over one eyebrow.

I said, "Sondra, would you mind calling me Don? My mother calls me Donnie."

She tapped the tip of my nose with her finger and cocked a freshly drawn eyebrow. "Maybe I'll just call you—Buck."

"I could be trained to respond to that."

"Mmmm. I'll bet you could—Bucky."

We were on the couch. A lamp with a two-watt lightbulb burned in the corner. The phonograph was playing the sound-track from *The High and the Mighty*. She poured me what she called a martini. It was bright red. She lit a Gauloise and we told each other about ourselves.

Sondra described her "tragic childhood," which did, in fact, sound difficult and ugly: seventeen years in an Adirondacks crossroads called Sneeds Pond, with fundamentalist Baptist parents who kept telling her she was "abnormal" and "not right" and locking her in her room with a Bible, a football, and a photo of John Wayne.

"Did you play football, Buckie?" She examined my thighs and calves.

"In high school," I said. "And off and on in the army."

"Ooo, which army? Whose side were you on?"

"Ours. Though I once met Jane Fonda and she said I was making a mistake."

"Tacky bitch. Where does *she* get off!"

"History will treat her more kindly than some."

Having checked out the shape of my legs, she moved on to my chest, a long, smooth hand sliding up under my turtleneck. She said, "Did you see *A Bridge Too Far* on TV the other night? Liv Ullman was too—*aloof*. She's so un*womanly*. Sean Connery, though—God, what a man! You could have played him, Bucky."

I thought, Christ, Sean Connery must be sixty by now. I said, "How old do you think I am, Sondra?"

"Thirty—nine."

120

"Not bad. You only missed by a year."

"Thirty-eight?"

"Yup."

"You have great nipples—for a man."

Was she a *lesbian,* too? I'd heard that about some of the famous starlets. She hiked up my shirt and ran her tongue around a nipple. I felt the heart under it begin to pump faster.

"Sondra—look, if we could just talk about some things for ten minutes, then I could be a lot more relaxed and we could really—"

She came up to my face and gave me a hard look. She said, "This is a social visit. You *said* so. It was your idea, Bucky. You wanna fuck, or you wanna fuck off? *Hey?*"

What would be would be. I said, "What do you think—sexy?"

She sighed and moved to the other nipple. I pulled her up and we sat kissing and feeling and massaging each other's legs and arms and backs and fronts while the record changed and the sound track from *An Affair to Remember* came on. She got my cock out of my pants and mouthed it for a while; I bent forward over her back, reached around, and got hold of hers. I wondered if Kim Novak was built like this.

We ended up on the floor, our garments soon strewn around us, kneeling and facing each other, kissing each other's faces, she massaging my cock and balls, me with a middle finger working into her warm, prelubricated anus.

"Bucky—baby—baby—Bucky—you've found my weakness."

We stood together and she led me into the bedroom by the finger. She flung the chenille bedspread aside and we fell onto the sheets. I was on top of her and she said, "Wait—more grease." The romance of the gay life.

She groped my cock with a palmful of Vaseline Intensive Care lotion—I was afraid I was going to come and in order not to I had to think about Eric Severeid—and then I got some of the stuff on my fingers and lubricated her asshole, which opened at my touch like a baby's mouth.

Her legs came up in the air, as if sprung into their natural position, and I eased myself into her, and felt her working her

121

sphincters like miraculous strong hands. Then we were moving together, she saying *ohhhh, ohhhh, ohhhh* into my ear, me grunting and sighing, and thinking from time to time of Eric Severeid.

After a long, wonderful time her face convulsed, tears ran down her cheeks, and she began to moan, "Oh, Donnie—Donnie, love me—love me real good, Donnie!" and suddenly it hit me. Oh Christ, I thought—this was no longer Sondra the movie star pumping and humping under me anymore, but this sad, fucked-up human being whispering and sighing and weeping into my ear was in fact the hopeless, unloved boy, now the lost, unlovable man, Harold Snyder of Sneeds Pond, New York.

I was panicking, having second thoughts, trying to decide whether or not I could go through with it, when Harold began to moan, "Ohhhh—*ohhhhh*—Yes-s-s—*Yes-s-s-s*—"

I hesitated, stopped, slid it out.

"Oh, don't stop, Donnie! Donnie!" He was grabbing wildly, trying to find it. I shook my ass around, evading him.

My mouth was at his ear. I said, "First, Harold—you've gotta tell me something."

"Donnie—Donnie, what's the *matter?* What did I *do?* You were making me feel so good—so—so *loved*—"

That was it. I collapsed onto him. I wept into his neck—great gulping sobs that made the both of us shake and slide and make slapping sounds in each other's sweat. He threw his arms around me and held me tightly for a minute, or five, or ten, until the tension was gone and we both lay still. We lay like that for a long while, breathing together.

I said, "It's okay, Harold. I'm sorry. I had a cramp."

He kissed my eyes and stroked my head. "Oh, Donnie—poor Donnie—"

I was hard again. Modern ideas about the human brain to the contrary notwithstanding, I've always thought the damn thing had a life of its own.

We began again, taking it slower and easier this time. We'd build, ease off, build again, ease off again, then ride away, up, and up, and up. And, in fact, Harold Snyder—Sondra the cleaning lady, the unrisen star and dirty-mouthed shrew—

turned out to be, in bed, a strong, sweet, knowing, graceful, warm-hearted homosexual man.

At eleven-fifteen, after a second go-round, Harold smoked a Gauloise, I had a black coffee, and then I drove home.

Timmy had let himself in and was waiting in my apartment. He looked up from the copy of *The Nation* he was reading.

I said, "How'd the meeting go?"

He said, "Talky, but useful. How'd the immorality go?"

"Not talky, but useful."

"That's par."

"But not entirely lacking in redeeming personal value."

"Do you want to talk?"

"No," I said. "It'll wait." I hung my jacket in the closet. I removed my clothes and tossed them in the corner. "A shower."

As I went into the bathroom, Timmy got up to pick up my clothes. Not just a sarcastic Jesuit, but a sarcastic Jesuit *mother*.

When I came back, the lights were out and Timmy was in the bed, his clothes neatly folded beside mine on the big ledge of my bay window. I slipped in beside him in the hazy blue of the streetlight, and we rolled gently together.

I said, "We're very lucky. You and I."

"I know," he said. "We are. Let's keep it up."

There was an undertone of apprehension in his voice. There needn't have been. He should have known that by then, but he didn't. So I told him.

15

DURING BREAKFAST THE PHONE RANG. TIMMY WAS SITTING beside it and answered it.

"It's Harold," he said. "I think you've made a friend."

Harold made complimentary and affectionate comments that were good for my ego but not for my conscience. My brief responses were friendly but vague. Then Harold got to the point. "Donnie, I really shouldn't be telling you this, and you must never, *ever* tell Mike I told you. Will you promise me that?"

"I promise."

"Donnie, I—I really can't tell you what Steve saw that upset him so much, 'cause I don't think you'd believe it. *I* saw it with my own baby blues, and *I* could hardly believe it! So if you must, doll, you'll just have to see for yourself. He doesn't meet them at the side door anymore, it's somewhere away from the place. You'll have to follow him somewhere. Tonight, after closing. He goes Wednesdays, and either Fridays or Saturdays."

"Meet who, Harold? Who does Mike meet?"

"You'll see, baby. You'll see."

"Does Mike know that you know this, whatever it is?"

"Ohhh, no-o-o-o, Donnie, and you *mustn't* tell him. Mike's so liquored up and crazy these days he'd fire me, and I might be forced to hit Hollywood and break into the business. And, God, it's such a debilitating experience out there in these crude times we live in—air pollution, dyke agents, Joan Crawford's shoes getting sold off like scrap metal. Within ten years I'd marry a degenerate disco franchiser and OD on Baskin-Robbins and heart-attack pills. Donnie, I have to stay in Albany, where I can be me. In a place where a certain amount of *class* is still respected. No, I can't—I *cannot* afford to lose my job, Donnie. You do understand, don't you, bunny?"

I said, "I won't tell him, Harold. But I might want to talk to you again. After tonight."

Huff, huff. "Well, I should *hope* you'll want to speak to me again. Now that we're lovers. Bye the bye, love-buns, who was that who answered the phone just now?"

"That was my houseboy."

"Ha, I should have known! You older guys! Is he Filipino?"

"Eskimo."

"And you told me you weren't queer!"

"I swing both ways, remember?"

124

"You're a flawed masterpiece, Donnie, that's what you are. But what's a woman to do?"

"Tell me another thing, Harold. Did Mike know that Steve saw whatever he saw?"

"Yes, it was horrible. Steve confronted Mike the day after—Steve told me—and Mike was sloshed, as usual, and started screaming like a bitch. He even *fired* poor Steven—but then he changed his mind five minutes later. See, that's why I'm so scared; Steve was the hot jock, and Mike needed him, and anyways Mike always had a soft spot for Steven even after they broke up. Me, lovable as I am, I'm just a charwoman to Mike, and I can be replaced by any sleazy slut who walks in the door."

"Where were you when you saw—it?"

"In the DJ booth with Steve. It was a quarter to five, and Mike thought everyone had left for the night. But I was depressed about one thing or another, and I was hoping Steven might cheer me up—he had once before. But he wouldn't this time, the little faggot. Anyway, we did get to talking, though— Steven *was* a dear, dear man—and then we looked out and saw it. We just sat there then, scared half to death, until Mike turned the lights out and left, and we got out with Steve's key. It really blew our minds, Donnie. The pits, the absolute *pits.*"

I said, "Thank you, Harold. You've done the right thing telling me this. But you mustn't tell anyone else, okay? And I won't either."

"My lips are sealed, lover. Except when I'm with you. Then they are parted."

"Good. Thank you. One last thing, Harold. Do you know a guy named Frank Zimka? He's a hustler I think Mike has done business with."

"I know who he is, yes. He's weird. I've seen him around. Once with Mike."

"When did you see him with Mike?"

"Last summer once. Or twice maybe. I don't like him. When Zimka's down, he's a real depresso, and when he's on speed, he gets crazy. I heard one time he bounced a toilet seat off a guy's head. Some other whore who'd turned on to Zimka's trick."

"A toilet seat? Does he carry one with him, or what?"

"I wouldn't know the answer to that, sweet thing; I'm only saying what I heard. Donnie—Donnie, I had a wonderful time last night. You made me feel like—like—"

A nat-u-ral wo-man-n-n—

"—like a human being."

A wave of dizziness. I'd made a terrible mistake. This was going to be hard—impossible. I said, "Um. I'm glad."

"Till the next time, lover."

"Oh. Right. See you, Harold. Thanks again."

"It is *I* who am the one who is grateful."

"So long, Harold."

I hung up. Timmy looked up from his Wheat Chex, then down again.

I said, "Shit. I am made of shit."

"Come on now," he said. "You have your good points."

"Today my one good point is I'm beginning to understand this whole Kleckner-Blount-Zimka-Truckman phantasmagoria. I think."

"Right. As a detective, you're sterling silver. It's only as a human being that you're made of—clay. What do you think you've found out?"

I told him. He didn't finish his breakfast.

Timmy put on some of the clothes he kept in my closet and left for his office. I gathered up my notes, retrieved the two letters for Billy Blount from "I'm Here Again," stuffed everything in my canvas tote bag, and drove over to Central.

In the office I made another appointment with the Blounts at one. Low tea on State Street.

I was going over my notes again when Margarita Mayes called.

"Mr. Strachey, I've been in touch with Chris."

"She called me too, as you said she would. Thank you."

"I talked to her last night. She said I could tell you she'd be in Albany Saturday night, and would you come for brunch on Sunday? She won't tell you where Billy is, though; she said I should emphasize that. And if you go to the police, she'll deny all of these things. Will you come?"

"Well, that's certainly a lovely invitation. And I'll let you know—by Friday or so, if that's all right."

"That will be fine. Call me at the office. I'm not staying at the house. Someone tried to break in last night, and I'm staying with a friend in Westmere until Chris gets back. There have been so many burglaries lately. It's really quite frightening."

"Margarita—let me ask you a question. Have you been getting any more crank phone calls?"

A silence. "How did you know that?"

"Because another of Billy's friends has gotten them. Describe the calls."

"There's nothing to describe. Someone calls, and then listens, and then hangs up. There have been eight or ten."

"At your office, or just at home?"

"Just at the house. But I'm out of there now."

"Were you home during the break-in attempt? What happened?"

"I'd been asleep for about an hour," she said, "when the burglar alarm went off. I thought I heard a banging or thumping noise out behind the house, and I called the police right away. I was just scared to death, and I locked my bedroom door until the police came, in about five or ten minutes. They looked outside and found that our stepladder had been taken off the back porch and propped up under the kitchen window. The policemen helped me put the ladder away and said I was safe with the burglar alarm working and to keep everything locked up and not to worry. It frightened me, though; I could hardly sleep at all last night, and I'm not going back there until Chris is home."

"Good. Stay with your friend until I've been in touch again, okay? You could be in danger if you're anywhere near that house, so will you stay away from the house until you've checked with me?"

"Yes, but—who's doing this?"

"I don't know. I think I know, but I'm not sure. When I know for sure, I'll tell you. And I'll let you know about Sunday."

"You can reach me at the office on Friday."

"I'll do that."

It was the goddamn phone book. Bowman should have

confiscated it. *I* should have taken it from Blount's apartment before some lunatic with a lethal contempt for Billy Blount's friends had gotten hold of it and used the listings-by-number directory to locate Chris, Mark, Huey, and—Zimka? He hadn't been bothered. I guessed I knew why.

I reached Huey Brownlee at his work number. "Huey, Don Strachey. Would you mind moving into my apartment for a couple of days?"

"Heh, heh."

"No, I won't be there. Sorry to say. It's all those phone calls you were getting—have you gotten any more?"

"Yeah, three last night. I was gonna call you. Fuckin' motherfucker. I'm just *waitin'* for him to show up, Donald."

"Huey, if you don't get out of there, you could be in for some trouble from a very dangerous screwball, the man who killed Steve Kleckner. Will you do it?"

"Say, you ain't shittin' me, Don?"

"I am not," I said, and he reluctantly agreed to move over to Morton Avenue. I gave him the address, told him where to find the key, and said I'd see him on the weekend.

I phoned Mark Deslonde at Sears. "Mark—Don Strachey, I have a funny question that isn't really funny. Have you gotten any weird phone calls in the last few days?"

"No, have you?"

"You haven't?"

"No, but I haven't been home. I moved in with Phil—Saturday night."

Another peripatetic gay male. The killer must have been having one hell of a time locating a victim at home in his own bed. I said, "Oh. It's that serious with you and Phil?"

"Yep."

"Well—I approve. Entirely."

"Entirely?"

I said, "Well, you know. But yes."

He said, "I know."

"Are you going to Trucky's tonight? I'll see you."

"We'll be there."

We'll. "Great. Us too. Look, do something for me. Whatever happens with you and Phil—and I do wish you all the best— whatever happens—I mean even if one of you has an attack of

128

second thoughts or whatever—do not move back into your apartment until you check with me. Will you do that?"

"Sure. I guess so. But why?"

"It has to do with the Kleckner killing. There's nothing to worry about if you just stay away from the apartment with your phone in it. Look, I'll explain it all in a few days. Will you just do what I say?"

Deslonde told me he would do what I said, although, as it happened, he did not.

I made coffee on my hot plate. I thought about going out for cigarettes. I went back to my desk. I looked up Frank Zimka's number and stared at it. I thought about calling him, but I concluded that I'd probably be tipping him off, so I didn't call. Instead I slit open the envelope Zimka had given me for Billy Blount.

The letter was handwritten on old, yellowing, three-ring notebook paper.

My Dear loving friend Billy,

I don't know where to get in touch with you, but the guy who is giving you this letter said he would give it to you. I miss you so much. Even though our relationship is quite strange, it has meant so much to me, as I told you many times. Is it an impossible dream that we will be together again one day? I don't think that is too much to hope for in this life, though sometimes I think it is, and I don't know what is going to happen to me. I guess I'm just a real crazy fuck-up. When I think about our relationship, I get depressed, but I am willing to continue it if the opportunity presents itself. I hope you are happy and healthy, and whatever befalls, remember that someone *loves* you. It makes me joyous just to be able to write that.

> With all my LOVE,
> Frank
> (Eddie, ha ha)

Eddie again. The name in the record shop and the name in the Blounts' letter to Billy. *Zimka* was Eddie? I had to talk to the Blounts, both senior and junior.

I phoned Timmy at his office.

"It looks as if I am going to Denver tomorrow. I'll know for sure by the end of the day."

"Did your friend in L.A. call back?"

"Not yet. But he'll come through. Harvey is relentless."

"Have you ever been to Denver? You'll go for it."

"I spent twenty years in Salt Lake City one summer, but that's the extent of my acquaintanceship with the mountain states."

"Denver's a nice town. And it's not called the Queen City of the Rockies for no good reason."

"A mile-high San Francisco."

"Hardly that, but still—nice. Lots of opportunities for immorality."

"In your ear."

"I hope you've spent a moral morning. If so, you're on your way. Did you know that after twelve years your soul heals, like your lungs after you've quit smoking?"

"What about immoral thoughts? Do they count? I had one awhile ago."

"Hey, *now* you've got the idea! Yes, they count. But not as much as deeds."

I said, "By the way, Mark and Phil are now living together. I called Mark to find out if he'd been getting funny phone calls like Huey Brownlee's. Margarita Mayes has been getting them too, and somebody tried to break into her and Chris's house last night. I suggested they stay away from their apartments for a few days, and that's when Mark told me. I'm worried."

"They're a good pair—it should work. Is it Zimka you're worried about?"

"I think so, yes. The only thing I'm sure of is they're all connected in some messy, volatile way—Kleckner, Blount, Zimka, Truckman, Chris Porterfield, Stuart Blount, Jane Blount—the lot. And then there's this Eddie—the wild card." I told him about the two letters, from the Blounts to their son, and from Zimka to Blount. "I'm seeing the Blounts at one. Maybe they'll clear things up, out of character as that might be for them." Then I told him what I had decided to do that night.

"Do you want me to go with you? And bring the Leica?"

"Yeah. I do. Wear your track shoes."

130

"Am I gay, or am I gay?"

Soon after I hung up, the mail arrived. There was a thank-you note on a little engraved card from "Mrs. Hugh Bigelow." A lapsed feminist. That was depressing, but I guessed everybody found a way. Also among the bills and clutter was an envelope with a check for two thousand dollars from Stuart Blount. I signed it over to the Rat's Nest Legal Defense Fund and stuck it in my wallet along with Mike Truckman's check.

At a quarter to twelve Harvey Geddes called from Los Angeles. He'd spent most of the night, he said, trying to track down someone with a current address for Kurt Zinsser of the FFF, and after driving from West Hollywood to Santa Monica to Venice and back to Hollywood again, he'd found it. I wrote down the phone number and the building and apartment number on a street in Denver. I told Harvey I owed him one, and he agreed.

I trekked up Central to Elmo's in search of nourishment to gird myself for a visit with the Stuart Blounts, of State Street and Saratoga.

16

"ANOTHER THOUSAND?" BLOUNT SAID. "WELL—I SUPPOSE.

You know your business, Mr. Strachey. Of course, I will be needing an itemized statement of expenses at some future point in time. For tax purposes, you understand."

We were seated in our customary places in the Blount salon, the missus sucking daintily on her long white weed, Blount père eyeing me gravely across his early-American checkbook. I'd thought about asking for twenty-five thousand but concluded that that would be pushing it. He forked over the grand, and I snatched it up.

"May I ask," he said, "where you'll be flying to tomorrow, Mr. Strachey?"

I said, "Caracas."

His eyebrows went up. Hers did not. She said, "We're being taken for a ride."

"I beg your pardon?"

"Stuart, he's playing us for a fool, and you're not stopping him."

I said, "I have the address where your son is staying. I received it from a contact in Los Angeles an hour and twenty minutes ago. I'll be with Billy tomorrow night."

"Billy's not in Argentina!" she snapped. "What do you take us for?"

I said, "Venezuela. Caracas is in Venezuela."

Blount said, "Mr. Strachey, really—how on earth could Billy have—"

"Who is Eddie?" I said.

She gave Blount an I-told-you-so look. He sighed, not so much at my question, I guessed, as at her look.

"Mr. Strachey," Jane Blount said, "have you ever heard it said that gentlemen do not read other gentlemen's mail?"

"I've heard it said, yes. Henry Stimson is usually credited with the line, or is it Liz Smith? Anyway, who is Eddie? Billy will tell me when I see him, I expect, so why don't you save me a small expenditure of energy and yourself the financial expense of my remaining an additional ten minutes in—Caracas. Okay?"

"Why must you know about Eddie, Mr. Strachey?" Blount said. "It is, I'm sorry to say, a private family matter."

"Because Eddie is a part of the puzzle. I'll know which part when I know who or what he is. The safety of three or more people could depend on my knowing."

Jane Blount shot smoke in the air. Her husband shifted in his chair and made an impatient face. "Eddie is a separate matter, Mr. Strachey. *Truly,* he is. You must believe that. He's got nothing to do with this situation Billy's gotten himself into. You have my personal assurance on that. Can you accept that? Can you?" He looked at me imploringly.

I said, "I might have if it weren't for the fact that Eddie's name has cropped up elsewhere in my travels."

They looked at me. Jane Blount said, "Where?"

"Does the name Frank Zimka mean anything to you?"

He said, "No."

132

She said, "Lord, no! *Zim*-ka? It sounds *Polish!*"

I said, "He's a friend of Billy's. An acquaintance."

"And he knows *Eddie?*" she said, looking queasy.

I said, "I'm one of the few people left in Albany who knows nothing about Eddie—*next* to nothing. Now, *who the bloody hell is Eddie?*"

I startled them.

She said, "He's—he's Billy's favorite uncle."

What shit. I said, "Tell me more."

"Stuart's brother Eddie—Billy and he were so close when Billy was young, it was quite touching, really. And then Eddie went away. He's in shipping, you see." Mistah Kurtz. "Uncle Eddie lived in the Levantine for many years, but recently he returned to this country, and Stuart and I thought he might exert his good influence with Billy so that Billy could *finally* be straightened out. So to speak. Don't you think there's good sense in that, Mr. Strachey? Some sound counsel from a wise and sophisticated and much-loved uncle?"

Straightened out. I thought about dropping the Sewickley Oaks business on them, but that would have been showing off, and in any case I had my own plans for that particular side of the equation.

"Well, why didn't you just tell me that in the first place? Is Uncle Eddie a leper? a syphilitic? a Pole? What's the big secret?"

Blount was sitting with his head back and his eyes squeezed shut. I'd have felt sorry for him if I hadn't known what a dangerous man he was.

Jane Blount said, "Uncle Eddie is—a socialist."

"In shipping?"

"Yes."

"Well, he's no idealogue."

"No," she said. "At least he's not *that*."

They were hopeless. I'd find out what I had to from my own sources, including their son, for whom there was evidence of sanity, even good sense. That sometimes happened in families.

I said, "When I see Billy tomorrow, I'm sure he'll be happy to hear about Uncle Eddie's being back. The news should make my job that much easier."

She took on a confused look. Her husband appeared as if,

while his wife and I chatted, he'd slipped on his death mask. I waited.

In her embarrassment Jane Blount turned surly. "Just bring Billy back here to Albany, Mr. Strachey. That's what Stuart's paid you a good deal of money to do. Bring Billy to this house—our home and his—and you'll be paid a cash bonus. You haven't asked for that, I know, but I feel confident that you will accept it." She looked at me as if I were the Lindbergh kidnapper.

I got up to leave, and Stuart Blount sprang to life. The missus excused herself, swooped into the foyer, deposited her ashtray in the maid's waiting mitt, and ascended the stairs. Blount walked me to the front door and out onto the stoop. He closed the door behind us.

He breathed deeply and said, "Eddie is an old school friend of Billy's. From the Elwell School. They were quite close." I guessed what that meant. "The boys have been out of touch for a number of years, and now Eddie is back in the area and Jane and I thought Billy might be more eager to come back to us if he knew we would reunite him with Eddie. Call it blackmail if you like, Mr. Strachey, but remember that we're doing it for our only son, whom we love very much. Is it all right now? Have I reassured you?

"You have," I said. "I'd like to meet Eddie. Could you arrange it? He might be able to clear some things up for me in connection with the killing."

He put his arm on my shoulder and spoke in a fatherly way. "Mr. Strachey, I appreciate the special interest you've taken in this matter, I sincerely do. But, truth to tell, don't you feel that that end of the situation would best be left to our police department? There are detectives who are paid good salaries to carry out the work that *you* seem to have taken on— at *my* expense!" He shook with mirth and waited for me to join him.

"I've been in touch with one of those highly paid detectives," I said, "and although the man does, I suppose, have his virtues—dedication, cleanliness, perhaps thrift—he definitely is on the wrong track on this case. My sorting through this Eddie business just might point us *all* in the right direction, the police included. And I can't put it to you too strongly, **Mr. Blount**, that a speedy resolution to all this lethal craziness could just possibly save people's lives. That *has* to be a part of what we're about here."

He gazed off into the park. I followed his eyes and saw a jogger stop and talk to a young man standing beside his bicycle.

Blount looked back at me and said, "No. I'm sorry, but I'll have to give you a firm no on that. It's Eddie's parents, you see. They've become friends of Jane's and mine, and I've given them my word. They are looking after Eddie's best interests, and I can certainly appreciate that. The boy has just moved back to this area and is working hard to establish himself, and his parents are quite insistent that Eddie not be brought into this extremely anxiety-provoking situation of Billy's. It *is* a separate matter, as I've pointed out, Mr. Strachey, and, I have to insist, an entirely private one. I'm sorry. The answer to your request is no."

The jogger and the bicyclist walked off together.

I said, "Eddie just moved back to this area recently? How recently?" I was confused again.

Blount said, "I simply am not at liberty to discuss Eddie's situation. I'm so sorry."

"All right, then," I said. "I'll do what I can with what I've got. I'll do it the hard way. I'll be in touch, Mr. Blount."

I left him standing there and walked up State Street.

I picked up the Rabbit on Central and drove down to the Dunn Bridge, across the river, and east on Route 20 toward Massachusetts.

The erratic weather had failed to bring out the colors of the foliage that year, and as I approached the Berkshires, the hills were drab even under the bright sky. When I reached Lenox after an hour's drive, a low cloud cover had slid in, and the place had a desolate November feeling to it, with Thanksgiving still more than a month away.

I got directions at a colonial-style Amoco station and found the Elwell School down the road from Tanglewood, which was shut down for the season, a chain across the gate with the big lions on posts. Like Tanglewood, the Elwell School was a disused turn-of-the-century estate, its monumental-frilly Beaux Arts main building looking like a miniature Grand Central Station. Most of the Berkshire prep schools had gone under in recent years—Cranwell, Foxhollow, the Lenox School—and Elwell had the look of a place clinging to life. A fancy sconce beside the main door rested on the gravel driveway, smashed, and had been replaced on the stone wall above it with a vertical fluorescent tube of the type found beside motel bathroom mirrors. An oval window had been filled in with plywood.

In the headmaster's office, I showed my ID to a pleasant woman in a cardigan sweater and said I was trying to trace the whereabouts of a dear old friend of my client. She led me down a high-ceilinged corridor and unlocked a door which led into a small, windowless room the size of a storage closet. This, she said, was the alumni office. I wouldn't be allowed access to the alumni files, but I was welcome to look through the yearbooks and newsletters. And if I found the man I was looking for, the woman said, the school would forward mail, provided it had a current address on file. She switched on the ceiling light and left me there.

I went through the 1971 yearbook, making a list of all the Edwins and Edwards. There were seven, as well as one Eduardo. Billy Blount was neither pictured nor mentioned as a graduating senior or as an underclassman.

Blount did show up in the 1970 volume, grinning sleepily and a bit warily at the camera—not, however, among the graduating class photos, but on a separate page at the back of the book for seniors who had not completed the school year. There were two other boys as well who had dropped out. One was a Clarence Henchman, of Westfield, New Jersey, who looked as if he were coming down with mononucleosis. The other nongraduating senior was Edwin Storrs, of Loudonville, New York. There was a hurt, frightened look in his eyes, and his blandly handsome teenage male model's face was that of a relatively fresh and unsullied Frank Zimka.

17

I WAS BACK IN ALBANY BY FIVE. I CONSIDERED SETTING UP another quick meeting with the Blounts. Either they had concocted an elaborate lie and had fed it to me coolly and systematically, using their great goofy sense of theater, or their friends the Storrs of Loudonville had lied to *them* about the present whereabouts and condition of *their* son Eddie, or there was another explanation that might boldly present itself once I could sit down with Billy Blount, the one figure in the whole cast of characters who knew things the rest of us didn't. I'd be seeing Blount within twenty-four hours, and I decided to forgo another session of drawing-room farce with the senior Blounts and wait until I got to Denver.

I drove out to Timmy's on Delaware and let myself in, then phoned my service to let them know where I was. I'd had one call during the afternoon, from Sergeant Ned Bowman of Albany PD, with the message, "Not Trailways either, pal. See me."

I called my own apartment to see if Huey Brownlee had gotten in all right. He said he had and asked if I minded if he invited a friend over. I said I didn't mind. I felt a little spasm of jealousy in my thighs and frontal lobes, but nothing heavy and it didn't last.

Timmy came in just after six. I gave him the two checks, one from Truckman for two hundred and one from Stuart Blount for two thousand.

"*Blount* is the anonymous donor? Holy mother! Well, you never know."

I said, "Make sure he and the missus receive a thank-you note. They're attentive to the social niceties and expect others to respond in kind. Have the alliance mail it to his office."

"Done. This is terrific. They'll make a great addition to our fat-cat hit list."

"Mm."

"Before we go to Trucky's tonight, a bunch of us are

137

dropping by the Rat's Nest. Do you want to come along? Nordstrum needs the business—he's strung out and afraid he's not going to weather this thing financially. We can buy his booze and cheer him up."

"I don't know—oh, I guess so. That place is liable to grate on my Presbyterian sensibilities."

He'd been getting a beer from the refrigerator. He stopped and stood there with the refrigerator door open. "Tell me about your Presbyterian sensibilities," he said. "I want to hear this. How do they work? Describe them. First ethical, then esthetic."

"That's too fine a distinction for me to make. To me it's all one big ball of wax."

He said, "That's about it." He shut the door, popped the tab on his Bud. "You'll trick people and use people, Don, but when it comes to a little mindless fucking around, where everybody's motives are up front and nothing of emotional consequence gets invested, you put on your big moral floor show for the uplift and edification of the sinners." A swig of beer and a muttered, "Damn Protestants."

"Oh, is that what I just did? I must have missed it. I would have described what I just said as an expression of mildly queasy indifference. Anyway, I haven't seen *you* trotting out there to Nordstrum's blurry grotto to get your pants pulled down by some inky form with trench mouth and cold hands— somebody's idea of a fun evening in the suburbs. Or have you?"

"Of course not. I might go to hell."

"Ahhh."

"But that's not the point. We were talking about you and your bizarre double standard."

"You mean Harold Snyder. *He's* what this is all about. That really got to you, didn't it? I'm never going to hear the end of it, *never*. When you're seventy-seven and I'm seventy-nine—"

"Eighty."

"—whatever. When we're both tottering on the brink, you're going to be reminding me, aren't you? You'll have it put on my goddamn gravestone: 'Donald Strachey—1939–2009— Once Fucked a Drag Queen.' If you're so worried about poor Harold's ass, go comfort her, take care of her. Put her in a convent, spend the night with her, get her a screen test. *You*

138

figure it out. *You* deal with her. Me, I'm sick of thinking about it."

"Don, it's not Harold's ass I'm concerned about, it's her *mind* you fucked. She's pathetic and vulnerable, and you used her in an extremely hurtful way. It's the worst thing I know of that you've ever done."

I said, "That's not the way it happened. Not exactly."

"What do you mean?"

I thought about it. I said, "I'm not telling you. But it's not *exactly* the way you think it was. I'll tell you about it—Christmas eve." I didn't know why I said that. He'd remember it, the bastard, and bring it up while we were trimming the tree; he had the memory bank of a Univac 90/60.

He said, "I'm prepared to take your word for it that the thing you did wasn't as cruel as it seemed—or as cruel as *you* seemed to think it was when you got home last night. It's you as much as Harold that I'm concerned about. I like you less when you don't like yourself."

"Timmy—I'll deal with this. I'll have to, I know. But you're not making it easier. You're coming on like Cardinal Cooke, and it's your least appealing side."

That got to him. He made a face and said, "Boy, could I use a shower." He went into the bathroom. Soon I heard the water running, and I decided that I could use one, too.

I'd been to the Rat's Nest once, just after it opened in midsummer. The place had been packed that night, with most of the revelers busy positioning themselves for a better view of the spaced-out nude go-go boy—"Raoul, from Providence, R.I."—as if they'd never seen a male body before. Not much had gone on in the back room that night; there'd been an itchy-tittery who's-going-to-go-first atmosphere that Timmy and I had been even more uncomfortable with than news of the goings-on that got started the following weekend.

Now the mood was different. The dancer—"Tex, from Pittsburgh"—was wearing gym shorts and a tank top, and could have been just another local shaking off some tension on the dance floor on a Wednesday night. During Stephanie Mills's "Put Your Body In It," Tex yawned.

139

There were only about thirty people in the place when we arrived at ten-fifteen; twenty or so in the main room, another ten in the murky back room, standing around in their jeans, or leather, or preppie outfits, like dummies in a gay wax museum. Timmy went off to the men's room, and I ordered two bottles of Bud from the back-room bartender, who was wearing tight white pants and red suspenders. I asked him if he expected any more trouble from the Bergenfield police, and he said no, Nordstrum's lawyer had said they'd probably have a temporary restraining order by the next morning.

I said, "What about tonight?"

He shrugged.

An odd, deep voice from behind me: "Hi there, lonesome stranger. Buy you a drink?" A deft finger between my buttocks. Oh Christ. I turned.

Timmy, working his eyebrows like Groucho. I pulled his face toward mine, then stopped. "Oh, it's you. They've really gotta put some lights in this place. Never know *who* you might do in here."

He said, "I'm Biff from Butte. Or, is it Beaut from Biff? Or, Butt from *Boeuf*. Whoever I am, wanna dance?"

We did, to Ashford and Simpson's "Found a Cure" and then Jackie Moore's "This Time, Baby." As a third number was starting, the alliance crowd came in and moved in a kind of raggedy undersea school across the dance floor and into the back room. We joined them.

Two of them had just met with Jim Nordstrum, the Rat's Nest owner, and his lawyer, who had assured one and all that right was on their side.

Timmy said, "Fine, but what about Judge Feeney?"

They said the lawyer had been vague about him.

Lionel the truck driver stumbled in, already in his cups. Lionel was a notorious barrel-chested, middle-aged sex maniac in work pants, leather, and a Hopalong Cassidy hat with a Teamsters button stuck on it who ordinarly hung out at the Terminal Bar in the wee hours but somehow had made his way out Western Avenue to what he must have heard was his more natural habitat. He moved through the dim green light uttering his famous ungrammatical greeting: "Hey, anybody wanna get blowed?"

140

Timmy said, "Are we supposed to raise our hands, or what?"

He came our way, and there were a few faint-hearted "Hi, Lionels" as people turned away from him. He swayed over and maneuvered himself onto a barstool.

Timmy said, "I think we should arrange a public debate between Lionel and Lewis Lapham. It'd make a terrific fundraiser."

I looked at him. "Who's the cruel one among us now?"

Sheepishly he said, "Yeah. You're right."

I could see his mind working. I said, "Okay, spit it out. Then that's all. What were you thinking?"

He said, "Well then, how about a debate between Lionel and George F. Will?"

"I figured."

A man of around my age in tan pants and a windbreaker got up from the bar and walked past us. He pushed open the fire door to my right and a uniformed police officer stepped through the opening. He was followed by a man who looked like a fireman wearing an auxiliary policeman's badge, then two others in work boots and army fatigues.

Timmy said, "Oh, look, it's the Village People!"

A second uniformed officer appeared through the doorway from the main room and walked to the bar. Lionel the truck driver turned toward him and glared. The first officer who had entered stood in the center of the room and instructed us to face the walls and place our hands against them high up. His tone was not menacing. It was that of a coach or gym teacher. He clapped his hands a couple of times, and I half-expected him to yell, "Twenty laps!"

The one who frisked me was the plainclothesman, the customer in the windbreaker.

I said, "Am I accused of a crime?"

"Shut up, faggot!"

I concentrated on a spot on the wall in front of my face and thought, don't do it. There's nothing to be gained. Don't do it. Later.

Now I knew.

He yanked out my wallet and had me hold it open to my driver's license while he wrote down my name and address.

Over my shoulder I saw two big men being led away, the bartender and Lionel the truck driver.

Jim Nordstrum came in from the main room and leaned against the bar, watching. The officer in charge glanced his way, then ignored him. When everyone had been frisked and our IDs taken down, the officer announced, "Everybody outta here! Get moving!"

People moved toward the exits as if a bomb had been discovered. No rebellious Stonewall queens, these.

Several of us gathered around my car in the parking lot and watched as other customers hurried to their cars and drove off. Lionel and the red-suspendered bartender were sitting in the backseat of a Bergenfield police department cruiser. The bartender stared straight ahead; Lionel was slapping the side of his head as if he had a bug in his ear. A third man, who'd been carrying a joint in his shirt pocket, we later learned, was hustled into the backseat beside them.

The officer in charge came out; Jim Nordstrum walked beside him, in handcuffs. As the officer opened the door of an unmarked sedan and shoved Nordstrum in, I walked over and said, "Jim, we'll call your lawyer." He looked at me with blazing eyes and nodded once. The cop, whose badge I could now see read Chief, said to me: "Your pal here attempted to bribe a police officer. That's a serious offense."

A minute later they were gone. We went inside, and one of the alliance officers phoned Nordstrum's lawyer. We rode back into Albany in charged silence.

18

TRUCKY'S, JUST AFTER MIDNIGHT, WAS JUMPING—MORE LIKE A Friday than a Wednesday night. I could never figure out how these people got up in the morning to go to work. Maybe they didn't; maybe they'd discovered a way to sleep for a living or were independently wealthy. Though few looked as if they'd managed either. I saw several faces of people who'd been at the Rat's Nest earlier.

Mike Truckman was at the door, just barely upright. As we came in, he pumped my hand and said, "Don, I wanna 'pologize about the other day, really I do. I'm under one hell of a lot of pressure, and sometimes I fly off the handle when I shouldn't. You won't hold it against me, right, buddy? Let's get together one day real soon. We'll chew this thing over and straighten it out. Real soon, you hear?"

I said, "How about if we talk right now?"

"Whazzat? Beg pardon?" Freddie James's "Hollywood" was banging out of the speakers at the far end of the bar. I saw Timmy move toward the dance floor with Calvin Markham. I leaned closer to Truckman and shouted, "How about right now, tonight?"

Ignoring this, he leaned into my ear and said, "The Rat's Nest was hit again tonight, j'hear that?"

I told him I'd been there when it happened.

"You *were?* Jesus, you weren't hassled or anything, were you? I'd hate for you to—get hassled."

"It was humiliating. I didn't like it. They arrested Nordstrum, and we called his lawyer. He's probably out there by now. Could we go back to your office for ten minutes?"

He looked at me bleakly from out of the caves of his eyes. "Oh God, what'd they get Nordstrum for, underage or some shit like that?"

I said, "He tried to bribe the Bergenfield police chief— according to the chief. I doubt whether that'll hold up. Unless it's true and the cop was wired. In Bergenfield the cops are probably lucky to get flashlights in their budget, though these days you never know."

"I gotta go," Truckman said. "I got this new kid mixing drinks. Listen, buddy, we'll talk soon, right? Be cool, now." He ducked under the bar and went over to a young man in a yellow T-shirt with a bottle of chartreuse liquid in his hand.

I watched them for a minute—Truckman glanced back at me once—and then I bought my draught and moved toward the dance floor. I ran into Phil and Mark in the mob around the

143

dancers and asked if either would like to dance. Mark said he would. We did. Then Mark danced with Timmy, I danced with Phil, and Calvin Markham danced with a tall black man with sorrowful eyes who was wearing a red T-shirt with white letters that said Rabbi.

When Sister Sledge's "We Are Family" came on, we switched again and I ended up with Timmy, and by the end of it some of the younger dancers were yelping and shouting and shaking their fists. These were gay men together, and it was Wednesday night.

Half an hour later we were standing by the bar when Timmy, seeing something over my shoulder, said, "Uh-oh."

I said, "What'd you say?"

He shouted it, over the music: "I said, Uh-oh. *Uh-oh*."

I turned. Harold Snyder was pummeling her way through the crowd toward us. She had on a low-cut dress the same shade of red as her martinis, big red hoop earrings, and a Veronica Lake wig. She was grinning and leading someone by the hand.

"Donnie! Donnie—you incredible *hulk,* you! I don't know what it was about last night, but you changed my *entire life!* You brought me *good fortune,* you fabulous Pisces!"

Timmy, Mark, Phil, Calvin, and the rabbi stared at Harold wide-eyed. Then they all looked at me.

I said, "Oh."

"Donnie, I want you to meet Ramundo. He's in show business in Poughkeepsie, and he's starting a dinner theater, and he wants to star me in the dramatic stage version he's writing of Barry Manilow's 'Copacabana.' Now, is that a part for me, or is that a part for *me!*"

We all exclaimed enthusiastically, and there were introductions all around. Ramundo, fiftyish, grandly mustachioed, and beaming in his powder blue velvet dinner jacket and ruffled orange shirt, kissed each of us on the lips and said, "Hoy."

More pleasantries were exchanged over Harold's unexpected entrance into what she now referred to as "the industry," and then Ramundo excused himself to "sloid over to the p-yowder room and frishen up."

"Where does Ramundo come from?" Timmy said. "Patagonia? Santa Lucia? Tibet?"

"Oh, I wouldn't know that," Harold said, adjusting her

Veronica Lake wig and looking at us with one eye. "Greene County, I think. Or San Francisco maybe—Ramundo is so-o-o cosmopolitan. I met him at the tubs."

I said, "The tubs?"

"This morning, Donnie. I always slip in around ten, then hang around for the noontime action. I'd just taped up my sign—I always hang a sign on my cubicle: Today Is the First Day of the Rest of Your Life—when Ramundo walked by and exposed himself. I pointed at his teensy-weensy, darling little hard-on and said, 'Ooo, it's Mister Bill! How are yew, Mister Bill?' and Ramundo looked at me and said, 'Don't talk anymore like dat—like a smutty lady. I am going to make you a *star!*' Well, naturally I thought that was just a line, but then after sex we talked, and he *meant* it. Even after he came. Can you *believe* it? Can you believe what's *happening* to this tired old cleaning lady?"

A day in the life. I said, "Will you be moving to Poughkeepsie then, Harold?"

"Yes, I've informed Mike that I'm resigning as his underpaid barf mop as of tonight. We're motoring down from the city after brunch tomorrow in Ramundo's mother's Chevette. I'll—" She looked at me. "—I'll miss you, baby."

Phil, Mark, Calvin, and the rabbi examined the walls. Timmy sipped his beer.

I said, "Well, it might not have worked anyway, Harold— us. Our life-styles are somewhat different." Though not all *that* different, I realized with a pang of something-or-other.

"That's the truth, Donnie, sad to say. I was thinking that very thought after you left last night. You're so—intellectual. Like your friends here. I'm more—of the earth. A people person."

Timmy said, "In this crowd an intellectual is someone who's seen *All About Eve* at least three times."

"Oh, really?" Harold said, looking surprised. "Well, I can relate to that." Then she gave me a troubled look. "Are you going somewhere tonight, Donnie? After closing?"

I said I was, but to forget about all that for now. I leaned down and kissed her and said, "Good luck, Harold. I wish you— continued good luck."

"And happy trails to you too, Roy." She gazed at me, and

just for an instant I again saw in her eyes Harold the yoo-hoo boy of Sneeds Pond, New York, trapped in a room with a Bible, a football, and a photo of John Wayne. She saw me see it, and she hugged me tightly.

When Harold pulled away, Ramundo had returned, and the show-biz couple went off to the dance floor to wow the country guys in from western Massachusetts, and to step on the other dancers' ankles, with a rhumba.

Mark, Phil, Calvin, and the rabbi left at one-thirty. Timmy had arranged to have the morning off from work, and we danced and hung around and ate popcorn until three-thirty, when we went out and drove my car across Western Avenue and parked in an abandoned Gasland station. I shut off the engine and we waited. The night was black and icy, and I ran the engine every ten minutes or so to warm us up.

"Any idea where we're going?" Timmy said.

"I think so. I hate to think it, but I think so. Is the camera ready?"

"Don't tell me then. Yeah, I'm set."

Just after four the last customers straggled out of Trucky's, across the road from where we waited. We could see the fluorescent lights go on inside.

At four-twenty Mike Truckman came out in a black peacoat and knit cap and lowered himself into his dark green Volvo. He pulled out of the parking lot and turned right onto Western, away from Albany. We followed.

We stayed a hundred yards behind the Volvo, which, with a drunk at the wheel, was moving slowly down the far right lane, sometimes edging onto the shoulder and then back onto the road again. There were few cars out at that hour—an airport limo, a bakery delivery truck, a couple of others—and we had no trouble staying with the weaving Volvo's taillights.

After a mile we passed the darkened Rat's Nest. Truckman drove on, keeping well within the forty-five-mile-an-hour speed limit. We passed chain motels and donut shops and fast-food joints. I accelerated slightly, so that by the time Truckman pulled off the road, we were just fifty yards behind him. I could see clearly that he'd turned into the parking lot of the Bergenfield police station.

146

I drove on by and pulled in on the far side of a "flavored dairy product" stand that was shut down for the season. We got out and walked through the weeds and debris behind the ice-cream stand. The Leica was strung around Timmy's neck, and I went first, feeling my way through the rubbish and dead vegetation. We passed the rear of a wholesale tire outlet and came within view of the police station, a small box of a building with gray corrugated plastic sides, a flat roof, and a pretty white sign in a "colonial" motif that said Police Headquarters—Bergenfield, N.Y.

We crouched behind a pile of tires. Sixty feet away, in a pool of light outside the police station's rear door, Mike Truckman was standing alongside his Volvo gesturing animatedly and shaking his head at the two men who stood facing him. From my encounter with them six hours earlier, I recognized the Bergenfield chief of police and the clown in the windbreaker who had frisked me and spoken rudely. Timmy eased out from behind the tires, adjusted his telephoto lens and light setting, and repeatedly snapped the shutter of the camera.

I whispered, "How's the light?"

"Good enough," Timmy said.

Still shaking his head, Truckman slid something from his jacket pocket and handed it to the chief, who held the thing in one hand and flipped through it with the other. Timmy got that, too. The chief counted out several bills and handed them to the guy in the windbreaker.

Truckman was saying something else, and now the chief was shaking *his* head. After a moment the police chief opened up his coat, and Truckman frisked him. The cop buttoned up his coat. The plainclothesman was next. Then Truckman nodded. Okay. No wire.

Truckman climbed back into his car and started the engine. We crouched low behind the tires as his headlights arced above us. He passed us and turned. I raised my head and saw the Volvo move back down Western toward Albany.

A second car engine came to life, and we saw the chief's unmarked Ford pull onto the highway and head west, away from the city. After a moment the third car, a silver-gray Trans-Am with black stripes, roared onto the avenue and sped off.

147

We walked back to the Rabbit under the cold stars and drove into town.

Timmy said, "I may throw up."

I said, "I can relate to that."

"Okay," he said, "but what's Eddie-Frank Zimka got to do with it? Or Blount? Or Kleckner?"

I said, "I'm not sure yet. Maybe I'll know tomorrow, in Denver."

19

THE RED AND ORANGE CONTINENTAL 727 FROM O'HARE CLIMBED out of the rusty haze over the Chicago suburbs and banked west. The tourist section was only half-filled; I had three seats to myself and did not have to sit like a mannequin in storage. The cheap seats in the four or five back rows were thigh-to-thigh with students and families on no-frill tickets, and when I walked past them en route to the lavatory they peered up at me like kittens in a box.

Chicken in brown jelly over Iowa, watery coffee across Nebraska, then southwest over the faded autumn fields and foothills until the Rockies loomed up off the right wing like Afghanistan.

By two-fifteen I had my bag in hand, had rented a Bobcat, and was in the car studying a map of greater Denver. I wanted York Street, in what the car-rental clerk had called the Capital Hill District, "the part of town where the city people live." That sounded right.

I drove west into the city on Colfax Avenue, found its intersection with York Street, then doubled back up Colfax and checked into a motel four blocks away. I phoned Timmy at his office in Albany and gave him the name and phone number of the motel. I put on my jogging gear, consulted my city map again, and headed back towards York. Denver, Timmy had told

148

me, was noted for its high, thin, filthy air. But on that day Denver was warm and odorless, and the mountains looked clean and serene off beyond the city skyline with its State Capital cupola and slab office towers a mile west of where I trotted along the sidewalk.

I turned up York, which was lined mainly with closely spaced, bulky old brick houses and, here and there, set close to the cottonwood-lined street, a newer three- or four-story apartment building of the California-nondescript style. The address for Kurt Zinsser was on a red brick Victorian manse with turrets and curved windows. I walked up the front steps and checked the big front door, which was locked. There were six mailboxes and buzzers, and I pressed the button under Zinsser's name. No response. I rang again. Nothing.

I jogged on up York, checking the parked cars along my route for Wyoming tags with a rental-car code. I saw none.

I cut right, then left up another street, and soon arrived at Cheesman Park, the big municipal swath of green I'd seen on my map. The still-fresh lawns sloped gradually down for a couple of blocks from where I stood, away from a granite neoclassical pavilion, from whose steps I had a dazzling view of the western sections of the city and the mountains beyond.

I rested for a while. I remarked on the weather to a chunky, sloe-eyed young Chicano, who walked me to his apartment, back toward York Street, and we had a Coors. He answered my questions about gay life in Denver—I wrote down the names of bars and organizations—and I told him about Albany. Our stories were similar, except homosexual Denver was much more populous, the gay mecca for all the Sneeds Pond boys from most of the plains states and half the Rockies. Boomtown.

In bed I became short of breath, and Luis said it was the altitude—it took a week or two to adjust. My inclination was to look for a calendar, but I didn't.

He said he hoped we'd run into each other again, and I said truthfully that I hoped so too but that it was unlikely, inasmuch as I'd be returning to Albany in a day or two. I gave him my Albany address, "in case you ever," etc. We kissed good-bye, and I jogged—ambled—back over to York Street.

I tried Zinsser's buzzer again, and again there was no

answer. It was five-fifteen. I walked back to the motel and took a nap, after asking for a wake-up call at eight.

I halved my exercise routine, showered, dressed, dined at Wendy's, walked back to the motel, looked up Kurt Zinsser's number in my notebook, and dialed it.

"Hello?" Chris Porterfield.

"Hi—Don Strachey. I'm in Cheyenne. How long does it take to drive down there—two hours, three?"

She hung up.

I drove the Bobcat over to York Street and parked across from Zinsser's building. In twenty minutes they came out carrying three suitcases. They moved quickly up the street, and I had to walk fast. I caught up with them as they were opening the door to Porterfield's Hertz car with the Wyoming tags.

"Hi, gang. Say it now, say it loud, we're gay, and we're proud." They looked at me as if I were a creature that had dropped out of the tree we were standing under. "Look, I'm Don Strachey, and all I want to do is talk. Really—"

Blount dropped his bag and bolted up the street. Zinsser, short, a bit portly, with dark angry eyes staring out over a Maharishi-style face full of hair, flung his suitcase down and came at me, one hand pushing into my face, the other grabbing at the fake fur collar of my bomber jacket.

As we grappled, I caught glimpses of Chris Porterfield standing there, suitcase still in hand, looking fed up, as if her bus were late. I kneed Zinsser in the groin, and as he doubled over cuffed the side of his head. As he went down slowly, I got behind him and whomped him in the seat of the pants with my gay clone work shoes. He grunted, and I took off up the street after Billy Blount.

At the first intersection I looked both ways and caught sight of him off to my right, a block away. I took off, gasping and wheezing and noticing a funny clamped feeling at the sides of my head. Blount hung a sudden left, and I broke into a full sprint. By the time he reached Cheesman Park, he had only half a block on me. We charged across the grass under the stars; on the mountainside, off in the distance, I thought I saw a huge,

150

lighted cross. I hoped it actually existed. My ears were screaming.

Beside some shrubbery at an exit on the far side of the park
from where we'd entered it, I caught up with him. I lunged and
brought him down. His fists flew, and he kicked and grunted,
"Motherfucker! Fucking asshole motherfucker!" He was strong,
but frantic—too frantic to know what he was doing—and when
I pounded my fist into his midsection, he curled up and
concentrated on getting his respiratory system functioning
again. I sprawled beside him and worked toward the same end.

He started to get up, and I shoved him down on his stomach
and fell on him. My mouth was at his ear, and I gasped into it
"You stupid shit, I'm trying to get you *out* of this fucking mess!
They want to put you back in Sewickley Oaks, and they're
using this thing to do it to you, and since you acted like a damn
fool and ran away, the only way you're going to stay out of that
place is to *help me find out who really killed Steve Kleckner!*"

I yelled it and he wrenched his head away, but he'd
understood me. He stopped squirming and lay unmoving except
for the heaving of his back as he struggled to get his breathing
under control.

After a moment he turned his face toward mine and said, "I
don't even know who the fuck you are!"

"Didn't Chris tell you?"

He looked like his photograph, except he'd shaved his
mustache, and the old black-and-white photo the Blounts had
given me hadn't brought out the high color of his smooth skin
or the depths of his black eyes. As we lay there panting
together, our faces nearly touching, I thought: Shit—again. I
thought about getting up and walking away and phoning
Timmy to ask him if he'd go away with me to an island
somewhere where we'd be the only men for hundreds of miles
around. Then I could do it—*thought* I could do it.

Blount said, "Chris told me you were probably okay, but
she didn't actually know you, and anyway you're working for
my parents, who are a menace to civilization. Isn't that the
truth? *Isn't it?*"

"The menaces hired me, yes, but I'm using their money to

151

work for *you*." A faint private smile on his face. "I'm damned if I know *what* your parents believe, but *I* do not believe you killed Steve Kleckner. Did you?"

He looked as if he'd have swung at me if I hadn't had his arms pinned down. "Of course I didn't!" He spat it out.

I relaxed my grip, and when he didn't move, I rolled off him and sat up. I said, "Then who did?"

"How the fuck would I know? Was I there when it happened?"

"I don't know, I wasn't there either. If you weren't, then where were you?"

"In the shower. You knew that. I heard Chris tell you Sunday night."

"And I believed it," I said. "I'm familiar with your after-sex habits. I know Huey Brownlee."

"You know Huey? Is he okay?" He rolled onto his side and studied me, his breathing coming back, the tension draining.

I said, "Huey's fine, no thanks to you. Huey and I were acquainted prior to all this. He's a good man."

A wistful look. "Yeah. He is."

"I've met Mark Deslonde, too. And Frank Zimka."

He looked at the ground and picked at a clump of grass. "Oh. How's he doing? Old Frank."

"He misses you quite a bit. I've got a letter from him in my car. And I've got some questions about old Frank."

The sound of voices calling. I looked up over the shrubs we'd tumbled down beside and could make out two forms moving across the park from where Blount and I had come in. "Bi-l-l-y—*Bi-l-l-l-yy*—"

"Your friends are here." He started to stand, and I took his arm. "Look, why don't we check in with them later. We'll talk first, and then I'll drop you back at Zinsser's apartment. We'll go to a bar I heard about. Ted's. It sounds nice."

"No. You know Ted's? No—anyway, no. They'll be worried." He got up. "It's okay. You'd just better be straight—what's your name?"

"Don Strachey."

"Well, Don Strachey, if you're a cop or something—if you're

152

fucking me over—Kurt has a lot of friends who won't take shit—"

"Am I alone, or am I alone? If I were a cop, would I come after a murder suspect with the Hundred and First Airborne or alone in a rented Bobcat? Which makes more sense?"

He waved and shouted, "We're over here."

They came trotting. They stopped about ten feet away, watching Blount for some signal.

"He's okay," Blount said. "It's cool. He'd *better* be." They all looked at me.

We were just twenty feet away from the street that paralleled the bottom edge of the park. I'd seen people stand up around the pavilion when I chased Blount across the grass, and one of them must have phoned the police. A cruiser pulled up.

"Everything okay here?"

I noticed that my jacket was ripped, and I gestured with my eyes to Chris Porterfield. She glanced at Billy, who nodded. She said to the cop, "Yes, is there some problem?"

"Somebody reported a fight. You see two guys run by here in the last ten minutes?"

"We just arrived, officer," Zinsser said. "There's no curfew, is there?"

The cop said, "Eleven o'clock. I'd watch myself in here, though. Lotta fags."

"Are they dangerous?" Zinsser said.

"Only if you bend over." We could see him shaking with delight. "I'd say *you're* safe, Miss." We guffawed heartily.

He drove away.

Zinsser said, "The law." He spat.

Back in front of Zinsser's apartment, I retrieved the two letters to Billy Blount from the glove compartment of the Bobcat. I'd retaped the flap shut on Zimka's note and carefully glued the one from the Blounts. I'd tell Blount, in due course, that I'd read the letters, but just then I needed to solidify his trust, misplaced as it may have been in that particular matter.

Chris Porterfield was in a snit. Her strong, big-boned face frozen in hurt anger, she stomped up the stairs to the apartment and charged into the bathroom, slamming the door. She'd asked how I'd found them, and when I said through a friend in L.A. who knew friends of Zinsser's, she didn't believe it. She thought Margarita Mayes had betrayed her.

Kurt Zinsser was still nursing the bruises I'd left on his tailbone and ego, though by the time we were seated in the apartment, he'd accepted me enough—he knew of Harvey Geddes—that he was lecturing me on the necessity of a reborn and expanded Forces of Free Faggotry. I couldn't disagree with him. Of all the radical movements that formed in the sixties, the FFF had to be among the bravest and most just. Zinsser talked about regrouping and mounting a "spring offensive." Meanwhile he was doing the work he'd been educated to do, as a data analyst in the computer section of a large hospital.

The apartment was spacious and calming, with high ceilings, lots of polished dark wood, and a fine parquet floor. The bookshelves were stacked with revolutionary literature from Marx to Fanon to Angela Davis. The more recent volumes were by authors of a milder outlook, and when I remarked on this, Zinsser muttered that not much else was available. New times.

Blount went into the bathroom with Chris Porterfield, and I could hear them talking but couldn't make out the words. From time to time she wept. I tried phoning Margarita Mayes, but when she didn't answer, I remembered she'd gone off to stay with a friend and I didn't know which friend. Maybe Porterfield knew, but she was the one who was pissed off and incommunicado. I decided to butt out; it was their problem.

Porterfield came out with wet eyes and began rummaging through the suitcase beside the daybed I was stretched out on while I waited for the household to regain its equilibrium. Blount stayed in the bathroom, and soon I could hear the shower running. I felt it happening again and casually rolled onto my stomach. Showers now. Hopeless.

Porterfield found a little vial of something-or-other. She said, "Who did you say you talked to in L.A.?"

I explained again.

She took the pills into the kitchen and I heard her turn on

the faucet. Sound of a glass filling, faucet off. After a moment, a phone being dialed. The kitchen door eased shut.

While Zinsser told me anecdotes of FFF exploits, Blount came out of the bathroom with a towel around his waist and went into the bedroom. I gave him time to dress, then excused myself from Zinsser, followed Blount into the bedroom, and shut the door behind me. I saw the two letters, from Zimka and the Blounts, lying on the East Indian print bedspread, unopened.

I said, "Let's talk."

"Beg your pardon?" He was standing barefoot in fresh jeans and a white T-shirt, noisily blow-drying his hair in front of a dresser mirror.

"Go ahead," I yelled. "I'll wait."

I sat in a wicker chair and read *The Guardian* while Blount groomed himself. After the dryer came a hot-comb, then some touching up with a pocket comb. Che Guevara at his evening toilet.

I said, "You're not going out tonight, are you?"

"No, why? I've gotta work tomorrow."

"Where do you work?"

"A record shop. Gay-owned, a friend of Kurt's. It's all under the table. I can't use my real name or Social Security number or I could be traced. Kurt knows about all that."

"What's your new name?"

"Bill Mezereski. Kurt picked it. Like it?"

I hoped Billy Blount was cleared soon, because I couldn't wait to tell Jane Blount of her son's Polish alias. I said, "Sounds workable."

"I'm just getting used to it."

"It looks as if you're cutting yourself off from your past entirely. Except for Chris and Kurt. That's too bad. I've gotten the idea there've been some good things in your life in Albany."

"That's true." He came over and sat on the edge of the bed across from me. "But do I have a choice? I'm *never* going to be locked in an institution again, *ever*, and I'll do anything I have to to avoid that. I mean *anything*." I looked at him. He said, "Well, almost anything."

I said, "You have a choice. Once we've found the person who killed Steve Kleckner and turned the Albany cops around and pointed them at the obvious, you'll be free to do anything you want with your life. You're twenty-seven, and if you've committed no crime, your parents can't touch you."

He sat back against the headboard. He said, "I've committed crimes."

Uh-oh. "Which?"

"Consensual sodomy. A class-B misdemeanor in the state of New York that'll get you three months in the county jail. For me that's three months too long."

"Don't be an ass. Let anyone try to prove it."

"I thought you'd been around, Strachey, but I guess not that much. It's been done."

He was right. And I thought I knew Jane and Stuart Blount well enough that I wouldn't put anything past them. There were others in my profession who'd take on the job of gathering evidence. It was rare, but it happened, and you always had to be a little afraid. Especially if you had people in your life like the Blounts.

I said, "There are plenty of people around who'll help you stay out of jail, me among them. My first concern, though, is keeping Kleckner's murderer from killing again. You can't argue with that, and you've got to help. You're the only living person who can."

His face tightened and he sat looking at his lap for a long time. Finally he said, "I know. I've thought a lot about that. Especially after Chris told me what happened to Huey. Chris and I talked about it. Kurt, too." He gazed at the bedspread.

I waited.

"I'm not going back," he said. He looked up at me. "Of *course* I want the killer caught, and I'll help you as much as I can. I'll talk to you. But I am *not* going back. Is that understood?"

I said, "Okay."

He fidgeted with the cuff of his jeans. He swallowed hard and said, "What do you want to know?"

"You're doing the right thing," I said. "You won't be sorry. The night it happened—begin at the beginning and tell me the whole thing. Minute by minute. Take your time, and don't leave anything out."

He reached for a pack of Marlboros on the night table and offered me one. I said no thanks. He lit one. I said, "I've been checking up on your habits, but I didn't know you smoked."

"I don't. Except about once a month."

One of those.

I asked him again to tell me the story of that night in Albany twelve days earlier. I wanted him to relax, so I suggested he begin with the events in his life that had led up to that night, and he did.

20

"By the time I met Steve Kleckner, I wasn't tricking a whole lot," Billy Blount began. "Maybe once every five or six weeks. I *used* to, when I first came out in Albany. I was nineteen then, and God, in the summertime when SUNY was out, I'd be in the park almost every night. I was really man-crazy then, and pretty reckless, and some of the people I went home with you wouldn't believe—kids, old guys, married guys, anything male. Sewickley Oaks was supposed to turn me straight, but when I came out of that place, I had the worst case of every-night fever you ever heard of.

"It wasn't just sex. At first it was, and I guess that was the most important part of it—I loved sex then, and needed it, quite a bit more than I do now—but after I joined the alliance in seventy, a big reason I wanted to meet people was to recruit them into the movement. That was probably part rationalization, I know—don't laugh—but at the time I was very serious about it. All the alliance people ever did was march up and down State Street, and I had this idea there were other gays in Albany who were ready to do more—maybe something like the FFF—and I was going to find these guys and get something

157

going. I never did, though. The people I met were too young, or too old, they thought, or too scared, or too fucked up. I did meet some nice people, though, and I had a couple of relationships with guys I saw pretty regularly until either the other guy moved away or one or the other of us just lost interest and stopped calling. You know how that works.

"Anyway, this went on for—God, five years. Almost every night I was on the phone to somebody, or in the park—or in the bars; I'd started hitting the bars pretty regularly by then, even though I'm not much of a drinker. One night the Terminal, the next night the Bung Cellar—Mary-Mary's it was back then—and the next night back to the park.

"It was a pretty messy and wild kind of life, I know, and I didn't really wise up until after I picked up some weird, awful NSU and it took me nine fucking weeks to shake it! God, the VD clinic tried everything—tetracycline, penicillin, Septra DS, the works—but for nine weeks whenever I pissed, it was like pissing needles. I always had these little plastic vials of pills in my pockets, and when I went dancing it sounded like castanets.

"It was really a very chastening experience, and after the NSU went away, whatever it was, I slowed down quite a bit. Maybe it was for the wrong reasons, but anyway I decided to start paying less attention to gay men's bodies and even more attention to their fucked-up minds. I tried to get the alliance moving—I was chairman of the political-action committee by then—but those guys are such a bunch of old ladies, I couldn't get them to budge. I wanted to zap the State Assembly and they wanted to put on luncheons. I saw that I was wasting my time with that DAR chapter they were running over there, so I dropped out. I almost went to California to join Kurt and the FFF, but they were having their own troubles by then and splitting up, so I decided to stay in Albany for a while longer.

"I was glad I stayed. I met Huey around that time, and then Frank. Also, I had a hot thing going for a while with a guy named Dennis Kerskie. He was going to help me start an FFF branch in the East, but unfortunately Dennis freaked out and took off for Maine to cleanse his intestinal tract, or some weird thing. Actually, it was just as well. Dennis could be pretty flaky, and I don't think he would have had the discipline for the things I wanted to do. I did meet Mark through Dennis, though, and I'm grateful for that.

"Anyway, by the time I met Steve Kleckner that night, I'd pretty much settled down. I was seeing Huey once a week—we had a nice, relaxed sexual friendship, nothing heavy—and I was seeing Frank once a week, but not too much else. Well, actually there was this one guy from Lake George I met in the park one night in August. Mark was staying at my place with a friend, so I took a chance and we went to my parents' place, and that turned into a very bad scene. Stu and Jane came home the next day unexpectedly and caught us smoking a joint in the front room without the vent on, and it got pretty ugly. After that I sort of swore off having sex with people I didn't know—it was just getting to be too much of a hassle—when Mark and I went out to Trucky's that night three weeks ago and I met this really neat guy. That was Steve Kleckner.

"It was funny—a couple of years ago I wouldn't have gone for Steve. He was sort of young and loose and goofy, and I usually went for more intense kinds of people, or guys who were savvy and cool, like Huey. But I guess somehow I was ready to just let go for a while and be a kid—I'd never done that when I *was* a kid—and I really fell for this happy-go-lucky young jock.

"At first I thought, oh Jesus, I really shouldn't. Not another involvement. I had the feeling right away that it might lead to something like that, and I was reluctant. My life was already going along pretty well—I had my job, which, shit job though it was, I enjoyed and it kept me solvent. And I had my friends, Mark and Huey—and Chris, who was always there when I needed her. And, of course, I had Frank, who gave me something nobody else could—I really don't want to go into that, if you don't mind; it's sort of embarrassing. Okay?"

I nodded. We'd come back to Zimka.

"Maybe all that sounds to you like kind of a crazy, fragmented life," Blount said, "but I was just thankful, even after nine years, to be out and on the loose and in charge of my own life. And anyhow, who is there really, gay or straight, who finds everything he wants in life in one place or in one person? I think it doesn't exist, and people who say they have it all—in a wife, or husband, or lover, or family, or great house or perfect job—those people are kidding themselves, and what they really mean is, they have the one or two things they want *most,* or that society approves of most, and to keep those couple of things they're willing to give up a lot of other things they'd love to have: variety, money, good sex, security, adventure, or whatever.

"Actually, I *did* have it all, in a way, even if it was spread all over town, and it would have been beautiful—damn near *perfect*—if I'd gotten my parents to accept me, too. That's the one thing I've never had, and—well, I guess that's the one thing I'm not going to have. You've met them, and you must have seen how hopeless they are. If I'd had a brother or sister, that might have taken some of the pressure off, but I didn't—I don't—so—what the hell. Fuck Stuart and Jane. Just—fuck 'em."

He sat silently for a moment. Then he reached for another cigarette and offered me one. I declined. He lit his, dragged deeply, and exhaled. He went on.

"So anyway, I'm cool, right? I went out to Trucky's that night with Mark, and we were going to dance and maybe meet some people we know and go get something to eat, to the Gateway or out to Denny's, and then I guess I had it in the back of my head that I might call Frank later and see if he wasn't busy.

"But I met Steve Kleckner instead. I'd seen him around some, mostly through the glass in the DJ booth, and I'd always thought he was attractive, but I really didn't know him and hadn't thought much about him. He was off work that night, though, out at the bar, and acting kind of mellow and funny and having a real good time, and one of the bartenders who knows me a little introduced us.

"We clicked right away. You know how it is, probably, when two gay guys who are physically attracted to each other meet, and each is sort of up—and *ready,* even if you don't know it—and you're both a little high, and there's this warm, *simpático* something that goes back and forth. You're trading lines and laughing at the same things, and you recognize in the other person's stories of his life a lot of the downs and hassles you have yourself, and you know he's understanding yours, and

160

then there's the sexual tension underneath it all that both feeds the closeness and makes it feel incomplete, and of course the atmosphere around you is saying do it, do it, do it.

"Well, that's what happened with Steve and me that night. We danced and drank and carried on and had a great time together, and then we left together to go do it, to make it complete.

"We left Trucky's around three. Mark had left earlier with this tall blond number he'd turned on to, and we rode into town in Steve's old junky-ass Triumph Herald. We had the top down, it was a warm night, and I remember the car making this awful racket, ka-bang, ka-bang, ka-bang as if there were firecrackers under the hood. Steve said it wasn't important, not to worry, the car always did that, something to do with a worn drive chain that would set him back three hundred to replace, and the car wasn't worth it, he'd just drive it till it quit."

The time had come to find out something. I said, "A question. Did you notice who left Trucky's around the time you and Steve left?"

He thought about it. Then: "No—I can't remember. Actually I was a little high, and I don't think I was noticing much of anything except Steve. I remember we sat in his car in the parking lot and kissed and messed around a little before we left. I suppose there were some people coming and going, but I don't remember who. Nobody hassled us, I know that."

"Then you wouldn't have noticed if another car had followed you?"

"Well, I supposed there wouldn't have been much traffic that time of night, but—no. I didn't. Jesus, do you think one *did?*"

"Yeah, I do. Do you remember seeing a big, new gold-colored car in the parking lot when you and Kleckner went out?"

"I don't know. Maybe. I just can't remember. Whose car would that have been?"

"Frank Zimka's—a friend of Frank Zimka's car. With Zimka in it."

"Frank? I don't think Frank was out that night. No, he wasn't. I saw him in the morning. I went there—after it happened. Or did he tell you that? I suppose he did. You seem to have a knack for getting people to tell you things they're not supposed to repeat." I lowered my head contritely. "I owe Frank money," Blount said, "for the plane fare. Chris has part of it. She'll mail it to Frank when she gets back to Albany. So it won't have a Denver postmark."

"Kurt taught you that?"

"That one I figured out for myself."

"What did you and Kleckner talk about during the ride to his apartment? It would have taken fifteen minutes or so. Did Steve mention that he'd been depressed over the past few weeks? His friends say he had been."

"You know, as a matter of fact, he did mention that. He said he'd been down and I'd helped him climb out of it—that made me feel good—and he said he wasn't depressed anymore. Just older and wiser."

"Why? What did he know that he hadn't known before?"

"He didn't say. I might have asked him—I probably did. But he just said something about the ways of the world and then dropped it."

"Was he afraid?"

"Of what?"

"Of what he'd learned. Of the person, or people, it concerned."

"No. Not afraid, I wouldn't say. Just sad. Sad when he talked about it, but not sad after and not before. Steve was just feeling too good that night for anything to keep him down."

"So you arrived at Steve's apartment."

"Yes. We went in, and at first we stood in the living room for a long time kissing and groping around. We were both really hot, I remember, but we couldn't seem to quit long enough to make it to the bedroom. You know how that is, right?"

"Right."

"Pretty soon our clothes were off, and we started back toward the bedroom. I remember Steve turned on the radio when we went by it."

"Disco 101?"

"Sure."

Sex music. The year before I'd gone home with someone who'd put on some old Nat Adderley records, and I was so

162

disoriented I could hardly remember where I was and what I was supposed to do. Though gradually it came back.

"So you made it to the bed. Were the lights on?"

"In the living room, a lamp, I think. There was some light coming into the bedroom from that. And in the bedroom, a blue light on the ceiling. I remember the blue light—at one point when Steve was groping around beside the bed for the grease, he reached up and pulled the light string with his toes. And then he left the light on. A very dim blue light. It was nice— Steve was nice—the *whole thing* was—" It hit him. He covered his face with his hands and silently shook.

I waited.

After a time he looked at me and said quietly, "You know, I haven't had sex with anybody since that night. I sleep with Kurt, and sometimes he holds me, but—" He shrugged. Tears slid down his cheeks.

I said, "Look—Billy—we could wait until tomorrow to do this. But it'll be better for you, I think, if we get it done now."

He wiped his face with his bath towel. "I know," he said. "Let's get it over with. I want to get this over with." He tossed the towel away, then sat with his face leaning against his open hand, his palm covering one dark eye.

I said, "There's a ground-level window beside that bed. Do you remember it?"

"Yeah. I do. I remember the breeze on my ass and my shoulders. It was a warm night, but by then I guess it had cooled off. I remember the window."

"There's a shade on the window. Was it up or down?"

"It was—the shade was down, but it was flapping against the windowsill—or the screen, I think there was a screen—and sometime, I'm not sure when, Steve reached over and put the shade up so that it wouldn't flap." His face went white. "Christ! Do you think somebody was—?"

I said, "Yes, I think someone was a few feet away from you and Steve, in the alleyway, watching and listening. And probably waiting."

Blount was breathing heavily now, angry, embarrassed, experiencing the fright and rage he'd have felt that night if he had known.

"After sex, then, you lay together for a time?"

"For a while. I don't know how long. He—Steve's head was on my chest. Yes, and then he fell asleep. I remember I had to move him off me when I went to the bathroom. I can't sleep, see, until I take a shower after sex. It's weird, I know, but—God, somebody was *out* there! All that time. *Jesus!*"

"How long were you in the shower?"

"A long time, probably. I do that. Then I sleep like a rock."

"You were planning to stay, to sleep with Steve?"

"Sure. I didn't have to work the next day. Of course."

"After your shower you came back into the bedroom."

He looked away, breathing hard again, and I could see him girding himself.

"Yeah. I came back then. I was starting to get back in bed when I saw it—the blood." There were beads of sweat on his forehead, and he blinked and repeatedly choked back the emotion as he described it.

"The sheet was up over Steve—I'd pulled the sheet over him because of the cool breeze when I'd gone into the bathroom, and it was still there when I got back. But the sheet was wet—*soaking wet.* All over his chest I could see this wetness, purplish in the blue light. At first I couldn't figure it out—I was dog tired, and I was still a little high. I thought, crap, what'd we spill, what *is* this stuff?

"Then I touched it, and somehow I knew right away it was blood, and I thought, oh shit, one of us has screwed up his rectum in some dumb way. But I thought it couldn't have been *me,* I'd just been in the shower and *I* was fine, and then it hit me all at once.

"I yanked the sheet away, and there it was—all this blood oozing out of Steve's chest. I got dizzy and I thought I was going to pass out. I just kept saying Steve, Steve, Steve, and I leaned down and I touched his face and shook his head, but all the time I was doing it, I could see he wasn't moving or breathing, and I knew he was dead.

"Then I just stood there looking at him. For a minute, maybe, or five, I don't really know how long, I stood there thinking what *is* this? What *happened?* I looked around the room, and it was the same as when I left it, except blood was coming out of Steve's chest, and he was dead.

164

"Then I guess I thought no, he *can't* be dead, and I started thinking a little, and I felt for his pulse. I felt his wrist, and under his jaw, and I couldn't find a pulse, and I was starting to feel his groin when I smelled it. The shit—Steve had shit himself. I almost passed out again. I sat down on the floor, and then—there was the knife. Whoever had done it had dropped the knife, and it was right there, wet and purplish in the blue light."

I said, "You didn't touch it?"

"No. I guess I was already thinking, without even knowing I was. In fact, that's when I *really* started thinking. I thought, they'll think I did it, everybody will, and I'll go to prison again."

"Again?"

"Sewickley Oaks. It's all the same. Except maybe in real prisons they don't strap you down and zap you till you think you're going to fly apart—muscles and bones and brains exploding all over the ceilings and walls. Or maybe in the *worst* prisons that's what they *do* do, Attica or in the South."

"They did that? At Sewickley Oaks?"

With a look of the most intense loathing, he nodded once.

I said, "What happened next?"

"I—I got dressed and I walked out of the apartment, up Hudson."

"When you left the apartment, was the window screen in or out? It's a portable, adjustable screen. I've seen it. When you left, where was it? Try to remember."

He tried, but he couldn't.

"But the screen wasn't on the bed, or on the floor where you could see it?"

"No. I don't think it was. No."

"What about the apartment door—when you went out. Open or closed?"

"It was locked. From the inside. I had to turn the bolt."

"Then you walked up Hudson."

"As soon as I got outside, the unreality of it hit me again, and I thought no, he *can't* be dead, and I thought maybe I'd been wrong and he was really still alive. There was a phone booth just a couple of houses up, on the corner at Hudson and Dove, so I called the police—started to call, but I didn't know Steve's address. I walked back to the apartment, memorized the address, and then went back and called. I said to go to the address, but I didn't say who I was."

"I know. It's on tape."

He grunted and shook his head. His T-shirt was soaked through with sweat, and droplets were now falling from his nose and chin.

"So you walked to Zimka's then? Up Hudson and through the park?"

"I knew I had to get out of Albany fast. I really didn't even understand what the fuck had happened, but I did know it was something horrible and I'd be blamed for it, and I had no choice but to run. No choice that I could see."

"And Zimka was home when you got there?"

"He was asleep. I had to bang on the door for—I don't know. A long time."

"How do you know he'd been asleep?"

Blount looked confused. "Because he said he was. He looked it. It was six in the morning. Did he tell you he wasn't?"

"No, he told me the same thing."

"But you don't believe it?"

"No. Maybe. I don't know."

"I don't get it. You keep saying suspicious things about Frank—you said he was in Trucky's parking lot that night when we left. Do you think *Frank* had something to do with—what happened?"

"Probably. It's not clear yet. Keep going. What happened next?"

"Frank borrowed a car and drove me to New York. I thought they might already be looking for me at the Albany airport, though I suppose they wouldn't have been watching that soon. Frank lent me the plane fare, and when I arrived out here, I called Kurt. I knew I could count on him, and I was right; he's been great. Look—what makes you think Frank is mixed up in this? Crazy old Frank. Frank is usually so whacked out he couldn't hurt a fly on downers."

I said, "Tell me about Frank. About you and Frank. Embarrassing or not, it's important that I know."

He looked away. "What's to tell? He's a trick—a friend I

trick with. I like him. He likes me. We get it off together."

"Jerk-off buddies? That's not the way Frank sees it. It's not the impression I get."

He looked at the wall and said nothing.

I said, "Eddie Storrs and Frank Zimka are the same person, aren't they?"

He sat there, his chest rising and falling, his face desolate—willfully empty, it seemed. He gave a choked laugh, then fell silent again. Finally, he looked at me and said, "No. They're not the same. Not really. The terrible truth is, there are two of them."

21

Billy Blount and Eddie Storrs, Blount told me, had been sixteen-year-old lovers at the Elwell School. Before then neither had known he was homosexual, just different somehow, and vaguely but deeply unhappy. In the presence of other male bodies, each had felt a disturbing, unresolvable tension whose source was unlocatable, baffling. The two sad, mystified boys became friends, and during a weekend visit to Eddie Storrs's home in Loudonville, they had been goofing off and ended up in the same bed—and it happened. Two weeks later they spent a weekend at the Blount home on State Street, and it happened again.

The two were terrified. At first they denied to themselves what was happening. They never spoke of it, tried not even to think of it, just did it. Then one night in Loudonville something snapped. Suddenly each professed his love for the other. They faced it, gave it a name, and let it pour out. The language they used was out of pop songs with half the pronouns transposed. It was explosive, glorious, liberating—and horrifying. In confronting their love, they also confronted something else: they were queer. A couple of cocksuckers. They were in love and magically happy—as at peace with themselves as they had been at war with themselves before—and at the same time they were frightened and wretched and ashamed of their true selves, which the other boys, and the world, would despise. They loved themselves and each other, and they despised themselves and, at times, each other.

Billy and Eddie contrived to meet in secret when they could—in the woods and fields around Lenox, in their parents' homes, in their own rooms at Elwell when their roommates were safely out on dates or off to hockey tournaments. Both boys' grades fell, and no one could explain why. When asked about this by their teachers and advisers or by their parents, both mumbled about how the curriculum "lacked relevance"— this was 1968—and the grown-ups shook their heads and muttered back about their keen desire to "establish a dialogue" with the boys. None, however, got established. You just did not tell people that you were a homo.

In fact, Billy and Eddie were spending most of their mental and physical energies on devising strategems for spending time alone with each other, and on the anxiety that resulted from their success with these ploys.

"This crazy life lasted for over a year," Billy Blount told me, "until the fall of our senior year, when the shit hit the fan. Some jerky kid from Danbury, Connecticut, caught us one Sunday night doing it on some mats stored under the gym bleachers. This kid never liked me; he was the type who smells a secret weakness in people, then baits you and tries to dig it out. When he caught us, I'd never seen such an evil, victorious smile on anyone's face. He walked straight over to the headmaster's house, and within three days our parents had been notified, and they came and got us. They told us that maybe we could go back to Elwell after we'd been 'cured.' We thought this was funny in a sorry kind of way, but we went along; we humored them. I mean, they were our *parents*. What did *we* know?

"The last time I saw Eddie was the day he left Elwell—I left the day after that. While our parents were with the headmaster and our roommates were in class, we shoved the desk against the door in my room and made love on my bed for the last time—what turned out to be the last time.

168

"As scared as we were, it was beautiful and very, very intense. It was one of the few times in my life when I've actually *made love* with a man, not just fucked with somebody for fun, or for connecting up with someone you like. We cried and held each other and said we'd love each other forever and ever, and no matter what happened we would find each other someday, and when that happened, we'd never let anyone come between us ever again.

"I remember Eddie bit my lip so hard it bled, and when he saw it, he made me bite him so our blood would mix, and that way we'd be a part of each other until we were together again. That seems pretty freaky to me now, but at the time it didn't at all, and I did it. And I'm not sorry. Eddie is the first person in my life who made me stop feeling like some kind of weird, dead robot and turned me into a human being with feelings I understood and wasn't ashamed of—or *shouldn't* have been ashamed of. Back then I didn't know I didn't have to be ashamed. No one told me. Everyone said the opposite. I suppose it would have happened anyway, the gay revolution. So many people were ready. But still—God bless the Stonewall queens!"

In lieu of a drink he raised another cigarette and lit it.

Now I understood—most of it. It was a story most gay men would understand. At Rutgers twenty years earlier I'd been in love with my best friend. He was straight, or so I assumed. And I'd been too frightened to open up to him, to declare my true feelings; the boy meant everything to me, and I was terrified that my revelation would end the friendship.

We parted after graduation, and at some point I moved and stopped answering his letters. Eight years later I thought I saw him—Jake, his name was—in a gay bar in Washington, D.C. The man turned out not to be Jake, though the resemblance was powerful; and the look-alike was an agreeable young man nonetheless, with a personality sufficiently bland and pliant that I could go home with him and seem to fulfill one of the great, unending erotic fantasies of my adult life. Afterward the Jake look-alike told me he'd never met a man with a sexual hunger as great as mine. I told him the truth of the matter, a mistake, maybe, and he was hurt. I never saw him after that.

I said to Billy Blount, "Frank Zimka is Eddie's look-alike, isn't he? You used Zimka. Regularly."

"Yes."

"And Zimka knew it and went along with it because he was in love with you and was willing to accept the humiliation in order not to lose you."

"Yes. I hadn't planned on telling him. I still don't know which would have been worse, telling him or not telling him. But I called him Eddie one night in bed. He asked me who Eddie was. And I told him. Not about the forced separation and Sewickley Oaks—that's always been very painful for me to talk about—but about Eddie's being my first great true love, who had left me and disappeared from my life. And then it began. Whenever I was with Frank, he became Eddie."

Blount had only dragged twice on his cigarette, and now he stubbed it out. He said, "I first saw Frank in the Terminal one night. I thought he was Eddie, and I nearly went crazy. When he wasn't—well, you know." I knew. "I didn't really plan on seeing him after that night, but—well, he went for me and gave me his phone number, and—one thing led to another."

I said, "Where is Eddie now?"

"I don't know. After Elwell, I was put in Sewickley Oaks, where I met Chris, and we became friends. She was in for the same 'abnormality' as mine. Margarita had been her lover, and when Chris was committed by her parents, Margarita ran away from home and made it out to L.A., where a year later she heard about the FFF. They rescued us and took us to L.A., where we stayed for six months until I called my parents, and they promised that if I came back to Albany, they'd get off my back. I came home, naively thinking I might find Eddie or at least find out where he was, but my parents would never tell me. They'd only say he was being 'rehabilitated,' as they put it, someplace out in the Midwest.

"I finished high school at Albany High, then went to SUNY, and for all those years I never heard from Eddie or a word about him. For a while, I'd thumb or bum rides out to the Storrs' place in Loudonville and try to talk to Eddie's parents, but they finally sicked the cops on me and I had to give up."

I said, "Read the letter."

"From Frank? I don't know whether I can handle that right now."

"No, the one from your parents."

"I can handle that one even less."

"I've read it," I said. "You'll be interested."

He looked at the letter warily, then at me. I nodded. He reached to the foot of the bed where the letter lay, picked it up, opened it, and read. He lay back and stared at the ceiling, the letter still in his hand. "They win the prize, Stuart and Jane," he said. "They win the fucking grand prize." He dropped the letter on the bed beside him.

Throughout our two-hour conversation—or rather Blount's extended monologs—the pieces had been arranging themselves and falling into place. There was one to go. I said, "Did Eddie Storrs ever hurt anyone? On purpose?"

Blount sat up straight and gazed hard at me. He said, "No—I mean, yes. Not after we'd become lovers. With me, Eddie really calmed down. But before that, yes. Eddie had a reputation for getting into playful kinds of fights—dorm scuffles and all—and then doing things that really hurt or were dangerous. Once he had a kid down and kicked him in the neck. Another time Eddie grabbed a nail file and—stuck a kid in the thigh with it."

We looked at each other.

"Was Eddie Storrs ever jealous of your friendships with other guys? Or didn't you have any?"

"Not after, but before, yes. When Eddie and I were just becoming friends, but before we'd figured out what was really going on, he always gave me a hard time about other guys I hung around with, and he'd act pretty rotten toward those people. In fact, one kid I sort of felt comfortable with some-times—I think now that he was probably gay—he was the one Eddie stabbed with the nail file." Blount's eyes got big, and he said, "No "

"Yes. Probably yes."

My mind went back to Albany. Huey Brownlee was at my place. Margarita Mayes was staying with a friend. Mark Deslonde was, as far as I knew, with Phil.

I said, "The phone."

Blount handed it to me across the bed. I dialed Timmy's number. It was 12:40 A.M. in Denver, 2:40 in Albany. He answered on the second ring.

"It's Don. I want you to go see Frank Zimka right away and

171

get him over to your place for the night, no matter what it takes. Are you awake enough?"

"Listen, I haven't slept at all. Where the fuck have you *been?* I've been calling your motel every ten minutes since midnight. A bad, bad thing has happened."

I said, "Zimka is dead."

A silence. Then, "How did you know? It just happened earlier tonight."

I said, "Wait a minute." I asked Blount for a cigarette, and he lit one for me. My hands were shaking, and the first drag on the Marlboro was like inhaling a medicated Brillo pad. I handed it back to Blount. I said, "Was he stabbed?"

Timmy said, "Yes. It happened at his place around eleven. Calvin was heading over to the park and saw the cops and commotion and checked it out and called me. They think it happened in the apartment, but Zimka managed to crawl out onto Lexington before he died. He must have been spaced out. He told the old woman who found him that a ghost had done it—the ghost of his own youth, or some crazy shit."

I said, "That's what he must have looked like to Zimka. Christ."

"*Who* must have looked like?"

"Eddie Storrs."

I summed it up for Timmy, then got Sergeant Ned Bowman's home number from Albany Directory Assistance. The operator said, "Have a nice evening." I woke Bowman up and told him where I was and who I was with. He said I was under arrest. Then I summed it up for him, and he replied that my story was pure fantasy and he wanted to see me first thing in the morning. I told him maybe later in the day, or century.

I called Continental and made two reservations through to Albany on a flight leaving Denver at 7:50 A.M. Blount heard me make the second reservation, for him, and he didn't object. Finally I called Timmy back with our flight number and arrival time.

Blount packed and wrote a note for Chris Porterfield, who was asleep on the living-room daybed. Kurt Zinsser was snoring beside her.

We took the Bobcat back to my motel, left word for a six A.M. wakeup, crawled into bed, rolled together, and slept.

172

22

BLOUNT TRAVELED AS BILL MEZERESKI, THINKING THE AIRLINE manifests were still being monitored. This was smart of him. For purposes of keeping Ned Bowman out of my hair, and to act cute, I traveled as Alfred Douglas—I figured Bowman had given up on that phantom—and as soon as we landed in Albany at 2:27 in the afternoon, I was taken into custody.

When the plane halted on the parking apron, the captain asked that passengers remain in their seats for just a moment; everyone sullenly obeyed. Two bulky lads in blue entered the aircraft and walked directly to seat 9-C. One said, "Would you come with us, please, Mr. Douglas? Detective Bowman would like to speak with you for a moment."

"Why, certainly," I said, shrugging cheerfully to the passengers around us. Blount sat frozen in his seat. I said to one and all, "Ah, what would Timmy say." As I got up, I kicked Blount's ankle. "Ah, *Timmy*."

They led me down the ramp and into the terminal wing. As we passed Timmy standing wide-eyed at the gate, I shook my head and rolled my eyes back toward the plane.

My escorts and I trudged up the corridor, past the metal detector, through a doorway, and up a concrete stairwell. In the airport security office I was shown a metal chair and instructed to sit in it. I smiled, and sat. Bowman arrived twenty minutes later.

"*His* name's not Douglas! That's Strachey! That's the asshole who—!"

Bowman turned and told a man in a gray suit and blue tie that he wanted the airport sealed off immediately.

"Sealed off?" the man said. "Why?"

"I'll explain later, Pat. There's a murder suspect who came in on that American flight from Chicago. I'll bet my mother's sweet name on it. He came in with this guy. *Al Douglas!*" He shoved at my chair with his foot and it scraped a few inches across the floor.

I said, "As I explained to you last night, Ned, the killer is in Loudonville. Or in Albany. Stuart Blount knows where, and so

173

do the killer's parents. Their name is Storrs. Billy Blount was with me in Denver last night. We can both prove it; we were both seen there by a Denver police officer. Frank Zimka was killed in Albany last night by the same man who attacked Huey Brownlee and killed Steve Kleckner. His name is Eddie Storrs."

The man in the gray suit said, "Ned, we can't just seal this place off—not just like that. There's just me and two officers here. We'll need help from the sheriff's office or from your department. Jeez, I'm sorry, but. . . ." He made an apologetic face.

Bowman had been watching me. I was trying to look confident and earnest but not too smug. He said, "Then let me use your phone, Pat. Can you do that this week, or will you have to make arrangements with the governor's office?"

The gray-suited man nodded toward the phone, turned, and stomped off.

Bowman phoned the DA's office and made noises about a "possible break in the Kleckner case" and asked that the assistant in charge of the case remain on call for the next twenty-four hours. Bowman said, "The Blount kid is back in town."

Then he called Stuart Blount and asked for a meeting. One was set up for half an hour later at the Blount abode on State Street. I was instructed to accompany him. I didn't object.

During the ride into Albany I repeated in detail what I'd told Bowman on the phone the night before, as well as everything else I'd found out over the past seven days and the conclusions I had drawn.

He said, "You misled me. You held out on me. You've committed a number of very serious offenses."

I said, "You are not just incompetent, you are willfully incompetent. I may file a taxpayer's suit. I haven't decided yet."

"You'd better redeem yourself in a hurry, Strachey. Your time has run out."

"So had you. So has yours. I have only your prejudices and intransigence to contend with. You've got a killer loose in your city."

"Thanks to you," he said. But he was only going through

the motions. He'd listened to my story, and he hadn't questioned it.

I said, "Where is Eddie Storrs?"

Bowman was beside me on the sofa, a foot of clean air between us so our thighs wouldn't touch and Bowman wouldn't have to arrest me for lewd solicitation. The Blounts faced us from their beautiful chairs and looked at me suspiciously.

"Have you found our son?" Blount said. "We'll tell him all about Eddie just as soon as he's in the sergeant here's custody. Is Billy in Albany, Mr. Strachey? I should think that for the expenses you've incurred in the past week—"

Now Bowman said it. "Mr. Blount, where abouts is this Eddie Storrs fellow? It might be helpful if I had a talk with him. Now I said *might*." He glanced at me. "I won't trouble the boy, just ask him a few questions that have been raised and are troubling my mind."

The missus gave me a steely look and went for her Silva Thins. Blount said, "Well, truth to tell, Sergeant, Eddie Storrs is in the process of rebuilding his life following many years of difficult psychological counseling. And in point of fact, I can't imagine a worse time to drag him into a complicated matter that can only, I should think, upset him and perhaps undo some of the good work that's been accomplished in regard to Eddie's life-style and much-improved mental outlook."

I caught Bowman's eye. He had the look of a man with a headache coming on. He said, "Where is the Storrs boy's family? Loudonville? Their names, please."

Jane Blount let loose. "Oh, *really,* Stuart—" She ignored Bowman and me and addressed her husband as if *he* were the one who was ruining her afternoon. "Stuart, I can't imagine what this is all about, but I have to insist that that boy's privacy be respected. After all these years of struggle and pain, and now with a new job and a lovely young wife—to have it all disrupted by dragging Eddie into this—kettle of fish! Well I, for one, will not abide it, and neither, I'm sure, will Hulton and Seetsy. It's all just too—deplorable!"

Bowman blithely pulled out a pad and wrote it down. Hulton Storrs. And Seetsy. Or Tsetse.

I said, "Eddie is married?"

"You wouldn't know about such things," Jane Blount snapped.

"I've read widely."

"You see, the thing is," Blount explained in his mild way, "Eddie Storrs has become a young man whom Jane and I are rather hoping will serve as a role model for our Billy, an example to emulate. Eddie is extremely happy and well adjusted in his new life, and we thought perhaps a short visit by Billy with Eddie and the nice girl he's married to would demonstrate to Billy just how fulfilling family life can be. It's not too late for Billy, and it's a life he might want to work toward. With professional help, of course. Jane's and my own example has never served that purpose, unfortunately, because we're older. It's the generation gap, if you get my meaning."

Bowman's words were, "The family is the bedrock of Christian civilization," though he looked at the Blounts in a way that suggested he might come to consider them exceptions to his rule.

I said, "Eddie Storrs killed Steven Kleckner. Last night he killed another man. He could—probably will—kill again. It's possible—likely—he's planning an attack on his next victim at the moment. Where is he?"

Bowman didn't move. Jane Blount gripped her ashtray. Stuart Blount looked at Bowman for help, saw that none was forthcoming, cleared his throat, and leaned toward us gravely. He said, "Hulton Storrs has invested forty thousand dollars a year for ten years in that boy's recovery. That is four hundred thousand dollars, only partially tax-deductible. Are you suggesting, Mr. Strachey, that in return for nearly half a million dollars, one of the finest rehabilitative institutions in America has turned Edwin Storrs from a faggot into a killer?"

"Your pal Hulton should have put most of his bucks into krugerrand," I said. "For a lesser amount he could have turned his son from a faggot into a wretched zombie with most of his memory blotted out. Mainly that's what those outfits manage to accomplish. But for four hundred grand—sure, that kind of money might come up with a killer. Apparently it has."

"Where's your evidence?" Blount said.

176

I explained. Blount scowled at his lap. Jane Blount sat bug-eyed.

When I'd finished, Bowman said, "It adds up. Where is he? Do you put us in touch with the boy's family, or do I waste thirty seconds tracking them down on my own?"

Stuart Blount removed an address book from his inside breast pocket and opened it. His wife got up abruptly and left the room.

Before we left for Loudonville, I used the Blounts' phone and called Timmy's apartment. No answer. I called his office; he was "out for the day." I checked my service and was given this message: "We're at a certain fitness center on Central Avenue." The tubs. Timmy probably had Blount locked in a cubicle with him and was reading aloud from Teilhard de Chardin.

I called Huey Brownlee, who was safe and just leaving the machine shop for my apartment, and then, at her office, Margarita Mayes, who said she was still staying with a friend in Westmere. Sears Automotive Center said Mark Deslonde had taken the day off and wouldn't be in until Monday. I phoned his apartment and got no answer; I thought, fine, he's still with Phil. I almost dialed Frank Zimka's number, and then I remembered.

During the fifteen-minute drive up Route 9 to Loudonville, Bowman was silent. I asked him if his police radio picked up Disco 101, but he ignored me. He'd phoned Hulton Storrs before we left Albany and arranged a meeting, but he'd held off explaining to Storrs the exact nature of the "serious matter having to do with your son Edwin" that Bowman said he wanted to "sift through." He sat in the driver's seat beside me, eyes fixed on the tarmac strip ahead of us. Once he said, "Goddamn Anglicans," and then he was quiet again. I supposed he was going to add Episcopalians to his long list of dangerous types.

Hulton and Seetsy Storrs lived in a commodious neo-Adamesque brick house on Hickory Lane overlooking a field of goldenrod. We parked on the gravel drive and rapped the silver knocker on the big white front door with a rising-sun transom over it.

"Chief Bowman, so *good* of you to drive all the way out here. I'm Hulton Storrs."

"It's Sergeant, thank you. This is Detective Strachey. Pleased to meet you."

Storrs was tall, thin, and stoop-shouldered in a tweed jacket, black turtleneck, and brown woolen slacks. He had a long face with dark vertical lines of age, and the eyes behind his horn-rimmed glasses were red with fatigue. He walked like a man working hard not to topple. Storrs led us into a large sitting room that ran the depth of the house, with french doors at the far end opening onto the back lawn. Three chintz-covered couches formed a U in the center of the room around a cream-colored rug. On one of the couches two women sat together, the older holding the younger one's hand.

"I've asked my wife and daughter-in-law to join us," Storrs said and introduced us to Seetsy Storrs and Cloris Haydn Storrs.

Bowman said, "Coricidin?"

In a high, sweet, little girl's voice, the young woman spelled it. She had on a pretty blue dress, pink lipstick, and yellow hair tied in a bun with a white velvet ribbon. A rumpled Kleenex stuck out of her clenched fist. The older woman looked up at us out of a worn, tight, politician's wife sort of face with frightened eyes.

We sat.

"My son has left home," Hulton Storrs said. "Have you found him? Is he dead?"

The women froze.

"No," Bowman said. "Why do you ask that?"

The women closed their eyes in unison and exhaled.

"Eddie sometimes suffers from a loss of memory," Storrs said. "He forgets who he is and where he is."

Bowman said, "That shouldn't be fatal."

"Oh, it isn't that," Storrs said. "The difficulty is, when Eddie has his spells, he sometimes ends up in the company of bad characters—people who might do God knows what. Hurt the boy. This has occurred in the past—once in Indianapolis and on another occasion in Gary, Indiana."

178

I said, "Your son's no boy. He's twenty-seven years old. He's a man."

"You don't know Eddie," Storrs said. "Eddie has only just begun to mature. You see, his development was retarded somewhat, slowed down, by a mental problem. You may or may not be aware that Eddie has spent most of the past ten years in a psychiatric rehabilitative center in Indiana. The boy has had his troubles, I'm afraid."

These people would have called the tiger cages at Con Son Island a correctional facility.

Bowman said, "Eddie may have committed a crime. It's urgent that I speak with him. Do you have any idea where he's gone? When did he leave?"

The two women clung to each other, looking wounded and well groomed, like a couple of Watergate wives. Storrs said, "Committed a crime? What do you mean by that, Captain?"

"Sergeant. It's Sergeant, thank you."

Bowman laid it out. As he spoke, the women wept and shook their heads. Hulton Storrs sat slumped with his chin on his chest, like another victim of the son he had "cured."

When Bowman had finished, there was a silence. Then Storrs looked up and said quietly, "Our plans seem not to have worked out."

Bowman said, "It sure looks like they haven't, Mr. Storrs. You and your loved ones have my deepest sympathy, I want you to know that. Now, sir, would you please tell me when your son left home, as well as the circumstances of his leaving?"

Hulton Storrs told us that his son had arrived home from his job as an "accountant-in-training" at Storrs-Lathrop Electronics in Troy the previous evening at six-thirty. He dined with Cloris in their "cottage," a converted stable on the grounds of the Storrs's estate. After dinner Eddie said he was "going for a ride" and drove off in his new gold-colored Olds Toronado. He'd "gone for rides" often in the past month, Storrs said, sometimes returning in the early-morning hours. Eddie's wife reported tearfully that the Olds was a wedding gift from the Haydns and that her husband "was just out of his gourd over that ace car of his."

Eddie Storrs had not returned at all on this morning,

though, and the family had been discussing notifying the police when Bowman telephoned. They thought Bowman would be bringing news of Eddie's whereabouts and condition, and feared that Eddie might have been harmed by "persons with masochistic tendencies," persons of the sort to whom he had been drawn during two month-long escapes from the Lucius Wiggins Psychiatric Rehabilitation Center in Kokomo, Indiana.

How these "masochists" were going to harm his sadistic son, Storrs didn't make clear. Maybe Storrs thought that in Indiana water went down the drain counterclockwise. It was the self-delusion wrought by love—or some grotesque permutation of love that I'd run into before but guessed I'd never understand.

At Bowman's request, the Storrs family led Bowman and me out to the young couple's cottage, where we discovered two knives missing from a velvet-lined wooden box of Sheffield cutlery. We also found—in a cardboard box full of Eddie Storrs's Elwell School mementos—a photograph of Billy Blount. The picture was taped to the front cover of Blount's phone book, the one stolen the previous weekend from his apartment.

Of the four phone numbers handwritten by Billy Blount on the back cover of the book, two—the first and second names, Huey's and Chris's—had penciled checkmarks after them, apparently signifying unsuccessful attempts on their lives. The third name, Frank Zimka's had been Xed out. The fourth name on the list, circled in red, was Mark Deslonde's.

23

I PHONED PHIL'S APARTMENT, WHERE DESLONDE WAS STAYING. There was no answer. I phoned Deslonde's apartment, where no one was supposed to have been staying. The line was busy.

It was five after seven. On Friday night Deslonde wouldn't

180

be going out until nine or ten. Bowman phoned Albany PD, and we raced out to the highway.

Bowman did a steady sixty-five on the two-lane road, weaving in and out of the Friday-evening traffic in his unmarked Ford. I said, "Haven't you got a siren on this thing, like Kojak? Christ!"

"Shut up."

We hurtled into the city, through Arbor Hill, up Lark, veered right and shot up past the park. Traffic on Madison was blocked off from New Scotland to South Lake. We eased around the barricade. Two Albany police cruisers were double-parked, blue lights flashing, in front of Deslonde's building, an old four-story yellow-brick apartment house. A crowd was gathering across the street from the building, and people were looking up. A figure sat perched on the fourth-floor window ledge in the center of the building. The figure was silhouetted against the light of the open window behind him, and at first I thought it was Frank Zimka, but of course it wasn't.

A fire engine and ambulance were parked up the street, and six men holding a safety net stood under the spot where Eddie Storrs was perched. The only sounds were from the crowd, speaking in subdued voices, and from the staticky sounds of the police radios. Twenty yards up the street, blocked in by the idling fire engine, sat the gold-colored Olds.

A patrolman explained to Bowman what had happened. "When we got here, Sergeant, the perpetrator—that guy on the windowsill—was in the hallway outside the Deslonde guy's apartment. When we came up the stairs, he must have seen us coming, and he opened up the window and climbed out there. He said not to get near him or he'd jump, so we backed off down the stairs and called the rescue squad. He's been up there for ten minutes, I'd say. An officer is in the stairwell behind the guy trying to talk him in, but he won't talk back, and if anyone gets near him he lets go of the window frame. That's about what we've got. You got any ideas? The captain's on his way."

Bowman said, "Where's Deslonde?"

"We haven't seen him," the cop said. "The door to his apartment looks like it's closed, but we can't get close enough to see for sure."

"Is there another entrance to the apartment?"

"The super says no."

"Get a ladder up to a side window," Bowman said. "And get a second ambulance out here. Cut through the window if you have to—but don't bust in, it'll be too noisy and might spook the jumper."

Bowman reached through the car window, pulled out his radio mike, and asked the dispatcher to dial Mark Deslonde's phone number and to patch Bowman through. We heard the clicks of the 434 number being dialed, and then the ringing. It rang twenty times before Bowman said, "Okay. Okay, that's enough."

He looked at me ruefully and shrugged. We stood there for a moment considering the possibilities, and then our eyes went back up to the figure on the ledge.

I said, "I'll get Blount. I'll need a car."

Bowman nodded and instructed a patrolman to take me wherever I wanted to go.

I said, "Ten minutes."

"In fifteen minutes," Bowman said, "we're going up there whether the kid jumps or not. The guy in the apartment comes first. There's no sign of him—he could be hurt in there."

We drove slowly up Madison until we'd rounded the corner onto Lake, then sped north toward Central and the baths.

I found them lounging on a cot in a closed cubicle, towels draped over their naked laps, surrounded by orange-juice cartons and Twinkie wrappers and looking sheepish. Teilhard de Chardin was nowhere in evidence. The ambiance did include, however, a certain distinctive combination of aromas.

I said, "We've found Eddie. You've got to come right now. Get dressed."

Timmy said, "No, first you're supposed to say, 'Holy smoke, I hope I'm not interrupting anything.'"

"Eddie Storrs is threatening suicide. Mark Deslonde may be in trouble. Hurry up. Move."

They moved.

A ladder was being raised up the right side of Deslonde's building from the narrow yard that separated it from an old

182

second-empire Victorian house. Eddie Storrs still sat motion-less on the window ledge in front. Billy Blount stood in the shadows of the autumn foliage and gazed up at him. Up the street a second ambulance moved quietly into position behind the first.

Phil had arrived. He was arguing plaintively with a uniformed police captain now on the scene who was not allowing anyone to approach the yard with the ladder except "family members."

I said, "He's Deslonde's best friend," and looked at Bow-man, who saw what I meant.

Bowman said to the captain, "He's the guy in the apart-ment's boyfriend, Lou. It's up to you."

"Family members only," the captain said blandly. He turned and walked away.

Phil started to lunge, and I stepped between them. Timmy and I wrestled Phil back into a yard across from Deslonde's building. He collapsed onto the ground and sat there, flushed, teeth clenched, his chest heaving.

Timmy stayed with Phil, and I walked back into the street where Bowman was standing. He said, "I make it a practice never to argue with a captain," and looked away.

I said, "That's not the way it happened. You were petty, and callous."

He looked back at me with hard eyes. "You people are going to make an incident out of this, aren't you? Blow it out of proportion."

I said, "I think so, yes."

"I'll deal with you later, Strachey. For a man who's broken as many laws as you have in the past week, you're acting pretty goddamned pushy with me. I want you to know I've just about come to the end of my rope with you."

"Do you want your defendant in the Kleckner case alive or dead?"

"Alive," he said. "It's expensive for the taxpayers but it's tidier on my record."

"Fine," I said. "I'll bring him down for you in return for an apology to Phil Jerrold, the guy you just fucked over in a particularly vicious manner."

He snorted and shook his head in disbelief. He turned toward the spot where Billy Blount was standing under a tree and gazing up at the man on the ledge. "Hey, come over here! You—Blount!"

Billy Blount walked into the middle of the street to where we stood.

I said, "Don't do what he says."

Bowman said, "Billy, you and I have got to go in there and say something soothing to your friend there. It might take awhile, so let's just relax and go up and sit on the stairs for a time and let the fellow hear the sound of your voice. Let him get used to it. Then we'll see what we can make happen. You got me?"

I said, "Don't go. Not until the sergeant here has offered an apology for his homophobic cruelty toward a friend of ours—a friend of Mark's."

In the side yard a patrolman with a tool kit strapped to his back was moving up the ladder.

"Come on, Billy, we've got to get that troubled lad safely onto terra firma. Let's go, kid."

Bowman moved toward the building. Blount stood still.

Bowman turned around, glowering. He said, "You're both under arrest."

We looked at him.

He said, "You, William Blount, for suspicion of murder. You, Donald Strachey, for aiding a fugitive from justice. I'm obliged to remind you that you have a right to remain silent, you have a right to—"

"Bi-l-l-leeee!" The voice sliced through the night. The crowd froze. The man on the ladder stopped and listened.

This time the figure raised one arm from the window frame. *"Bi-l-l-l-eeeee!"* The crowd gasped, and someone behind us said, "Oh, God."

Blount yelled, "I'll be right up, Eddie! Hang on! I'll be up!"

Blount trotted across the street, up the brick walkway, and into the building. A minute later two arms were wrapped from behind around the figure on the ledge. The figure began to turn as if on a pinwheel, and then it doubled up and disappeared through the window.

184

We charged into the building and up the stairs. Blount and Storrs were sitting beside a blue gym bag on the floor of the fourth-floor landing, their backs against the wall under the window. Blount was holding Storrs's hand. They hardly seemed to notice us banging on Mark Deslonde's locked door.

There was no response from inside the apartment. Two firemen bounded up the stairs with axes; Bowman and I and three patrolmen stood back. I could hear the radio blasting away inside. Disco 101—the Three Degrees' "Jump the Gun." After three well-placed blows the door splintered and fell away.

The living room was empty. The face of the man on the ladder was visible through the window. We moved into the bedroom and found no one. A second set of stereo speakers carried the roar of the music into the room where we stood. Bowman said, "Somebody shut that goddamn thing off!"

The bathroom door opened. Mark Deslonde stepped out in his nylon briefs and stared at us with the most astonished look I'd ever seen on a face.

I said, *"Jesus!* Are you all right? Where the fuck have you been?"

"I've been trimming my beard. What is this? What the hell is going on?"

"Trimming your beard? For an *hour?* For a fucking *hour?"*

Deslonde shrugged, tilted his head, and grinned.

24

"YOU'VE GOT A LOT OF NERVE COMING IN HERE, STRACHEY. Because we're such nice guys, the DA and I decided during the excitement last night not to go to the trouble of prosecuting you and your pal Blount, and now you waltz in here like you owned the goddamn city of Albany and start badgering me and asking for favors. I've run into some pretty deluded perverts over the years, but, Jesus' mother, you take the cake, Strachey, you surely do."

I said, "What a crock. You owe me a big one, and you know it. I just want to borrow the thing overnight. You'll have it back first thing Sunday morning. By noon, anyway. Or one."

He shifted in his chair and caused the holes and nodules on his face to move around. "I'd have to know your intended use for the device," he said. "That thing is worth a lot of money, and if it got damaged in any way, they'd make a note of it and take it out of my pension when that holy day comes, and that pension is already so piss-paltry the wife and myself will probably end up in some trailer parked by a meter on Central Avenue. Now, what the hell are you gonna do with it?"

"I can tell you this much, Ned. The device will be used in a manner your department will approve of entirely. I'm talking about law enforcement. It will be used to collect evidence against a felon. I plan to provide the DA with another warm criminal body for Judge Feeney to pounce on and gobble up. And if you'd like, I'd be happy to mention your name in connection with the apprehension of this disgusting public menace."

He cringed. "You can skip the last part."

An hour later, before I had lunch with Timmy at his apartment, I phoned Sewickley Oaks.

"This is Jay Tarbell, calling for Stu Blount. Mr. Blount's son William has been located, as you may know, and Mr. Blount wishes now to proceed with the boy's treatment. He would appreciate your picking up the boy late tonight, and I'd like to discuss the arrangements—the boy is rather distraught, I'm afraid, and might put up some resistance. I'm sure, though, that your staff can come prepared for any eventuality."

"Oh—I see. Well, Dr. Thurston has stepped out, but I know the doctor thought perhaps Mr. Blount might have changed his mind. I mean, considering what happened last night—we saw the TV reports, and we thought—"

"Not at all, not at all. The boy is no longer under suspicion of murder, of course, but, sad to say, young William is still queer as a three-dollar bill, so to speak, ahem. And you do have Judge Feeney's order in hand, do you not?"

"Oh, yes—"

"As well as the substantial first payment of Dr. Thurston's fee."

"Oh, certainly—"

"Well then, let's get on with it, shall we? Let's lay out a plan. Now I must tell you that young Blount has altered his appearance and that he has assumed an alias. I'll be calling later tonight with further details, but for now, let me just pass on to you Stu Blount's instructions. . . ."

Saturday night at Trucky's. After a warm-up at the Terminal, we drove out Western just after eleven. As we went in, Cheryl Dilcher's "Here Comes My Baby" was on. Truckman was at the door, drink in hand, and I told him I'd like to see him in his office, that I had an apology to make.

He smiled feebly and said, "Sure, Don, sure. Gimme ten minutes."

We ran into the alliance crowd and learned that the judge had denied a restraining order against the Bergenfield police, and that Jim Nordstrum, out on bail, was planning to close the place if it was raided one more time. Despite the absence of any discernible warm feeling for the Rat's Nest and its approach to gay life, there was real anger among the movement people over the sour indifference of the legal establishment toward the harassment of a place that detracted from the moral fitness of no one who chose not to go there. The human machinery of the law was smug and petty and substantially corrupt; that was what hurt. No one could figure out what step to take next, and I did not tell what I knew.

I went looking for Mike Truckman, found him, and ushered him almost forcibly into his office.

I said, "I did think you had something to do with Steve Kleckner's death, Mike. It was mainly because of the company you keep. And your booze problem didn't help—you've got one and you'd better do something about it fast. Anyway, I was stupid and wrong-headed, Mike, and I hope you'll forgive me."

He raised his glass, tried to smile, and set the glass down. "Forget it, Don. Shit, I guess you had your reasons. Let's pretend it never happened. I'm game if you are. We need one

187

another, all of us. Gay people can have their differences, sure, but when push comes to shove, we gotta stick together, right, buddy?"

"That's well put, Mike. Which brings up a painful but related matter."

He'd been glancing at the manila envelope I'd carried in with me, and now he watched me open it and spread the photos out across his desk. He sat blinking, his mouth clamped shut, and peered at them.

I said, "You know what you have to do, don't you? If you're going to get your head together and come back to us, Mike, you've got to start by dealing with this shit."

He managed to get his mouth open far enough to rasp, "Yeah. Yeah, I guess I know."

I took off my jacket and shirt. I removed the Albany PD microphone and wires and recorder from my torso and placed them on the desk alongside the photos of Truckman handing money to the Bergenfield police chief and his plainclothes associate, in payment for their raids on the Rat's Nest.

I said, "Before I show you how to work this thing, I'd appreciate your answering a couple of questions."

He blinked boozily at the display on his desk and said, "Oh, God."

I called Sewickley Oaks from a pay phone up the road from Trucky's. Then I walked back to the disco and danced with Timmy, among others, until closing.

The usual crowd was on hand—Phil, Mark, Calvin, the rabbi—and while most people were subdued at first, only just beginning to recover from the shocks of the past week, one by one each of us gave in to the New Year's Eve atmosphere that gay life can, with luck, produce two or three times a week. By the time Billy Blount arrived with Huey Brownlee at two-thirty, the mood was entirely festive, even celebratory. The DJ played "Put Your Body In It," and everybody did.

At four-forty Timmy and I crouched behind the pile of tires next to the Bergenfield police station. We watched while Mike

Truckman handed over a roll of bills. Timmy took more pictures. The three men lingered longer than they had the last time we'd watched this scene unfold; Truckman was making sure everyone's voice was recorded, that he got it all.

Truckman drove away first, as he had the last time; then the chief; then the plainclothesman, the asshole in the wind-breaker who'd frisked me and spoken disrespectfully during the raid at the Rat's Nest.

As the plainclothesman pulled his Trans-Am onto Western, two unmarked vans that had been parked nearby came to life and pulled into his path, blocking him. The man in the windbreaker jumped from his car cursing and sputtering, and we could make out the look of befuddlement on his face when the back doors of the vans were flung open and seven extremely large men in white jackets poured out and surrounded him. One of the big beefy fellows waved a document in the cop's face, and then they carried him off. He fought, but the straitjacket fit nicely. Within three minutes they were gone, and Timmy and I fell laughing raucously into the pile of tires.

Epilogue

Eddie Storrs was locked up again, this time forever. Stuart and Jane Blount fled back to Saratoga. Chris Porterfield returned to Albany; Timmy and I had a nice Sunday brunch with her and Margarita Mayes, and they sold us a February vacation trip to Key West. Billy Blount moved in with Huey Brownlee, at least temporarily. Mark Deslonde—who had gone back to his apartment that Friday night to pick up some belongings and gotten distracted by his mirror—moved in with Phil permanently. And I moved in with Timmy.

Late on the first night in my new home, I said to Timmy,

"One thing. When you and Blount were in that cubicle at the tubs that day—what did you two do all that time?"

"Oh, fucked and whatnot. Blount was worried about his sexuality. He said he needed reassurance. Why do you ask?"

"Oh, just wondering."

Some Jesuit. This wasn't going to get easier.

❏ **BETTER ANGEL,** by Forman Brown. Written in 1933, this classic, touching story focuses on a young man's gay awakening in the years between the world wars. Kurt Gray is a shy, bookish boy growing up in small-town Michigan. Even at the age of thirteen he knows that somehow he is different. Gradually he recognizes his desire for a man's companionship and love. As a talented composer breaking into New York's musical world, he finds the love he has sought. This new edition contains an updated epilogue and black-and-white photographs from the author's life.

❏ **BI ANY OTHER NAME: BISEXUAL PEOPLE SPEAK OUT,** edited by Loraine Hutchins and Lani Kaahumanu. Hear their voices as more than seventy women and men from all walks of life describe their lives as bisexuals. They tell their stories — personal, political, spiritual, historical — in prose, poetry, art, and essays. These are individuals who have fought prejudice from both the gay and straight communities and who have begun only recently to share their experiences. This groundbreaking anthology is an important step in the process of forming a new bisexual community.

❏ **BROTHER TO BROTHER: NEW WRITINGS BY BLACK GAY MEN,** edited by Essex Hemphill. The late black activist and poet Essex Hemphill followed in the footsteps of Joseph Beam with this anthology of fiction, essays, and poetry by black gay men. Contributors include Assoto Saint, Craig G. Harris, Melvin Dixon, Marlon Riggs, and many newer writers.

❏ **CAPTAIN SWING,** by Larry Duplechan. Johnnie Ray Rousseau's life is at its lowest ebb. The love of his life was killed in a hit-and-run accident, and now he's been called to the deathbed of his hateful, homophobic father. There he meets Nigel, his second cousin, who looks like mortal sin in Levi's and a tank top and who offers a love that Johnnie is none too sure he ought to accept.

❏ **CHARLEYHORSE,** by Cecil Dawkins. Charley was born wanting things she was not supposed to want: horses, spring calving, flying planes, and driving combine harvesters. Charley runs a ranch half the size of a township, but it's not enough. When Juna, a new schoolteacher from New York, moves in, Charley finally has a chance at what she wants — but first she has to deal with her eccentric and manipulative mother.

a

❏ **CODY,** by Keith Hale. Steven Trottingham Taylor, "Trotsky" to his friends, is new in Little Rock. Washington Damon Cody has lived there all his life. Yet when they meet, there's a familiarity — a sense that they've known each other before. Their friendship grows and develops a rare intensity, although one of them is gay and the other is straight.

❏ **CRUSH,** by Jane Futcher. It wasn't easy fitting in at an exclusive girls' school like Huntington Hill. But in her senior year, Jinx finally felt as if she belonged. Lexie — beautiful, popular Lexie — wanted her for a friend. Jinx knew she had a big crush on Lexie, and she knew she had to do something to make it go away. But Lexie had other plans. And Lexie always got her way.

❏ **DEATH BY DENIAL: STUDIES OF SUICIDE IN GAY AND LESBIAN TEENAGERS,** edited by Gary Remafedi. A federal study found in 1989 that teenagers struggling with issues of sexual orientation were three times more likely than their peers to attempt suicide. The report was swept aside by the Bush administration, yet the problem didn't go away. Here are the full findings of that report and of several other studies; they document the difficulties faced by teenagers who are coming out and propose ways to ease that process.

❏ **EYES OF DESIRE: A DEAF GAY AND LESBIAN READER,** edited by Raymond Luczak. Coming out is hard enough already. But it becomes a new challenge altogether when one can't take communication itself for granted. Here, for the first time, lesbians and gay men who are deaf tell about their lives: discovering their sexual identities; overcoming barriers to communication in a sound-based world; and, finally, creating a deaf gay and lesbian culture in a world that is too often afraid of differences.

❏ **HAPPY ENDINGS ARE ALL ALIKE,** by Sandra Scoppettone. It was their last summer before college, and Jaret and Peggy were in love. But as Jaret said: "It always seems as if when something great happens, then something lousy happens soon after." Soon her worst fears turned into brute reality.

❏ **A LOTUS OF ANOTHER COLOR: AN UNFOLDING OF THE SOUTH ASIAN GAY AND LESBIAN EXPERIENCE,** edited by Rakesh Ratti. For the first time gay men and lesbians from India, Pakistan, and other South Asian countries relate their coming-out stories. In essays and poetry they tell of challenging prejudice from both the South Asian and gay cultures and express the exhilaration of finally finding a sense of community.

❏ **NOT THE ONLY ONE: LESBIAN AND GAY FICTION FOR TEENS,** by Tony Grima. Many lesbians and gay men remember their teen years as a time of isolation and anxiety, when exploring sexuality meant facing possible rejection by family and friends. But it can also be a time of exciting discovery and of hope for the future. These stories capture all the fears, joys, confusion, and energy of teenagers coming face-to-face with gay issues, either as they themselves come out or as they learn that a friend or family member is gay.

a

ONE TEACHER IN TEN: GAY AND LESBIAN EDUCATORS TELL THEIR STORIES, edited by Kevin Jennings. Gay and lesbian teachers have traditionally dwelt in the deepest of closets. But increasing numbers of young people are now served by teachers who are out and proud. Here, for the first time, educators from all regions of the country tell about their struggles and victories as they have put their own careers at risk in their fight for justice.

THE PRESIDENT'S SON, by Krandall Kraus. D.J. Marshall is the handsome, gay son of a popular president. But as the reelection campaign begins, D.J. finds himself cut off from his father by ambitious advisers who are determined that no scandal should threaten their power. Soon D.J. realizes that he has no one to trust. No one except Parker, the beefy Secret Service agent who is taking an unusual interest in D.J.'s personal life. But just how far can Parker be trusted?

REFLECTIONS OF A ROCK LOBSTER, by Aaron Fricke. Guess who's coming to the prom! Aaron Fricke made national news by taking a male date to his high school prom. Here, told with rare insight and humor, is Aaron's story about growing up gay, realizing that he is different, and ultimately developing a positive gay identity in spite of the prejudice around him.

REVELATIONS, edited by Adrien Saks and Wayne Curtis. For most gay men, one critical moment stands out as a special time in the coming-out process. It may be a special friendship or a sexual episode or a book or movie that communicates the right message at the right time. In this collection, twenty-two men of varying ages and backgrounds give an account of this moment of truth. These tales of self-discovery will strike a chord of recognition in every gay reader.

SCHOOL'S OUT: THE IMPACT OF GAY AND LESBIAN ISSUES ON AMERICA'S SCHOOLS, by Dan Woog. America's schools are filled with gay men and lesbians: students, teachers, principals, coaches, and counselors. Author Dan Woog interviewed nearly 300 people in this exploration of the impact of gay and lesbian issues and people on the U.S. educational system. From the scared teenager who doesn't want his teammates to know he's gay to the straight teacher who wants to honor diversity by teaching gay issues in the classroom, Woog puts a human face on the people who truly are fighting for "liberty and justice for all."

SOCIETY AND THE HEALTHY HOMOSEXUAL, by George Weinberg. Rarely has anyone communicated so much, in a single word, as Dr. George Weinberg did when he introduced the term "homophobia." With a single stroke of the pen, he turned the tables on centuries of prejudice. Homosexuality is healthy, said Weinberg: Homophobia is a sickness. In this pioneering book, Weinberg examines the causes of homophobia. He shows how gay people can overcome its pervasive influence to lead happy and fulfilling lives.

a

❏ **TESTIMONIES,** edited by Karen Barber and Sarah Holmes. More than twenty women of widely varying backgrounds and ages give accounts of their journeys toward self-discovery. The stories portray the women's efforts to develop a lesbian identity, explore their sexuality, and build a community with other lesbians.

❏ **TOMBOYS! TALES OF DYKE DERRING-DO,** edited by Lynne Yamaguchi Fletcher and Karen Barber. For many people, "tomboy" is virtually a synonym for "lesbian," and there is, in fact, considerable overlap between the two categories. This collection of stories, essays and photographs examines and celebrates tomboyhood and its meaning for those tomboys who grew up to be lesbians. Readers will delight in both the commonalities and the varieties of experience revealed in these tales told with humor, attitude, nostalgia, longing and, above all, love.

❏ **TORN ALLEGIANCES,** by Jim Holobaugh, with Keith Hale. Jim Holobaugh was the perfect ROTC cadet — so perfect that ROTC featured the handsome college student in nationwide ad campaign. But as he gradually came to realize that he is gay, he faced an impossible dilemma: To serve the country he loved, he would have to live a life of deceit. His story dramatizes both the monetary waste and the moral corruptness of the military's antigay policy.

❏ **TWO TEENAGERS IN 20: WRITINGS BY GAY AND LESBIAN YOUTH,** edited by Ann Heron. Twelve years after compiling *One Teenager In Ten,* the first book ever to allow dozens of teenagers to describe what it's like to be gay or lesbian, Ann Heron asked for stories from a new generation. She found that their sense of isolation and despair runs every bit as deep as a decade ago. *Two Teenagers in 20* combines these new voices with many essays from her first book. This book will greatly ease the way for teenagers just now coming out and will help the adults who seek to support them.

❏ **UNLIVED AFFECTIONS,** by George Shannon. After the grandmother who raised him dies, eighteen-year-old Willie is eager to leave everything behind as he clears out her house for auction. His tenuous sense of family and self is shaken to the core as he reads a hidden box of letters written to his long-dead mother from the father he'd never known. A father who he'd been told was dead. A father who'd never been told he had a son. A father who'd been searching for his own sense of self and family as a gay man eighteen years before.

❏ **YOUNG, GAY, & PROUD!** edited by Don Romesburg. One high school student in ten is gay. When *Young, Gay, & Proud!* first appeared in 1980, it was the first book to address the needs of this often-invisible minority. In this revised edition the editor has reworked the book to make it newly relevant to the issues faced by gay teens in the mid '90s, issues such as: Am I really gay? What would my friends think if I told them? Should I tell my parents? Other sections discuss health concerns, sexuality, and suggestions for further reading.